Until the War is Over

Until the War is Over

Rosemary Goodacre

hera

First published in the United Kingdom in 2020 by Hera

Hera Books
28b Cricketfield Road
London, E5 8NS
United Kingdom

A CIP catalogue record for this book is available from the British Library.

Print ISBN 978 1 80032 160 1
Ebook ISBN 978 1 912973 33 0

Printed and bound in Great Britain by Clays Ltd, Elcograf S.p.A.

To my husband, Ian,
still adjusting to having a writer in the family.
Also to Elaine Everest, tutor at The Write Place Creative
Writing School at Hextable, and to my group of writing buddies
there. They have given me so much help and encouragement,
and together we have enjoyed often hilarious social events.

Chapter One

'Will you be ready soon, darling?' Edmond Derwent asked his wife, Amy.

'Yes!' Their baby daughter, Beth, was growing sleepy as she completed her feed. Amy set down the soft, warm little bundle in her cot and buttoned up her dress. It was nearly time to set off for today's event in the church hall.

She combed the dangling curls of her blonde hair before reaching for her best hat with the velvet trim. She slipped her arms into her coat, then scooped up Beth once more and wrapped her in a thick blanket for her first outing, for the day was cold. Her heart surged with pride as she looked at her sleepy baby. It was the first Saturday of 1918 and some family and friends would be meeting their daughter for the first time.

'Let me carry Beth for you,' Edmond said as she approached the stairs, for she needed to hang on to the banister. Her bad leg was still a considerable handicap. She walked with a limp because her broken ankle had been badly set in France at a hospital overflowing with casualties, and she could only make slow progress.

He took hold of his daughter, his blue eyes bright, for he too was still overwhelmed with joy at Beth's arrival on

New Year's morning. He was tall, and thinner than when they had married. With clothes concealing the lung injury he had sustained near Ypres, he was still a good-looking man, though strain occasionally showed in his face.

'How will we all get in the motor car?' he asked as his father joined them in the hall. With his mother, and sister, Beatrice, there would be five of them, besides the baby. 'I'd better walk.'

'No, I'll have time to make two trips,' Pa said valiantly, for he was without a chauffeur now the man had joined up. As Amy had grown closer to Mr Derwent, Edmond's father, she had started calling him Pa.

'I don't mind walking,' Edmond said. 'I'm recovering every day.'

Amy admired his optimism but he still got breathless easily.

'You're not that fit yet,' Pa said. 'It's nearly two miles to the village. I'll drive you two and Beth first, for everyone will want to see her.'

His wife bustled into the hall, wearing one of her huge feather-trimmed pre-war hats. Amy called her mother-in-law Ma, but that lady was often standoffish, only warming a little lately, with the arrival of her grandchild.

'If only the day were milder,' Ma said.

Amy gasped as Pa opened the front door. It had been snowy for two days, but now sunshine illuminated the drive, shining on the bare branches of the ancient beech trees, sparkly white against the blue sky.

'It's like fairyland!' she said. She supposed Beth was much too young to appreciate the magical scene.

Pa's tall figure was still unbent as he walked resolutely to the car. He drove them down to St Stephen's, the old stone church in Larchbury village, where Amy's uncle, Arthur Fletcher, was vicar. She felt a glow of anticipation as they hurried past the church, through the slush along the path to the hall.

At the door to greet them was Uncle Arthur, wearing his dog collar with everyday clothes. 'Your news is marvellous,' he told them. Beth was stirring now.

Beside Uncle Arthur were Aunt Sophie, in her best dress, and the upright figure of James, her cousin. He had not managed to get Christmas leave but now he was home. Since she had last seen him he had grown a moustache. He eased back the corner of Beth's blanket to take a better look, and beamed at her.

'How lovely to meet a new member of our family!' he exclaimed.

Tables and chairs were arranged in the hall, which was lavishly decorated with foliage, mostly branches of pine from the Derwents' forest.

Amy's parents were sitting at one of the tables, and Father rose to hug her. He was brother to the vicar. As she sat down with them, Mother reached across to kiss Beth's cheek. Others welcomed them, smiling at the new arrival, who slept on.

Her friend, Florence, in her familiar brown winter coat and smartest hat, greeted them from the same table. She had already visited Amy to see little Beth.

The hall was half full, and many parishioners were soberly dressed. Recent church services had included prayers for the outcome of the war, and Uncle Arthur struggled to keep his sermons optimistic. 'We must keep faith,' he would reiterate to a weary congregation.

Soon Edmond's parents and Beatrice arrived. She was wearing her fur-trimmed coat and her smile looked a little forced. At church the previous Sunday, she had been the centre of attention, when her engagement to Lieutenant Charles Shenwood had been the latest news. Amy realised now their Beth had seized her limelight.

'They might have held the event in the vicarage.' Beatrice looked disgustedly at the paraffin heaters, which were not always adequate, and the hard wooden chairs.

Uncle had considered using the large reception room in the vicarage, but was uncertain how many parishioners would attend. While some welcomed the festive diversion, others found little to celebrate.

'I'm so glad Aunt Sophie had her brainwave,' Amy said.

The vicar's wife had proposed that the afternoon should celebrate the Women's Working Party, who sent comforts to the troops. They and their families were encouraged to attend.

'And we'll have young men to tell us how the work is valued by the soldiers,' Aunt Sophie had told them when she had planned it in December. 'You'll speak to them, won't you, Edmond? And I think James will be on leave by then.'

'I'm glad they invited you to speak too,' Edmond said to Amy. 'After all, you've nursed in France.'

She nodded, only slightly apprehensive. Hadn't she always maintained that women's opinions should be valued?

Pa chose the table next to theirs, and allowed Ma and Beatrice to sit down first. Amy preferred to sit with her parents and Florence. Besides being Amy's oldest friend, from school days, Florence had been engaged to her brother, Bertie, before he had been killed on the Somme. Amy had not fully recovered from the loss, and probably never would. She pitied Florence, still often submerged in grief. Even now Amy's parents regarded Bertie's fiancée as practically part of the family.

Amy's spirits rose again as Mother took baby Beth into her arms. How relieved she had been when Mother had arrived to hold her hand through the final stages of Beth's birth! The baby opened her eyes, gurgled a little and then settled again. Father, smart in his newest suit, admired his grandchild.

Amy unbuttoned her coat. 'Do I look all right in this dress?' she asked. It was her blue woollen one, two years old. 'I couldn't get into my newer day dress.'

'Of course, dear.' Mother's hair had been fair once, like Amy's, but was turning paler now.

Margaret Leadbetter, an enthusiastic member of the Working Group, came to their table. 'Congratulations on your good news!' she said, admiring Beth. Her husband, the headmaster, followed her to their table to greet them. Amy's father taught in the senior section of the village school, and Florence taught a junior class. Mr Fletcher and Miss Clifford were both popular teachers.

As a few more villagers arrived there were other families they knew and two women interested in joining their group. Coughs and colds were keeping some members away, she had heard.

'Arthur might have fitted everyone into the room at the vicarage after all,' Amy's father said. Few people had removed their coats in the chilly hall.

The vicar climbed the few steps to the platform and formally greeted his guests. Then, to their surprise,

5

Edmond's father got up and followed him. 'May I call upon you all to wish the vicar a very happy fiftieth birthday,' he announced, in his loud, confident voice. Most of the visitors gasped with surprise, previously unaware of the occasion, then they burst into applause.

'Our vicar and his wife generously decided to hold a party for the Women's Working Group, instead of a private party for a select group of friends and family,' he told them.

'It was a wise decision,' Amy's father said to the others on his table. 'With the news from Flanders there's so little to celebrate.' After more than three years of fighting, hardly any families were unaffected by the terrible losses.

'We must all offer our congratulations to Amy and Edmond, on the birth of little Beth,' Uncle Arthur said. 'They are like a symbol of hope, of life carrying on in spite of all the horrors.' Other guests turned to them and clapped their hands.

Amy basked in their good wishes. Once she had been regarded with disapproval by some villagers, when her direct action with the Suffragettes had been discovered. Now, following her war work as a nurse, she felt accepted once more.

In a pause while some latecomers arrived, James fetched another chair and joined their table, smiling.

'I'm glad they approved your leave,' Amy said.

He was less plump and had grown up noticeably in the past year, while working as an orderly at the Front. 'How are you both now?' he asked.

She had last seen him while she was nursing in France, before she was sent back to have her baby. At that time Edmond had still been seriously ill in the hospital in Ypres.

'Much better now,' she reassured him. *Edmond is recovering, though he'll never be entirely fit*, she thought. *My ankle is better, but it still feels stiff and my walking is impaired, but all the same...* 'When I wake up now and we're both together and have a beautiful daughter, it seems like a miracle,' she said.

'I wish I hadn't been invalided out,' Edmond said. 'I keep thinking of the poor chaps in the Front Line.'

'But you nearly died!' Amy exclaimed. 'Your lung may never heal fully. You've made your contribution.' She understood how he felt, though, for she had joined the Voluntary Aid Detachment and nursed troops in London and in France before her pregnancy and injury.

'This afternoon we'll be hearing from some brave young people who have served at the Front,' Uncle Arthur said now. She knew he was determined the women of the Working Party should realise how much their contributions were appreciated. 'I'd like to call upon Edmond Derwent to begin.' He sat down on one of the chairs arranged on the platform.

Edmond walked forward and climbed the steps to the platform, less nimble than he had once been. Conversation stopped as the guests waited respectfully for him to speak. The Derwents were a prominent family in the village, and with his brave struggle to overcome his wound, he had gained their admiration.

'This time last year I was in France, in the Somme area,' he said, standing very upright in front of them, in his khaki army uniform, with one hand on Uncle Arthur's chair. 'It was bitterly cold, with frequent snowstorms, and I can tell you all we were very thankful to receive the socks and gloves and balaclavas you fine women knitted

7

for us. Imagine what it's like to go on night patrol when it's frosty!'

Ma and Beatrice exchanged self-congratulatory glances. Ma remarked loudly on their determination to contribute to the war effort by joining the Working Party. Amy recalled the way they missed sessions there when they felt it essential to visit the shops or their dressmaker instead.

'It was a happy day for us, every time a bundle of comforts from home arrived,' Edmond went on. 'And the cakes our families sent, of course – they always cheered us.'

'Thank you for telling us that,' Uncle Arthur said. 'Now may I call on your wife, Amy, to share some of her experiences working in France as a nurse. You take a seat here on the platform, Edmond – I'll invite questions shortly.'

Amy went up and looked out over all the familiar faces. She knew what she must say.

'It's vital that we have a good supply of bandages,' she said, for the Working Party prepared and packed dressings. 'Some days lots of casualties arrive…' She stopped short of telling her audience about the groaning patients, waiting on stretchers to be allocated a bed; she must not become too graphic for gentle listeners, like Mother. But at the Front sudden emergencies would arise.

From where she was standing on the platform she could detect a delicious savoury smell of soup. Although the hall was warming up, something hot and nourishing would be very welcome. 'It's essential we practise good hygiene on the wards to aid recovery,' she said. 'We need to replace dressings regularly.'

'Thank you, Amy. And now, as my son James is home on leave, he can tell you about his work as a medical orderly.'

There was less obvious enthusiasm as he joined them on the platform. People still remembered that he had not volunteered to fight, and had taken a position as an orderly only when conscription loomed and he might otherwise have faced jail for refusing to fight.

He hesitated. 'Edmond and Amy have covered several important points already,' he said. 'Regarding the medical dressings, there are sometimes delays to the transport. We need to maintain a good stock so we don't run short.' He seemed to be considering what to say next. 'And don't forget, the men love to receive letters from home. Time passes slowly for an invalid, and news of loved ones will raise his spirits.'

His father stood up. 'Thank you, James. Now, are there any questions?'

The three of them sat apprehensively, wondering what their audience might ask.

Mr Leadbetter rose to his feet. 'Is there any hope of victory in the near future?' he asked. It was what they all wanted to know, but no-one else had dared enquire. Newspaper reporters implied that the war would not grind on for much longer, but they had been repeating that since 1914.

Edmond stood up. 'I believe there are causes for optimism,' he said. 'The Americans have joined us now, and should reach Europe in large numbers this spring. And we have our new vehicles, the tanks, which can move fast across muddy terrain.' He had heard from friends who were still serving how effective they could be.

Aunt Sophie got up from a chair near the platform. 'Thank you all for your contributions,' she told them. 'Whenever I attend the Working Party I shall be certain I'm helping the war effort. Now then, I'll see if the refreshments are ready.'

She went to the kitchen area but did not return, so Amy suspected they needed to wait a while longer.

'Can anything be done to make life easier for the invalids?' Uncle Arthur asked them.

'Hospitals hold concert parties for convalescents when they can find entertainers,' Amy said. There had not been a concert at her hospital.

James got up. 'We had a patient who was a cavalry officer,' he said, 'so we cheered him up in the classic fashion.'

'How did you raise his spirits?' the vicar asked. Edmond was smiling as though he knew what the answer would be.

'You have to take his horse to see him. We arranged it.'

They took a horse on to a ward? Amy was incredulous.

'It was in the autumn, and the officer was in a tent,' he explained. 'Mind you, the horse was a great brute, almost seventeen hands he must have been, and the tent nearly collapsed around them.'

Their audience could not help laughing at his comical account.

Aunt Sophie returned. 'We're just going to serve the meal,' she announced.

Amy exchanged glances with Edmond and James. They had conveyed the importance of the Working Party well, she felt. They followed the vicar down from the platform and returned to their table. As they passed

Edmond's parents she noticed Ma was looking bored. A smart friend of Beatrice had joined her table to admire her engagement ring, with its cluster of diamonds.

Mother got up and passed Beth to Amy, before following Aunt Sophie to the kitchen, to help serve the meal. Mrs Johnson, the good-humoured charlady, followed them. She helped Mother once a week and also came twice weekly to the Derwents at The Beeches, as Ma was struggling to manage with fewer servants than before the war.

Beth was still sleeping peacefully. 'It must be cheerless in France now,' Amy said to James. 'I suppose it's quiet at least.' There was seldom fighting in the depth of winter.

'We've still got lots of wounded to tend.'

Uncle Arthur said *grace*. As plates of hot carrot and coriander soup were brought around Amy fell quiet, remembering some of the brave men she had nursed, particularly ones who had not survived. She held Beth firmly with one arm, while sipping the tasty soup.

James's eyes lit up as he turned towards Florence. 'It's lovely to see you,' he said.

She nodded her head in a token reply, looking uneasy. He had grey eyes like Bertie's and Amy supposed the resemblance was disturbing.

Beth was waking up now and Florence, who had finished her soup, took her in her arms, her soft hazel eyes focussed on the baby.

'Will you and Amy go on living at The Beeches with your parents?' James asked Edmond.

'I want to be fit enough to go back to university this autumn,' he replied. 'If I can't fight any more I can at least continue my science course at Cambridge. I only completed the first year, before the war. We plan to find a little house so Amy and Beth can come too.'

If only it all works out, Amy thought. She longed for him to be well enough to fulfil his plans. The Beeches was much grander than the little house where she had grown up with her parents and Bertie. She should be grateful for her lovely home, but Ma and Beatrice still made her feel inferior. At least Edmond was there with her now, but how she yearned for a time when they could settle in their own little home!

'So when do you have to return to France?' Edmond asked James.

'They only gave me four days here, so I need to set off tomorrow. I'll be back there in a field ambulance all too soon.'

Florence looked up suddenly. 'It's all very well for you,' she snapped uncharacteristically. 'You're not actually fighting.'

'You're right, I'm only an orderly.' He looked at her directly. 'The work is hard, though, and worthwhile.'

Florence made no reply but her mouth was a tight line. She rocked Beth gently in her arms. Amy was concerned at her implied criticism.

'The orderlies do valuable work!' she cried. 'They prepare patients for surgery and dispense drugs. I've seen James at work escorting casualties and helping at the hospital in Ypres.'

She had not told anyone, not even Edmond, that her cousin was keeping a war diary.

An awkward hush fell on the table. Even Father seemed disconcerted. It was the first time Amy had seen him look at Florence disapprovingly.

Then Aunt Sophie brought chicken pie and mashed potato for their next course. She hovered by their table, neatly but simply dressed.

'If only James could stay longer,' she said. 'I hope he receives his share of the comforts we send, so he can keep warm in his quarters, in the middle of winter.'

'Some of the buildings are makeshift,' Amy said. The previous winter she had been in France. 'You just get used to wearing extra clothes under your uniform.'

She congratulated Aunt Sophie on the successful event before she bustled off to serve more meals.

As soon as they had finished their main course, Florence gathered up their plates, saying she would help serve the portions of apple pie. As she left she was looking a little embarrassed, as though sensing she had gone too far.

'Florence shouldn't have spoken to you like that,' Amy said to James. She had never before felt so angry with her.

'It's about Bertie, isn't it?' he said with resignation. 'I understand very well. She's not the only one around here to think I'm a coward. The man she loved died fighting, and she still misses him dreadfully. I've taken a less dangerous option.'

Florence took less trouble now with the clothes she wore, and arranged her light brown hair very plainly. Amy could not remember when she had last relaxed into her sunniest, dimpled smile.

'I'm sure that's how she thinks,' Edmond said. At first he too had been critical of James, for being determined not to fight, but his view had changed. 'I saw enough of the vital work orderlies do at the Front to value them.'

'I confess I have feelings for Florence,' James said, his eyes straying towards her as she served plates of dessert to a nearby table. 'She's sweet and pretty. But her heart has been broken, and I'm a little younger than she is and not much of a catch. I can't blame her for not encouraging me.'

'She's entitled to keep you at a distance,' Amy said, 'but she needn't be unpleasant.'

Beth was becoming fretful as her next feed was due. Amy asked Pa if he could drive her and Beth back to The Beeches.

'Certainly,' he said. 'I'll come back later for the others.'

Florence brought their plates of apple pie. 'I'm afraid I have to leave now,' Amy told her, passing Beth to Edmond while she did up her coat.

'I need to leave shortly,' Florence said. 'My sister is visiting us.'

'Allow me to escort you back,' James said.

'That won't be necessary,' she said quickly. 'It's hardly any distance.'

He looked mortified but accepted her wishes.

'Thank you for your lovely celebration,' Amy said to her uncle as she prepared to leave.

'If I'd known for sure that your little one would be here in time I could have planned it so you and Edmond and Beth were at the centre of the celebration!'

'No, focussing on the Working Party was a wonderful idea.' She tucked the blanket tightly around Beth and followed Pa outside. The sunlight had faded and it was growing chilly.

Chapter Two

Larchbury, January 1918

'How do you occupy yourself, when you're not teaching?' Sarah, Florence's older sister, asked her.

She realises that time drags for me during the school holidays, Florence thought. *At least we begin again on Tuesday.* 'I read a good deal,' she said, 'and practise on the piano.' She herself felt she was taking root in the house, as though preparing for inevitable spinsterhood.

On Sunday, Sarah had to return to Wealdham. 'Monday's a day I'm normally at home,' she said. 'It's such a trial having to do all the washing myself, now my laundry maid has left to work in a shop.' So many jobs were available for young women now the men were away fighting.

'How have you managed?' their mother asked in a concerned tone. Her grey hair was held tightly in a bun and she was wearing a check dress with white cuffs.

'I managed to persuade Mrs Taylor to do an extra half day to help me out,' Sarah said, referring to her other maid.

Sarah's hair was light brown, like Florence's, arranged on top of her head. She was growing plumper as the years passed. She had sons of ten and twelve, who had stayed at home with their father.

Florence's attention wandered as her mother and sister shared further domestic details. Sarah's house in Wealdham was smaller than her home, but laid out similarly. Both had parlours which were meticulously clean and well-polished. Here, the coal fire flickered cheerfully in the hearth, with its surround of Delft tiles. Soon they would remove the Christmas foliage from the walls, and everything would be almost exactly as it had been in 1914. Few social events took place at this stage of the war, and the general air of despondency was oppressive.

–

When Sarah had set off for home, Florence decided to walk over to The Beeches to see Amy. She put on her brown coat and her plain felt hat.

On her dressing table she still kept the photo of Bertie, in uniform, taken in 1915 before he left for France. How proud and confident he looked, and how jolly and entertaining he had always been. Had she imagined that his silly cousin James was interested in her now? How could he ever think he could replace her fiancé?

All the same, she felt a shade guilty now about the way she had spoken to James, and was anxious to make her peace with Amy.

She set off along their drive, where shrivelled shrubs appeared through the remaining patches of snow, and walked along the High Street, then turned on to the narrow road towards The Beeches.

When she arrived, Chambers, the butler, admitted her and led her into the drawing room, where Amy and Edmond were sitting with his mother and sister.

'Hello, Florence,' Amy said. There was a little hesitation in her greeting. *She didn't like how I spoke to James yesterday*, Florence thought.

Amy rang for Janet, the maid, and asked her to bring tea and cake to the nursery. Florence followed her friend upstairs.

The little nursery was freshly wallpapered in a pale blue floral design. 'It's tricky finding somewhere to entertain visitors,' Amy said. 'Our other room has our bed in it, and just a very small sofa. The conservatory isn't particularly attractive at this time of year.'

Florence chose the upright chair, so Amy settled in the rocking chair, and Beth slept on in her cot, beneath its frothy lace canopy.

Janet knocked and came in with a pot of tea, and some Christmas cake left from seasonal celebrations. She was thin and probably in her thirties. She bustled round in her usual energetic fashion, pouring them tea and serving the cake.

After the maid had left, Amy was quiet, a serious look on her face. Florence's stomach lurched. She could guess why her friend was angry.

'You were horrid to James yesterday,' Amy said forcefully, her blue eyes piercing. 'If you'd been out in France, like I have, you'd know how hard the orderlies work. They do essential duties.'

'I suppose so. Perhaps I was harsh with him.'

'Sometimes they organise baths for the men and help with the delousing. They look after the isolation cases as well. And you don't hear them complain.'

'I'm sure you're right,' Florence said. 'But they're not risking their lives like the fighting men, are they?'

'Not so much,' Amy said, 'but you do hear of orderlies being killed or injured when they go near the Front to evacuate the wounded.'

Florence winced. 'I'm sorry I was outspoken,' she said. She could not bear it if Amy stayed angry with her.

'Remember how we used to campaign for votes for women before the war?' Amy said.

'Of course – you even got sent to jail for taking direct action!' She was not likely to forget that incident, or the way it had disrupted Amy's wedding plans.

'James has principles, the way we have,' Amy went on, clattering her teacup as she set it down on the tiny table. 'His conscience won't let him fight. He's entitled to uphold his beliefs, the same as we are.'

'If you put it like that, I suppose I should respect his views,' Florence said, thoughtfully. 'But there's something else, too. I think he's growing sweet on me. I noticed it the last time he came on leave, in the summer it must have been. He made a point of greeting me after church, and once he came to my house and asked if I'd like to come for a walk. I made an excuse of having to visit a pupil.'

Now Amy's expression softened. She put her arm round Florence.

'It's all right,' she said. 'I understand you can't forget Bertie and don't return James's feelings. No-one expects you to spend time alone with him if you don't want to. Just be gentle with him, that's all.'

'I feel mean now, for the way I spoke to him.' Florence's mind was troubled. 'Should I write to him, do you think? No, that might make it look as though I was encouraging him... Tell you what, if I write a little note, apologising for speaking harshly, and saying I respect his principles, could you put that with your letter, next time you write to him?'

'Of course, that would be fine.'

Beth was waking up, making little murmurs. Amy pulled back the quilt, picked her up and passed her to Florence for a cuddle. *She's going to forgive me,* Florence thought. *And I really should have accepted James's right to have a mind of his own. He's stuck to his ideals even when it's brought him hostility.*

—

'Let me help you,' Edmond begged his father a few days later. 'I'm tired of being an invalid.'

Amy found him increasingly restless. 'My friend, Katherine, is coming tomorrow,' she reminded him. 'You can help me entertain her.'

Beatrice was away for the day, visiting a friend, but his parents were taking coffee with them in the small morning room.

'I'll do that,' Edmond promised. 'But Pa, I can at least help with your paperwork for managing the forest. I can add up a column of figures as well as anyone else.'

'Very well,' Pa said. 'I can certainly do with some assistance. But you're to stop if you get tired.'

The room was at the back of the house, and through the window Amy could see the forest up the hill, the pines dark green in the thin winter sunshine. Their plantation was the family's source of income.

'Did you manage to get another forestry worker?' Amy asked Pa.

'I've approached two men who retired just before the war began, and they've both agreed to work a day or two each week. Walter is competent to act as a manager when he can come.'

When conscription had started in 1916, some of Pa's best men had been called up.

'At least they let you keep Ross to do the heavy work,' Edmond said.

'I should think so!' Pa said. The war had brought him many concerns and his hair and moustache were entirely grey now. 'There's a high demand for wood. How do they expect me to produce it without the manpower? Apart from the old men working part time, I've got two remaining men in their fifties, and two youths too young to join up yet. I couldn't manage without Ross. We need to keep the forest well maintained. The trees near the wide path need trimming back to provide an adequate fire break before the weather warms up.'

Amy knew that in the horrifying event of a fire starting, perhaps through a lightning strike, the break might contain it.

They finished their coffee and Edmond got up eagerly to follow his father back to the study.

Amy had fed Beth and left her asleep in the nursery. There, as here, Janet had lit a fire to drive away the chill. Ma looked up from her book. As usual she was stately in a smart blue dress and elegantly piled up grey hair.

'How long is your nursing friend staying tomorrow?' she asked in the grudging tone she was less likely to use when Edmond was there. He had not previously met Katherine but he had encouraged Ma to agree to her visit.

'Just until late afternoon,' Amy said, hoping the weather would be mild enough to go out. 'She's got a week's leave and she's visiting her aunt and uncle who live around ten miles from here. I've scarcely seen her since I left St Luke's hospital for France, so it will be lovely spending time together.'

'You'd better come with me to see Cook. You must realise how hard it is now to provide meals suitable for guests.' Ma was always complaining about wartime shortages.

'I promise you, Katherine will be happy with whatever is served for lunch,' Amy said. 'She's from a fairly well-off family, but she's been at St Luke's for two years now. You should see the food served in the nurses' hostel – mostly slurpy stews and overcooked vegetables. She'll be grateful for anything decent to eat.'

Ma looked unconvinced.

'I'm sure it won't be a problem,' Amy said, as she followed Ma to the kitchen.

Elsie, Mrs Johnson's sixteen-year-old daughter, who accompanied her mother to work there two days a week, was chopping carrots messily on the table. Cook, plump and grey-haired, looked up from peeling apples. Amy knew she had a nephew fighting in Flanders. She toiled without complaint, even after their regular kitchen maid had left to take a position at the inn, replacing a man who had gone to fight.

She smiled at Amy when Ma asked what she planned to serve. 'Your guest is another nurse, I gather. I'll do my very best for her. I'll make one of my pies.'

'Thank you – that'll be perfect.'

'It won't be a game pie, like before the war, but we should run to veal and ham.'

–

Edmond woke up next morning as Amy was feeding Beth. The familiar pain and tightness in his chest reminded him at once of his wound. There was the dismal feeling, whenever he woke, that his chest was deformed now and he would never be entirely fit again. Then he would look at his wife beside him, lovely in the dim light, and realise how fortunate he was.

He still had disturbed nights, less now from the pain but more from recollections of his experiences at the Front during the Somme and the Ypres offensives. More than once Amy had said she had woken to find him thrashing around and rambling in his sleep. Sometimes it still seemed strange that he was no longer in danger every day. He had to make light of his haunting memories.

'How's Charles?' Amy asked Beatrice after the mail had arrived with a letter from him.

'He's fine, and he's been promoted to Captain – isn't that wonderful?' Her green eyes sparkled. 'I always knew he was an outstanding officer.'

'Captain! I must write to congratulate him,' Edmond said.

'You were in the running for promotion before you got wounded, weren't you?' Amy reminded him.

'I was mentioned in despatches...' His mind returned to the vulnerable young men in the trenches. He had done his best to maintain morale as he led them into battle.

Soon Katherine arrived, brought over by her uncle and aunt in their chauffeur-driven car. They were a friendly couple who asked after Amy and her husband before setting off again.

Amy hugged her friend and introduced her to Edmond and his family. He greeted her warmly as he shook her hand. Ma and Beatrice looked over the newcomer. Katherine's curly dark hair was neatly arranged and when she had taken off her outdoor clothes she was wearing a smart cream-coloured woollen dress. As she thanked the family for inviting her, he could tell the other women approved of her refined accent.

Janet brought them coffee and ginger cake.

'Where's your little Beth?' Katherine asked and Amy explained that she was asleep in the nursery but promised to bring her down soon.

Katherine turned her attention to Edmond. 'I've heard so much about you,' she said, looking him up and down. 'Are you making a good recovery still?' As a nurse she would recognise that his complexion was a reasonable colour now and his breathing not too laboured. 'Were you slightly built before your injury?'

'Yes, I've always been quite slim.' He was determined to minimise his health problems. He kept as active as possible, trying not to betray how tired he sometimes felt. He would only slow down if he was beginning to get out of breath, for Amy was sure to notice and be concerned. There had been that setback in late October, when they had visited George, their former gardener, who was home on leave. He lived in the industrial area of Wealdham, the nearest town, and the foul, smoky air had hampered Edmond's breathing, leaving him weak for days afterwards and impeding his recovery.

'His weight went down a lot from the trauma of his injury,' Amy put in, 'but five months have gone by and he's making progress.'

'I was very fortunate to be operated on by Mr Westholme, an extremely well respected surgeon,' he told

Katherine. He was the father of Amy's friend, Lavinia, and had been in Ypres at the time. 'And he actually brought Amy from the hospital where she was working to see me. It made a huge difference.' Seeing her and hearing that she was expecting their child had given him so much to live for.

'Have you seen a doctor lately?'

'I've seen Doctor Stanhope, the local man, and he's pleased how well my lung is healing. In about a month I've got to go back to the specialist in London for a check-up and I'm sure he'll be pleased with my progress.'

–

Ma need not have worried about the food, Amy thought, at lunchtime when Katherine expressed her appreciation of the veal and ham pie. They chatted about St Luke's, where they had both worked as new recruits to the nursing arm of the Voluntary Aid Detachment, and where Katherine still worked.

'It was a struggle to learn the ropes when we were training,' Amy told the others. She remembered Katherine's shock at the conditions in the hostel, after leaving her comfortable home, and alarm at the injuries they had to tend.

Katherine was a little less plump than when she had started nursing. 'Wasn't I helpless at first?' she remembered with an embarrassed smile. 'I'd never even made my own bed, let alone anyone else's.' At one time Amy had been afraid she would leave during her probationary period, but her friend had found the resolve to persevere. Edmond listened, fascinated.

After lunch they returned to the easy chairs in the drawing room. Beatrice had shown little interest in Katherine's account of her work at the hospital. Now she told their visitor how she longed to marry Charles when he came on leave, showing her a photo of her fiancé, tall and smart in his officer's uniform. 'Isn't he handsome?' she said, and Katherine smiled as she agreed.

'Katherine is engaged too,' Amy said. 'Is your young man still in the Ypres area?' she asked her friend.

'No – Laurence is on his way to the Italian Front,' she replied. 'He came on leave before he left for Italy, and that's when he proposed!'

Amy smiled. 'The weather should be better there.'

'Not necessarily,' Edmond told them. 'I gather the Front Line runs through the mountains towards the Austrian border.'

'I'm relieved to hear there's not much going on there at the moment,' Katherine said.

'It sounds like an improvement on Ypres,' said Edmond.

'I'm still on the list of nurses prepared to serve abroad,' Katherine said. 'I don't know how soon they'll send me. Some women have to leave for France at very short notice. Of course I'd love to be sent to Italy, but we can't choose.' She looked thoughtful. 'I'm competent enough to be useful now. It'll be strange to be so far from my family, though. I won't get many opportunities to go home on leave. While I'm in London I love heading home for some decent food and a rest.'

Amy was fully involved now with helping Edmond with his recovery, and looking after Beth, but for a moment she remembered her time at the hospitals in

London and in France, nursing soldiers. There had been many shocking sights but she was thankful she had done her duty there while she had the opportunity. Her delight in seeing the luckier ones make a good recovery had only been spoilt by her awareness that they would be sent back to the trenches.

Soon Amy took Katherine to the nursery. She pulled back the little blue and pink patchwork quilt and lifted Beth out of her cot. 'Hello, sweetie,' she said, kissing her daughter before passing her to Katherine.

'Oh, what a darling child!' cried her friend. 'I know how you and Edmond have struggled, after he was so badly wounded, but I can't help envying you now you're together, and with a baby too. One day I'd like to settle down with Laurence and have children. If only the war ends soon and we can do that – it would be sheer bliss!'

'Oh, yes – I do hope you get the chance before long!'

'It's what we plan, in our letters.' She passed Beth back to Amy. She looked around at the cosy nursery. 'Are you content, living with your in-laws?' she asked.

'Pa has always been kind to me, but Ma thinks Edmond could have found a wife with a higher social background.' She was, after all, only the daughter of a schoolmaster.

'I can tell you've supported Edmond through his recovery,' Katherine said. 'They must be grateful for that.'

'Yes, they are. But I don't know if Beatrice will ever really accept me.'

'Why's that?'

Amy sat in the rocking chair and began to feed Beth. 'I never told you about my activity with the Suffragettes, did I?'

'No…' Katherine's deep blue eyes stared at her in fascination.

'I daresay you won't approve.'

'I'm in favour of votes for women,' Katherine said earnestly. 'Now we're working so hard in the war and taking on some jobs men used to do, they shouldn't deny us the same rights.'

'I thought you'd agree about that,' Amy said. 'The thing is, in the summer before the war I joined some others in taking direct action. One of my friends broke into the cricket pavilion and we wrote slogans on the walls.'

'Oh, my goodness, did you?' Her eyes widened. 'Were you found out?'

'Only about a year later. I was arrested on what should have been my wedding day and sent to jail for a week.' It was the overbearing Colonel Fairlawn who had used his high rank to influence the magistrates to send her straight to prison, even though Edmond was leaving for France within days.

'Oh, Amy, how awful! I never would have guessed that you'd been in trouble with the police.' Amy was thankful to see her amused smile. 'But you must have lived it down now.'

'When I first reported to start as a VAD the matron nearly didn't accept me, because my misdemeanour had been in the local paper, but it's largely blown over, now I've done war work. A few people can't resist reminding me of my guilty past from time to time. Beatrice was to be my bridesmaid and she was horrified when she saw me arrested. I don't think she'll ever forgive me.'

'How mean of her!'

'After that we weren't able to get married till Edmond came on leave, and I think Beatrice tried to persuade him not to go through with it. She refused to be my bridesmaid.'

'How dreadful.'

'Luckily Edmond's cousin, Vicky, took her place.'

'Does Beatrice still dislike you?'

'She stays civil in front of Edmond but she's very cold towards me.'

Amy had hoped they could take a gentle walk into Larchbury, with Beth in her perambulator, but it was still very cold, so they took Katherine for a short stroll round the gardens. A chill wind was ruffling the shrubs.

'Your leg isn't quite right yet,' Katherine remarked as Amy limped along.

'No, but it's better.' It would have been more accurate to say that she was becoming accustomed to walking with a stiff, distorted ankle. In some ways it was convenient, for it encouraged Edmond to walk slowly when he was with her, so he was less tempted to overexert himself.

'You have lovely grounds here,' Katherine said, looking from the garden to the forest on the hill behind the house.

'It's less well cared for now the original gardener is away fighting,' Edmond said.

'But it's beautiful, especially in summer,' Amy said.

As they went to visit Edmond's horse, Wanderer, in his stable, they discussed the possibility of Amy having another operation to get her ankle reset.

'I might consider it, if the war is over some day.' If her operation had been hastily done it was because most of the patients in the Ypres hospital were men who had been injured in the fighting, so were a much higher priority.

She had not told Edmond that her accident had occurred while she had been trying to escape the unwelcome attentions of Captain Wilfrid Fairlawn, the colonel's son. At the time Edmond had been in the hospital, fighting for his life after being wounded. She had attempted to complain about Fairlawn's behaviour, though. Peter, Edmond's brother, was one of the officers at High Command who had pursued her allegation, but they had so far failed to bring him to justice.

Soon they went back indoors to take tea and shortbread with the others. Janet drew the blue velvet curtains in the drawing room as dusk began to fall.

Pa began asking Katherine more about her work at the hospital. Amy guessed she was being careful to avoid any alarming details. She told them of the special services and entertainments arranged for the soldiers over Christmas, and how they had blown up old rubber gloves to look like balloons.

Soon after it was time for Katherine to leave.

'I wish you could have stayed longer,' Amy said.

'I'll spend a last evening with my uncle and aunt,' she told Amy and Edmond. 'Then I'll go back to London tomorrow and begin work again the day after. We've still got a lot of casualties there.'

They were all quiet for a moment. Amy guessed that the others, like her, were wondering how much longer the Front in Flanders would remain quiet.

'Next month we have to go to London for Edmond's check-up,' Amy reminded her. 'It's not at St Luke's, but it's only a couple of miles away.'

'Do meet me if you can,' Katherine said. 'Tell me what day it is and I'll try to arrange some time off.'

'We might call on my aunt Louisa and stay overnight,' Amy said. 'She lives nearby.' It would be splendid to see her friend while they were there.

The young women embraced before Katherine set off in the car her uncle had sent for her.

'I enjoyed meeting her,' Edmond said.

'I'm glad you didn't talk much about the Front while she was here,' Amy said as they went back indoors. 'I worry so much about her young man.'

'He's in Italy now. Let's hope the fighting there won't be as intense as we saw round Ypres.'

–

Amy saw Florence less often when she was back teaching in the school. 'James asked me to thank you for your note,' Amy told her after church one Sunday. She had sent it enclosed in her own letter. 'He seemed pleased you understand him better.' She wondered if he was still managing to keep his secret diary of what he observed of life near the Front Line.

'I realise now that his work is gruelling and worthwhile,' Florence said. 'I believe he's motivated by his principles, not cowardice. I'm glad I wrote.'

Florence had invited them back after church to her family home nearby, and her father had promised to drive them back to The Beeches in time for their luncheon. They were sitting in the Clifford family's comfortable parlour, with its well-polished furniture, large bookcases and good quality piano.

Amy removed Beth's thick shawl and cuddled her as they talked.

'About Bertie,' Edmond asked Florence gently, 'did he ever tell you that if he didn't return you should find someone else to love?'

'No – he never suggested that could happen. He knew I couldn't bear to face the idea of losing him.'

'I think Bertie was too optimistic to consider the possibility,' Amy said.

'I discussed it with Amy,' Edmond said. 'Only after the Somme, though. Losing men from my unit, and losing Bertie, brought home the dangers, so I had to face the question.' He turned to Florence. 'I know he'd have wanted you to be happy,' he said earnestly. 'To honour his memory, of course, but make a new life for yourself.'

Her expression was bleak. 'I can't imagine loving anyone else,' she said.

'I understand,' Amy said, putting her arm round her. They should not expect her to transfer her affections lightly.

Florence's parents came to join them. 'You'll take a glass of sherry with us, won't you?' her father asked. He was a well-built man with thick glasses who was the local solicitor.

They accepted, and asked after Florence's sister, several years older than her, and her shopkeeper husband, who was slightly too old to have been called up.

'Is the Westholme girl still nursing in France?' Mrs Clifford asked Amy.

'Yes – Lavinia's out there. I've just had a letter from her,' Amy said. 'I haven't seen her since I left France – I do hope she comes on leave soon.'

'I suppose she's at the hospital near Arras, where you used to nurse?' Florence asked.

'She's been transferred to the large hospital at Ypres, where Edmond was treated. The weather there isn't as bitter as last year, she says.' Lavinia had been delighted at her news of Beth's birth and had sent her a coat and bonnet she had knitted.

Amy, Florence and Lavinia had all belonged to the Suffragette movement back in 1914. How long ago that seemed now, so much having happened since. Lavinia, who was a little older than they were, had been very active in the movement. Florence and Amy had admired her and stayed friends ever since. The militant activities had mainly been suspended for the duration of the war, while Suffragists concentrated on doing war work and helping refugees.

'Have you heard?' Florence asked. 'There's a bill going through Parliament called the Representation of the People Act, aiming to give women the vote!'

Mrs Clifford's eyebrows rose at the idea. Amy knew Florence's parents had not approved of her Suffragette activities. They knew their daughter had been there when Amy got into the cricket pavilion and chalked slogans, and were thankful that Florence had not taken any active part. They suspected that Lavinia might have been there, but only Amy had been caught.

'Yes – wouldn't that be wonderful!' Amy said. 'Do you think they'll approve it?'

As they drank their sherry they discussed the topic for a while longer, with Florence's parents reluctant to accept that such an event could happen. Then Mr Clifford drove them back to The Beeches.

Chapter Three

London, February

Edmond's check-up was scheduled for a Saturday in the middle of February. He would be seen at the hospital in mid-afternoon, so they arranged to spend the night at Aunt Louisa's little house in west London. From there they could easily visit St Luke's hospital, where Amy had once worked, to see Katherine. Then they could take a cab to the hospital where Edmond had been nursed when he had first arrived back from Ypres.

They offered to go by train but Pa insisted on driving them to Aunt Louisa's. Amy had carefully packed everything Beth might need, thankful that she was a robust baby, likely to adapt well to the journey. Happily the weather was milder now.

Katherine telephoned them the night before. 'I've been sent to help at another hospital nearby for a week or two,' she told them, 'but we can still meet up.' They arranged to leave their luggage at Aunt Louisa's and then meet Katherine in a little café she knew for lunch.

They set out with Pa early in the morning and he dropped them off at Aunt Louisa's house. She greeted them delightedly and made the acquaintance of Beth.

'How are you, Auntie?' Amy asked.

'Fine. I'm having to work harder to keep the house in order because I can only get a maid for a few hours each week. They all seem to want to work in factories these days.' Her hair was fading from golden to grey, like Mother's. 'I've joined one of those Working Parties now to knit comforts for the troops.'

Aunt Louisa went on to ask Edmond about his recovery. She had always liked him. Back in the summer of 1914, which seemed so distant now, Amy and her mother had been visiting Auntie at the seaside when she and Edmond had met, having previously known each other only as children. On that momentous day shortly before the outbreak of war they had first begun to fall in love.

'I hope you don't mind that we're meeting a friend for lunch,' Amy said. It would save her aunt the trouble and expense of providing all their meals. She seemed content as they would have the evening together.

Aunt Louisa suggested she looked after the baby while they went out to lunch. Soon they were sitting in the little café, between tables occupied by families, couples and uniformed servicemen. Katherine joined them and they ordered some meat pie from the limited range of dishes available.

'Where've you been sent to work?' Amy asked her friend.

'The hospital in Chelsea, where they have the pensioners. Several of their nurses are off sick at present.'

Amy remembered the problems there were with keeping civilian hospitals well-staffed as well as the ones for war casualties.

Katherine undid her tweed coat but kept on her attractive hat with a feather.

'You're not in uniform!' Amy said. 'Have you wangled the whole day off?'

'I'm on nights,' Katherine said, yawning.

'Heard any more about serving abroad?' Edmond asked her.

'No. I imagine they'll send me if the fighting begins in earnest again. I've heard from Laurence recently, though. He's settling in well in northern Italy. The Front is quiet at the moment and he's with the reserve troops, not up in the mountains.' She showed them a picture of a smiling young officer with a dark moustache. As always, Amy was anxious for her friend's young man abroad.

When their meal arrived it was tasty though less plentiful than sometimes, now there were shortages. Amy enjoyed it, while half distracted wondering what the doctor would say that afternoon. She had the impression Edmond was making a good recovery, but she worried that he would never recover fully from the damage to his lung.

'I'll need to go back to my aunt's and feed Beth again before we go on to the hospital,' Amy said. They just had time to finish their portions of sponge pudding.

'Why don't we meet here again tomorrow, and bring Aunt Louisa?' Edmond proposed. 'Will that suit you, Katherine? We'll bring Beth too.'

They checked the café would be open the following day, which was Sunday, and Katherine set off back to her hostel.

Edmond hailed a passing cab.

'We could walk back to Auntie's,' she objected.

'I know – we'd just about have time – but I don't want to arrive at the hospital looking tired out,' he said.

Aunt Louisa was happy with the arrangement to take lunch out the following day.

–

After Amy had fed Beth they took another cab to the hospital and followed the signs to the clinic where Edmond was to be examined. He looked unconcerned, but he must surely be at least as anxious as she was that all was well, or at least as good as it could be.

Soon the consultant was examining him. His thin chest was still misshapen where debris from the shell had hit him, but the bruising had disappeared now and the scars were fading.

The doctor sounded his chest. 'You've made good progress,' he said, looking at him seriously through his glasses. 'My colleague, Mr Westholme, has put your chest in order very competently. I'll get them to take an X-ray to confirm that nothing more needs doing, and send it to your local doctor, when I have it.'

'Thank you!' Edmond looked at his most perky.

'However,' the consultant went on with a stern expression, 'the capacity of your right lung is significantly reduced. You'll always have a degree of disability, and will be prevented from undertaking any strenuous activity.'

'My wife takes good care of me,' Edmond said. 'She used to be a VAD nurse. She's making sure I get fresh air and exercise.'

The doctor smiled at Amy. 'He certainly looks as though he's been well looked after,' he said.

'Will I be fit enough to go back to Cambridge in the autumn?' Edmond asked urgently.

'As an undergraduate?' He looked dubious.

'I'll go with him and make sure he gets good meals and enough rest,' Amy said.

'He'll certainly need some support. Well now, Lieutenant Derwent, I can't make any promises. When would you need to apply for your place?'

'In the spring.'

'We'll make you another appointment around Easter time and see if you're fit enough.'

Amy's spirits were lifted, but only up to a point. As she sat waiting with him outside the X-ray room she had a disturbing vision of Edmond setting off determinedly for university whether or not he was sufficiently recovered.

–

Aunt Louisa had managed to acquire a chicken for dinner. 'I had to beg the butcher for one,' she said. 'I told him that it's for a wounded war hero.'

She had prepared it with some cabbage and turnips, and they enjoyed a merry meal. Afterwards they sat in Auntie's tiny parlour and played some card games. Amy fed Beth before going to bed just before ten, as she and Edmond usually did. Her aunt had borrowed a cradle from a neighbour and Beth was soon sleeping there contentedly in their room.

Edmond followed Amy wearily into bed and for a few moments they lay there drowsily in each other's arms. Then suddenly there were loud noises: the sound of aircraft, followed by gunfire.

'A raid!' Edmond cried and they rushed to the window and peered out at searchlights and aircraft in the distance. 'I think they're approaching from the south.'

Beth woke up and began to cry.

There was a knocking at their bedroom door. 'Come down to the basement at once!' Aunt Louisa cried shrilly.

Amy slipped her arms into her wrap and scooped up Beth in her blanket. Edmond followed them as Aunt Louisa, in curlers and a dressing gown and holding a candle, led them down to the ground floor. Edmond held Beth while Amy negotiated the rickety steps down to the cramped cellar. As her aunt lit more candles Amy could make out sacks of coal, a rack of bottles and a crate of root vegetables. They could still hear the sound of aircraft.

'I've never heard them this close before,' Aunt Louisa said. She found Amy an old chair and settled in the other one herself. Edmond held the dark curtain to one side and tried to peer upwards through the tiny window.

'Come away from there!' Auntie said.

'Yes – don't take any risks!' Amy echoed. She remembered occasionally seeing one of the sinister great Zeppelin airships passing in the distance when she had been working in London.

Edmond sat down on one of the coal sacks. 'I read that the Huns sometimes try to hit one of the main stations now,' he said.

'But our planes are attacking the Zeppelin,' Amy said. Beth was settling again in her arms.

'The Germans don't use Zeppelins any more,' Edmond told her. 'Lately they've been flying Gotha bombers.' She remembered now: it had been in the newspapers.

'Our airmen got some better ammunition,' he went on. 'They started hitting the Zeppelins so they burst into flame.' In the dim light there was a grin on his face.

Amy stared at him. 'You're not usually so bloodthirsty.'

'Dropping bombs is worse than fighting in the trenches,' he said. 'Even if they're aiming for the docks they often hit civilians. Women and children get killed.'

The noise was growing louder still. For a moment Amy wished she could actually watch the battle between the planes.

'Heavens!' cried Auntie. 'It sounds as though they're almost overhead.'

Beth began whimpering.

Suddenly an enormous explosion rang in their ears and made the house shake. A metal bucket and a cake tin fell off a shelf, their clatter barely noticeable in the racket. Beth was crying now but at first the others were all too shocked to speak.

'That sounded very near here,' Aunt Louisa said, trembling.

Amy coughed; the air seemed full of dust. The sound of the explosion was still ringing in her ears, but she could also make out the noise of the planes and gunfire.

She cuddled Beth and kissed her, trying to calm her.

'Poor darling,' Edmond said. 'Not seven weeks old and she's caught in a raid.'

Soon Beth was settling again.

'There'll be casualties,' Amy said. 'They'll take some of them to St Luke's, and perhaps to the hospital where Katherine's working now. She'll be on duty. I really should go along to help.'

'You'll do no such thing,' her aunt protested. 'The raid is still on. Remember you're a mother now and that's where your duty lies.'

Amy held Beth close. Auntie was right, but all the same… She could picture the wreckage in the streets, like in Arras or Ypres.

Gradually the sound of the aeroplanes diminished. When they felt certain the raid was over they went back upstairs to bed. Amy blew out the candle and held the curtain to one side. In the distance a building was on fire. A fire engine drove past, its bell ringing loudly.

She went to bed but found it hard to sleep.

–

A little before first light she fed Beth. 'I'm going along to see where the bomb fell and offer my help,' she told Edmond.

'Then I'm coming with you,' he said, getting out of bed.

'You don't need to come – I'm the one who's trained!'

'I've given first aid to wounded men.' He started to get dressed.

Her aunt, still in her dressing gown, passed her on the landing and tried to persuade them not to go.

'We have to, Auntie. If there are lots of casualties they'll need extra help.'

She gave in and agreed to look after Beth.

They put on their coats and went out into the chill grey morning. There was a smell of cordite, and dust and smoke were visible, perhaps from half a mile away. They set off in that direction, Amy limping and Edmond plodding beside her.

A young man approached on his bicycle. 'They've hit the hospital!' he cried.

'Which hospital?'

'The one with the pensioners.'

Amy tried to walk faster. 'That's where Katherine's working. She'll be in the thick of treating the wounded.'

As they approached the smoke they could see wreckage in the street. It looked as though one side of the hospital had been demolished. There were ambulances and a fire engine nearby, and she could see doctors and nurses stooping to tend casualties who were lying on stretchers in front of the hospital.

Amy remembered that she had wanted to watch the raid as a spectacle. 'It looks quite dreadful,' she said guiltily. 'It's hours since the bomb fell and they're still picking people out of the wreckage.' She had seen men with terrible injuries in Flanders but she had not witnessed the aftermath of a raid within hours of its taking place. The fact that the stricken area was in London, close to where her aunt lived, made it even more shocking.

As they drew nearer they could see piles of rubble, broken doors and fixtures, and shattered glass. Men in the uniform of orderlies were carrying patients on stretchers towards an ambulance. Some victims were sitting by the roadside, mostly on chairs or a bench, huddled under blankets, some of them still trembling with shock. They would be ones with minor injuries, waiting for treatment, Amy reasoned. She looked around but could not see Katherine; probably she was nursing other patients inside the remains of the building.

She approached a young woman wearing the cape and hat of a VAD nurse. 'I'm trained as a VAD,' she told her. 'I've come to help.'

'Come and see sister.'

'I've seen service in Flanders,' Edmond said. 'I can do first aid.'

The sister looked weary and was pleased to see them. 'Go and help the group with minor injuries,' she told them, furnishing them with a basket of dressings.

The group with lesser injuries included pensioners and hospital staff. Amy was relieved Katherine was not among them. She began to pass from casualty to casualty, assessing their state. Towards the middle of the group was an elderly man whose pallor alarmed her. He was holding a piece of bandage to a wound on his arm and she could see that it had become saturated with blood.

'Sister!' she cried. 'This man needs urgent attention.'

Sister asked a senior nurse to examine him. She called for a stretcher and sent the injured man off to an ambulance. 'We're sending severe cases to St Luke's,' she said.

Amy rejoined Edmond who was still passing along the row of patients, checking that no-one else needed emergency attention. It was easy to understand that the first response to the disaster could be chaotic, and how severe cases might be missed, especially at night. They chatted to the casualties, who seemed encouraged by their arrival.

'Are you a nurse?' an old man asked her.

'Of course she is! Can't you tell by the way she checks us over?' replied another man before Amy had the chance to reassure them that she was qualified to help.

Then they got to work. Edmond went ahead, cleaning wounds with antiseptic, then Amy dressed them carefully. Sometimes they asked one of the regular nurses if the patient might have medication to relieve the pain.

A young nurse had splinters of glass in her leg.

'I've got a friend who's working here,' Amy said. 'She's called Katherine and she's been sent here from St Luke's. Do you know if she's working on one of the wards inside?' By now she should have gone off duty, but in the emergency she would have been required to stay.

'Katherine? I don't know her. I can't tell you, I'm afraid. They've been deciding if the hospital is still structurally sound, and it seems some of the wards can still be used. It was the north-east wing that was hit.'

'I hope they shot down the buggers!' cried the man sitting next to her. 'Sorry, ladies, excuse me for using that word, but those Huns don't deserve to live.'

They went on from patient to patient until they had examined nearly all the casualties. Edmond was working hard but Amy was growing anxious that he would overtire himself. 'It's time to take a rest,' she said, leading him to a space on a bench. Reluctantly he sat down next to an old soldier. Amy saw the man offering Edmond a cigarette and reminded him that he was not to smoke. Soon Edmond was telling the man how he had become injured at Ypres.

There was the sound of concerned voices behind Amy. Another two severely injured victims had been pulled out of the rubble, one of them a child. As soon as she had finished her allotted task she went and helped tend to them so that they were ready to be taken off by ambulance.

At last an orderly brought out some mugs of tea. 'Take a break, Nurse!' the sister told Amy. She took a mug for herself and one for Edmond, sugared them, and joined him. He shuffled along the bench so she could sit down.

'This was a major raid,' Edmond said. He turned to his new-found friend. 'Do you know if there were any fatalities?'

'I gather there were – among the staff, and the poor children of one of them, who were living here.'

'Remember what I was telling you,' Edmond said to Amy grimly, 'even children aren't safe any more.'

She had experienced a feeling of pride at helping in the crisis, but now it faded into gloom at the losses.

Along the pavement opposite, a well-dressed family were walking purposefully, probably on their way to church. They paused to stare at the stricken hospital before continuing more slowly, as though distressed at the plight of the casualties.

Soon the sister walked briskly over to where Amy and Edmond were sitting. 'Thank you, both, you've been a great help. We'll send off the group with minor injuries soon. They'll be fitted in somehow at St Luke's for now, or in emergency accommodation if they don't need a bed.' She paused to take a gulp from her mug of tea.

Amy stood up to speak to her. 'I've got a friend called Katherine working here,' she said. 'Katherine Harris – plumpish with dark hair. She's been sent over from St Luke's. Do you happen to know what ward she's on?'

The sister's smile had disappeared. *I'm being foolish*, Amy thought, *they're not going to give her a break to meet me, especially not when they're dealing with an emergency. Oh, and we were going to meet her for lunch – I don't suppose there's much chance of that. She might be off duty by then, but she'll be exhausted.*

'Katherine Harris, you say?'

'Yes, that's her.'

The sister took her arm. 'Nurse, I'm extremely sorry to tell you, but she died in the raid. She was killed outright – there was nothing anyone could do.'

44

Amy swayed and Edmond got up to catch her other arm.

'That's simply dreadful, Sister,' he said.

'No!' Amy cried, dizzy with shock.

The sister went on standing with them while Amy tried to come to terms with what had happened. She felt wretched and weak but tried to control her reaction; she must not become hysterical. Hadn't the sister enough to deal with, without having to prop up a grieving young woman?

'Your friend was crushed by some masonry,' the sister said. 'Her neck was broken.'

Amy clutched at Edmond. 'Have you notified her family?'

'Yes, of course, a telegram has been sent. It was all very distressing.'

'Where is Katherine now?' she ventured.

'In the morgue… Do you want to see her?'

'Yes.'

Edmond went with her as one of the VADs led her into the main wing of the hospital, still standing, though some areas were roped off. Concerned-looking men were assessing the damage, as though deciding whether parts of the hospital needed to be demolished. As she continued, Amy barely noticed the corridors they passed on their way to the morgue, which was unusually full. Katherine's pitiful remains were shown her. Her eyes were closed and, were it not for the bruising and the strange angle of her head, she looked as though she might be sleeping.

'I can't believe it!' Amy cried.

Edmond held her tightly. 'I'm so sorry, darling. She was a fine young woman.'

She stood there for a while longer, trying to wipe away tears that would not stop flowing.

'Had we better be getting back to Beth and your aunt?' he said.

'Beth – oh, goodness – she's due a feed!'

They hurried out of the hospital. An ambulance was just driving off.

Amy limped along as best she could with Edmond, as though in a dream. 'I can't accept it's happened!' she said. 'I was so worried she would lose her young man in a battle in Italy. She never even made it abroad as a nurse. How could she get killed herself, here, in London?'

Chapter Four

After learning of Katherine's death none of them had any inclination to go out to lunch. Auntie served them the remains of the chicken, but no-one had much appetite.

Auntie was absentminded and nervous. 'Look at that crack down my parlour wall!' she said.

It was a fine crack, barely perceptible. 'Do you think the bomb did that?' Amy asked.

'Yes – remember how the house shook as it landed!' She sniffed. 'I shouldn't grumble, I suppose. The houses nearer to the blast will have much worse damage.'

'Yes – there are lots of windows missing, and some chimney stacks have come down.'

'You'd better have a builder look at your wall and patch it up, just in case it's unsafe,' Edmond said.

When Pa arrived to collect them they were at least able to tell him the good news of Edmond's encouraging report from the hospital, but the loss of the dedicated young nurse hung over them.

'I must write to her parents,' Amy said when she arrived back at The Beeches. 'And to her uncle and aunt, as I've met them.'

During the days that followed the weekend with Aunt Louisa, the memory still resonated, with its shocking end.

Katherine's parents lived in Kent, and two weeks later Pa drove them over there to attend her funeral. Amy had to feed Beth discreetly in the car and leave her with Pa while she and Edmond attended the service. She had managed to fit into a dress she had worn when mourning Bertie, and Edmond wore his uniform. It was a moving occasion, attended by several of the staff from St Luke's, some of them nurses who Amy had once worked with. She gathered that Laurence was in northern Italy with his unit, unable to obtain leave.

Afterwards she assured Katherine's family how valuable her work had been, and how she would miss her.

'It seems the planes that came over that night were larger than the Gothas,' her uncle said, his brow wrinkling. 'They used a new type of large bomb.'

'So I read,' Edmond said.

Amy had heard that too. It was not much consolation to know that only the one aircraft had inflicted losses.

'Another Gotha attacked the following night,' Katherine's uncle went on. 'It hit St Pancras station and lots of people were killed.'

They stayed a little longer. Amy still felt numb when she remembered Katherine's smile as she had talked of her plans for her future with Laurence. They travelled back to The Beeches, sick at heart.

Next day she went to Sebastopol Terrace to see Mother, who had received a fretful letter from Aunt Louisa. 'She's nervous about the crack in her wall,' she told Amy, scratching her head, 'although her builder says it's not in a dangerous state. And she says she doesn't sleep well at night now from fear of another raid.'

'Poor Auntie!'

'So we've invited her here to stay,' Mother went on. 'We've got enough space.'

'How long for?'

'Till the end of the war, I suppose.'

So a few days later Aunt Louisa arrived at Amy's parents' little house, with the most essential of her belongings. 'I feel much safer here,' she told the others.

When Edmond's X-ray was ready it confirmed the consultant's view that his lung was mending as well as could be hoped.

The memory of the sudden loss of her friend continued to disturb Amy.

–

Florence was attending lacemaking classes, run by Madame Rousseau, one of the group of Belgian refugees they knew. Amy and Florence had been part of the team helping them after they had first fled to Britain in 1914. Now Amy began going with her friend to the classes in Wealdham. She looked forward to their Saturday outings, with Florence helping her get on and off the train. Edmond was content to mind Beth.

One Saturday in early March Florence phoned to say she had a bad cold and would rather stay at home.

'I'd still like to go,' Amy said. She was getting a little more confident at walking, and Madame Rousseau lived near Wealdham station. Pa drove her to Larchbury station for the early afternoon train, and arranged to meet her as usual when she returned on the train that arrived at about half past four.

She passed a pleasant afternoon improving her skills, manipulating the bobbins carefully to move the strands of cotton around the pins according to the pattern. She loved watching the intricate design gradually appearing. She chatted happily to the other woman who was learning the process. Madame Rousseau was stout and grey-haired, and her black-haired daughter, Yolande, looked grown up now. These days most of the younger Belgian men had joined up to return to Flanders to fight the enemy, and the women and children were becoming more settled in Wealdham.

Madame Rousseau always refused to let Amy and Florence pay for their lessons. 'You're making progress, I can see that,' she told Amy. She spoke English with only a faint accent now.

'I want to make a panel of lace for a dress for Beth's christening,' Amy told her. 'Goodness, is that the time? The afternoon has rushed past. I must go and catch my train back.'

–

It was cool and cloudy as she walked the short distance to the station, thankful she was around a mile away from the river, with only a faint whiff of the foul air around the factories. She took her place on the usual platform. The stationmaster was walking along, speaking to the few waiting passengers. 'Where are you going, Miss?'

'Larchbury.'

'They've just phoned from up the line. The train's broken down. They're sending another one, but it'll be a good half hour getting here. You might like to go in the waiting room.'

She retreated there, with another two women who were engaged in conversation and paid little attention to her. She took out the scrap of lace she had completed, admiring its even pattern. Edmond would be interested to see it.

She wondered if she should make a telephone call to The Beeches to tell them she was delayed. But the train had been late before, and Pa had not minded waiting. When it was due she went out on to the platform.

'It'll be a while longer,' the stationmaster told her when she had been waiting for several minutes.

'Perhaps I should phone to say I'll be late.'

'Better not leave the platform. I'm not exactly sure how long it'll be.'

It would not do to miss it. She waited, sometimes pacing awkwardly along the platform, wishing she had phoned when she had first heard it would be late. The other women were complaining about the delay.

When they finally heard the approaching train she had been waiting for over an hour. She climbed into a second class carriage as best she could, hanging on to the door, and sat down. Poor Pa, if he had been waiting all this time. The other women got into her carriage, but alighted at Alderbank.

At last she reached Larchbury, as dusk was falling. She gave up her ticket to the collector and went outside, but there was no sign of Pa or the car. She remembered vaguely that besides meeting her train he had to collect Beatrice from a friend's house.

There was the sound of another train arriving from the opposite direction.

'Mrs Derwent?' The stationmaster had recognised her and followed her outside. 'Your father-in-law was waiting, but we told him the train was delayed. He had to go off on another errand, and said if he wasn't back you were to take a cab.'

'Thank you.' As she made for the solitary cab a woman hailed it and it drove off.

Amy stood wondering what to do. She could telephone Edmond, but she did not want him to rush out and tire himself walking to the station and back. She could wait for the cab to return, or walk back by herself.

It's already past the time to feed Beth, she thought. She turned up the collar of her coat and set off along the High Street towards The Beeches. It was dark now, and before long she was regretting her decision. Her walking was slow and tiring, and it was over a mile to the driveway to The Beeches.

Behind her she could hear footsteps, a man's footsteps, she judged, determined not to look round. In front of her the road was empty in the early evening. *If only the street lights were on*, she thought now it was getting quite dark, but the blackout had been extended beyond London. And when she reached the turning for The Beeches the narrow road would be even less likely to have familiar passers-by.

The footsteps seemed to be getting closer. Echoing from the buildings, they were heavy steps of a large man. She tried to hurry but it was no use; she could not reach any speed with her bad leg. She felt her heart beating as unwelcome thoughts invaded her mind. A man was pursuing her, and she was suddenly paralysed with fear, remembering her ordeal in Ypres the previous summer.

She had been on her way to the nurses' hostel there when he had come out of a bar and seized her, urging her to spend the evening with him. She shivered at the memory of Wilfrid Fairlawn's hot, beery lips and his hand ranging over her breasts.

She remembered breaking free and running through the rubble-strewn street with his lofty figure pursuing her. Then she had lost her footing and sprawled among the loose stones, landing heavily on her ankle. He had started to run towards her, and it was probably only the approach of a vehicle that had made him give up.

But now I'm in Larchbury, she told herself. Can I call on someone? But my parents and uncle and Florence all live in the other direction.

The streets are familiar, she tried to reassure herself, and any minute now I'll meet someone I know.

It did not help. The memory of that evening, when she had been at Wilfrid's mercy, made her feel clammy and faint.

Back then he had left her in pain, alone in the dark street, unable to pull herself to her feet. Only the timely arrival of a pair of nuns had brought about her rescue. They had summoned an ambulance and she had been taken back to the hospital, desperate with worry that the fall might cause her to miscarry her baby.

Now, in Larchbury, as the footsteps pounded behind her, her feet were barely doing her bidding. What if she lost her footing and fell?

The steps were catching her up, as though the man was determined to reach her. Now he was right behind her.

'Mrs Derwent?' She stopped, alarmed at the man's voice, trying to think who it might be.

'It's me, George.'

She turned and looked at the man, in his private's uniform. There was just enough light remaining to make out his friendly, familiar face: of course, he was the former gardener from The Beeches, who they had last seen in the autumn, when he was on leave.

'Are you all right, Mrs Derwent? I didn't mean to startle you.' His voice was deep but gentle.

'Yes, thank you. How nice to see you.' She struggled to speak to him normally.

'I'm on leave again. They can't usually spare men now there might be a major offensive. They only allowed it because my cousin's recently died near Passchendaele.'

'I'm very sorry to hear you've lost him,' she said, stricken. 'Did he live with your relatives in Wealdham?'

'Yes – I've spent most of my leave with them. But Mum and my sisters are back here in Larchbury now – they managed to find a cottage we could afford. I'm thankful to be back. I've just had a pint in the Station Tavern with an old school friend who's been invalided out of his battalion.'

Amy remembered the tiny, grimy house near the factories in Wealdham that they had visited in the autumn. The smoky air had given Edmond his relapse. How glad she was that George's mother and sisters no longer had to live there.

'How's Mr Edmond getting on?'

'He's much better, thanks.' She was still trembling a little from her fright.

Just then she heard the noise of a car coming down the road towards them. As it slowed down she recognised their family car.

'Hello, Amy,' Pa said, getting out. 'Sorry I wasn't at the station to meet you. Is that you, George? How are you doing?'

They exchanged news for a minute more, then Pa opened the door for Amy. 'Are you all right?' he asked her.

'Yes, thank you.' She had not quite recovered from her scare.

'You shouldn't have tried walking back on your own. Well, it was good to see George. He's a much better gardener than his brothers.'

His younger brother, Henry, had taken over for a while before he also had left to fight. Then Joe, the youngest, had taken his place.

Amy struggled to compose herself as Pa drove her back to The Beeches. Why had she become so nervous, simply walking through Larchbury? The memory of Wilfrid Fairlawn's manhandling of her in Ypres was haunting her still.

I must overcome this, she reasoned. *I was becoming independent when I was nursing in London, sometimes walking back after dark by myself to the hostel. I can't let my experience with Wilfrid leave me frightened to be alone.*

–

Edmond was interested that George was back in Larchbury, though only for a few days. *I must try to see him before he goes back to France,* he thought.

Amy was quiet that evening, almost as though something was troubling her. 'Was the walk back becoming too much for you?' he asked her.

'No – well, I was becoming a little tired, I suppose.'

She had been by herself after dark, he realised, but it was not like Amy to be upset by that.

On the Sunday he went to speak to George after church. 'Let's go and take a pint together in The Farmers,' he suggested to the young man. It was the inn in the middle of the village.

He bought them glasses of beer. 'What happened to your cousin?' he asked. So far as he knew there was little activity at the Front. Perhaps the man had caught one of the fevers going round.

'It was an accident.' George's face was sombre. 'You know what the roads are like out there. He was travelling in a wagon when it turned over and he was thrown out.'

'What a dreadful waste of his life!'

'At least it was quick.'

Another pointless death, Edmond thought, but now he himself was not fit to fight he felt he must at least talk to men on leave, allowing them to unburden themselves of disturbing memories.

When they had finished their pints he went to buy another round.

The bartender looked dubious and went out to the back, returning with Mr Spencer, the innkeeper.

'Don't you know you're not supposed to treat another man to a drink now?' he asked sternly.

'Sorry, I'd forgotten.' It was a wartime regulation, intended to discourage drunkenness. The beer was watered down too, Edmond had heard. Did Mr Spencer know he had already treated George to one drink, he wondered. 'May I just buy George one? He's a soldier on compassionate leave.'

'Very well, Lieutenant Derwent, just this once.'

He and George sat companionably discussing the trenches. They were still waterlogged, George told him, and lately they had become infested with insects. The men had got trench foot, open sores and fungal infections that could even lead to gangrene. Edmond listened patiently.

They changed the subject when other customers came and sat nearby. George asked after Beth and he was pleased to tell of her progress.

Pa soon arrived, to drive him home, and they both shook George's hand and wished him good fortune as he prepared to return to the Front.

As Pa drove him back Edmond's thoughts were elsewhere. They had recently received a letter from Peter, with mention of his work for High Command, investigating disciplinary matters. *But that's not all he does*, he thought, recalling his brother's revelation at Christmas about his secret visit through a tunnel to occupied Belgium. He and Peter had not confided this mission to anyone else in the family. *What's he really doing now*, Edmond thought. *Is he still undertaking clandestine activities, vital but highly dangerous?*

Soon they were joining the family for luncheon. Amy remained a little subdued at times, he found, but would not admit to anything being wrong. He supposed she must still be upset at the sudden loss of Katherine.

Chapter Five

Flanders, March to April

For a few weeks in the depth of winter Charles Shenwood had been billeted in a house, but now the brief respite of living within four sheltering walls was over. The privates had taken turns in maintaining the trench, while those not on duty had sometimes managed to find barns to sleep in.

The trench had not improved in his absence. There was the familiar sickly smell of mud. The cold seemed to gnaw into his bones. There were two beds in his dugout but for the moment he seemed to have it to himself, though another officer was expected. The men, if they were lucky, would be able to sleep between their night time duties in funkholes in the trench wall.

The sound of artillery was noticeable; it seemed the spring offensive would begin in earnest one day soon. It was late afternoon, and the men were beginning to return from inspecting and repairing the barbed wire. Charles had little time to distribute his few belongings around his bunk. He took Beatrice's framed photo from his knapsack and positioned it carefully on the crudely made shelf. With her beautiful face smiling at him he felt slightly more settled.

The gas curtain fell back at the entrance as another officer came in and saluted, followed by an orderly carrying his kit.

'First Lieutenant Bentley reporting for duty, Sir!' The red-haired officer saluted him.

Charles had met him before somewhere. Probably they had both joined the battalion in 1914. 'You're back from the hospital, I gather,' he said. 'Take a seat.'

The newcomer sat on the edge of the free bed. 'Thank you for escorting me, Fletcher,' he said to the orderly. 'I can manage now.'

'Fletcher?' Charles stared at the young orderly. He had the feeling he had seen him before, too, but in some civilian capacity. 'I know you, don't I? Where have we met before?'

The orderly smiled shyly. 'At my cousin's wedding, Sir,' he replied. 'You were best man when Amy married Edmond – Lieutenant Derwent.'

'Yes, of course. I remember you – you were an usher, weren't you?' Both times, he was tempted to add, but he stopped himself from reminding the young man of the first occasion. As usher he had had the unenviable task of telling the wedding guests that the service would not take place as the bride could not, after all, attend. Poor Amy, being arrested on her wedding day.

'I know Lieutenant Derwent!' exclaimed Bentley. 'We shared a dugout for two years, till he got severely injured. Is he recovering well?'

'Yes, Sir,' said Fletcher. 'He's been very brave, and he's becoming more active now, though he'll never be fit enough to fight again.'

'That's tremendous. For a week or two we didn't know if he'd survive.'

A new recruit arrived with a mug of tea for Charles, who sent him off to fetch two more. 'Everyone well in Larchbury?' he asked Orderly Fletcher. 'Amy had a little girl, didn't she?'

'That's right, Sir. Both doing well. And I believe you are to be congratulated, Sir? I hear you're engaged to Beatrice Derwent.'

'That's correct. We became engaged at Christmas.' He still found himself beaming whenever his good fortune was mentioned. 'Heaven knows when I'll next get leave, but we'll get married just as soon as we can.'

The other mugs of tea arrived. 'Are you fully fit now, Bentley?' Charles asked.

'Much recovered, Sir,' he replied. Charles had been promoted to a higher rank than his. 'I got shrapnel in my leg at Passchendaele but I'm pronounced fit to face the enemy again now. Though I don't expect to be playing football much in the near future,' he added.

The army hospitals got men back into battle if at all possible. There was conscription now, but every man was needed.

'I'd best be getting back to the ambulance, Sir,' Fletcher said, saluting him. 'We need to return to the hospital.'

'Good to have met you again.'

As Fletcher went out the sound of the artillery was louder and they could hear the men chatting and grumbling as they crowded into the trench.

'The food here isn't too bad,' Charles told his new comrade. 'Private Barnes does the best he can with what we're given. In the summer he used nettles to flavour the meals.' By now he would be starting a fire in the trench wall. 'He makes a reasonable maconochie.'

'What, the soup?'

'No, he'll make a stew from scratch. There's not much chance of getting fresh beef, or even horsemeat, but he'll put in a tin or two of corned beef, and there'll be some winter vegetables.'

'That sounds more edible than at my last place, where it was mostly beans.' Bentley was unpacking, and there was a photograph of him with his parents.

'You got a sweetheart at home?' Charles asked him.

'No, Sir, no-one special… Your fiancée is a lovely looking young woman, if I may say so, Sir.'

'She is, isn't she? I must write to her and tell her we're back in the Line… without alarming her, of course.' He was due to receive a letter, for Beatrice wrote at least once a week. Very probably it had arrived at his old quarters after he had left.

'I managed to spend a weekend in Paris last month,' he said. 'I bought Bea a new shawl, very stylish. I feel sure she'll love it.'

His letters caught up with him a few days later. Beatrice was thrilled with the shawl he had sent her. She was concerned about his wellbeing, though when she asked after his meals her questions suggested she imagined him living in some kind of hotel. She had little real understanding of what trench warfare was like. She chatted on about a trip to London to see a school friend and visit the theatre, and told him about her new hat. The letters from his mother and elder sister were much the same. They had both assured him that Beatrice was going to make a fine addition to the family.

Occasionally he wondered about her. When Amy was mentioned he could not help remembering the occasion when Beatrice had refused to be her bridesmaid, after Edmond's first wedding day had ended so disastrously. The two young women were so different. Amy was a schoolmaster's daughter, who behaved in a refined manner but thought for herself. Bea had the traditional polish and accomplishments of a young woman brought up to be an ornament in society. She did not have modern ideas like Amy, or any inclination to take on serious war work. But when he looked at her delicate features, and the slightly coquettish smile which seemed just for him, he would not have her any other way. She was exactly the kind of feminine figure for whom they were fighting.

As he folded her letter and added it to some others, a man arrived at his dugout with a message from the major. He and Bentley were summoned to a briefing.

They and the other officers crowded round in a dugout which did the service of a makeshift office.

'The Huns are on the move!' They had all noticed that the artillery to the east was becoming louder. A spring offensive was inevitable. He had almost given up hope of a swift victory, but since they were destined to fight they must get on with it.

'Make sure all the men are prepared to move up the line as soon as orders come!' commanded the major.

They knew better than to question their orders in front of him. 'How soon do you think the Americans will start arriving?' Bentley asked as they returned to the dugout.

'I don't know,' Charles replied, deciding they could drop pretences when they were together. 'The Germans have made a treaty with Russia and stopped fighting on the eastern Front. The Huns will have reinforcements now.'

It was like a deadly version of one of those childish games, like Musical Chairs, he reflected. Each time the music stopped one of the players was eliminated. An officer friend had been killed on the Somme, and Edmond had been gravely injured at Passchendaele. If you were still in the game when the music continued, you wondered if you would stay lucky, or whether next time you would be out.

—

By the beginning of April the enemy had begun their advance and his unit was being moved elsewhere. Their guns were being hauled by horses but this time they had managed to secure a train to transport the troops.

As Charles surveyed the passing flat Flanders country-side memories of their recent attempt to defend Arras preyed on his mind. They had seen battle for a few days and once again he had lost comrades and seen others with severe wounds being despatched in ambulances. The German artillery had proved resistant to their efforts.

The train slowed down and clattered through a local station. The men were curious where they were headed. Those most aware, veterans of several journeys around Flanders, could tell they were proceeding west.

'Our Front Line's become too extended,' Charles told them. 'We'll leave some of the forward posts so we can concentrate on the most strategically important areas.' It would not do to call the move a retreat.

'Won't we go south to protect Amiens?' asked a junior officer.

'Other troops are headed there,' Bentley replied. They had heard the New Zealanders were marching towards the Somme to protect the vital railhead.

The young man wearied of his questions and took a pack of cards from his pocket. Some of the others joined him in a lively game.

Besides the valuable men with combat experience they had new recruits, some very young, many of them conscripts. Their training had been hurried. Unlike the blithe young men of 1914, they were usually aware that challenges lay ahead, but it was hard to predict how individuals would react when they suddenly found themselves in the Front Line.

Charles took out his cigarettes and most of the men lit up. He inhaled the smoke thoughtfully. Early that morning, as they marched towards the station, they had passed a military hospital. Some orderlies had been loading equipment into a vehicle. Others had been carrying stretcher cases to an ambulance, while nurses assisted the walking wounded. *They're evacuating the hospital*, he had realised.

They went on travelling west, heading towards the Channel.

–

Lavinia sat in the ambulance cab with Private Petch, the driver, for the back was filled to capacity. She and Emily took turns to sit inside with the wounded men. They had started out early that morning, and struggled along the rutted roads, through the dim, drizzly April day. There was the sound of artillery fire from a little behind them.

'This is the most vulnerable part of the journey,' Petch told her. 'The Huns hold the high ground near here and can see anything that passes along the road.'

'They won't actually target us, will they? They can see the red crosses on the vehicle.'

'They're aiming at the army vehicles, at least I hope so – they're supposed to respect hospital transport.' He was a skinny young man who had been serving for two years now and conveyed their situation in a matter-of-fact way. If he was anxious he concealed it effectively.

Evacuating their hospital had been a new challenge for Lavinia, but she knew she had better not mention it in her letters to Amy and Florence. There was panic in the air as the Germans advanced, but she suspected the British papers might not yet be revealing the gravity of the setback.

They were in a long convoy of vehicles heading westwards, anxious to make good progress because the Germans were not far behind. There was another burst of fire and the sound of shells landing nearby.

The ambulance lurched suddenly and churned into some mud. Petch strained on the wheel but the vehicle would not move properly. He swore. 'Sorry, Nurse,' he said. 'I'll have to get out and see what's wrong.'

He climbed out. The road was wide enough there for other vehicles to overtake, so at least they were not holding up the convoy.

'I'll need to change the confounded wheel,' he told her.

Alarm swept over her. Shells were still landing around them. If the Germans decided to ignore wartime conventions they were sitting ducks. She climbed out of the cab.

'I'll help you,' she said, her shoes beginning to sink into the squelchy mud.

'Can you manage?' he asked.

'Yes – I've done it before.'

She helped him ease off the damaged wheel. 'Surely we weren't hit?' she asked. The attack was coming from the other side.

'I should have been more careful to check the wheels before we started out,' he said, 'but there was such a scramble to get going this morning.'

Emily looked out of the back door. 'What's going on?' she asked, a trace of alarm in her voice.

'We're just changing the wheel,' Lavinia said, trying to keep an appearance of calm. 'Tell the men we'll be on our way again soon.'

She helped Petch position the replacement wheel. The drizzle was turning to sleet now and water was dripping down her neck. As soon as her hands were free she turned up the collar of her coat.

Army vehicles were continuing to pass. No-one seemed inclined to stop and help, and it was hard to blame them when they were under fire. Petch had to secure the new wheel now. There was a heavier burst of fire and when she looked up she was thankful that they and the ambulance were still intact.

'Let me give you a hand.' One of the other vehicles had stopped and at last another driver had taken pity on them. He took over from Lavinia, though she stayed in case they needed any further help. At last the wheel was fixed. They thanked their helper and climbed back inside the cab. Their assistant waited beside the road to be sure they were able to continue.

Petch started the ambulance and they sighed with relief as it began to get up speed. 'As soon as we've left this dangerous stretch we should stop, so I can help Emily check the men's condition,' she told him.

'Right ho, Nurse.'

Sporadic artillery fire pursued them for a while longer, but at last they were out of immediate danger and able to pull over at the side of the road. Petch lit up a cigarette.

Lavinia got out and joined Emily inside the ambulance. The most severely injured man seemed to be holding his own. They took temperatures, gave injections and passed round glasses of water. Emily was one of the nurses from the hospital near Arras who had worked with Amy a year earlier. She was a short, small-framed young woman, but she was a hard worker.

'This is the second time we've been evacuated,' said Thompson, a young recruit who had been wounded in the leg almost as soon as he had reached the Front Line. 'Are we retreating? Will the Huns take us away as prisoners of war?'

'Might be the best thing, to be out of this bloody war! Let's surrender.' Davies had a painful arm injury and was constantly complaining.

'You'll do no such thing!' Lavinia cried, shocked to hear such words.

The others were quiet, as though considering his suggestion.

'I've nursed some Germans,' Emily told them, 'and I can speak a little of the language. I've heard them talking about what happens to British prisoners. They send them to Germany in cattle trucks and treat them as slave labour. They get half a loaf of bread to last them five days.'

'Seems like we'll have to go on fighting,' said a more resolute comrade.

Another started singing '*Pack Up Your Troubles in Your Old Kitbag*', and soon someone was joining in.

Lavinia exchanged glances with Emily. She had never before heard defeatist talk. 'I'll relieve you now,' she said. 'Would you rather ride in the cab or squash in here?'

'I'll go in the cab, for some fresh air.'

'I'm just going for a quick word with Petch,' Lavinia said. She returned to the cab through the drizzle.

'Can you spare a cigarette?' she asked him.

He lit it for her and she drew on it gratefully.

'What happened to your motorbike?' he asked her.

'I had to leave it in Ypres.' She sighed. 'I'm hoping one of the men who isn't assigned to escort any wounded will drive away on it for me, instead of taking a train. If he doesn't end up at the same place as us, he'll need a day's leave so he can ride it over to wherever I am, and take a bus or train back.'

'I suppose that might work, when we find a new hospital.'

'Do you think you'll reach Cassel by dusk?' she asked him. 'I'd like our dangerously ill man to see a doctor as soon as possible.'

'I'll do my best, Nurse.'

There was no time to lose. She took another couple of puffs of her cigarette as she walked to the back of the ambulance, then stamped on the remainder and went to take over from Emily. Once they had changed places the ambulance started again.

Chapter Six

Larchbury and Flanders, April

Towards the end of March the bitter news came that the fighting had started again. Edmond had the impression the Germans were gaining ground rapidly.

They celebrated Easter. 'Just think, last year we were at Béthune,' Edmond said. They had both been serving in France and had managed to get leave to spend together.

'What a delightful weekend that was!' Amy said.

He agreed that it had been a memorable break, until, as they returned to their stations on the Monday, they had seen men on the move towards Arras for the next outbreak of fighting.

In the week following this Easter, Edmond had his next appointment at the hospital. He would be seen in the early afternoon.

Amy accompanied him again, less buoyant than usual, disturbed by the memory of their final meeting with Katherine. Pa drove them to London and they grabbed a quick lunch in a café before keeping the appointment.

Edmond was seen by the same doctor as before and tried to remain calm as the specialist applied the stethoscope to his chest.

'You're making progress,' came the verdict.

'I can tell that!' he said gleefully. 'I can walk much further now without becoming breathless. Reassure my wife I'll be well enough to resume my studies at Cambridge in the autumn.'

The doctor smiled behind his glasses. 'I can tell you're impatient to be active...'

'I certainly am. With so many others at the Front it's especially frustrating to be sitting around at home.'

Amy looked at him anxiously.

'Of course I love being at home with you, dearest, but I need an occupation,' he pressed.

'I daresay you'll cope with university if you take things calmly,' the doctor said.

'I'll apply as soon as we get home,' he told Amy and Pa as they left the hospital.

Aunt Louisa had given them her key and asked them to take a look at her house, so they drove along her street. Her little home was chilly but looked just as it had before.

'She was afraid it might get damaged in another raid,' Amy said. 'She can't stop thinking about that night.'

'I think there are fewer raids now,' Pa said.

–

One day not long afterwards Pa took Edmond to Cambridge, to see the Principal of his College about resuming his studies. He had proposed making the journey by himself, but it meant travelling across London between trains and would be tiring.

'You're not quite well enough for that, son,' Pa had said and insisted on driving him there and back. They set out the day before the appointment and spent the night in a hotel.

On the day of his interview, Amy was at The Beeches, wondering how it was progressing. In late afternoon she was sitting in the drawing room with Beth, singing her a lullaby before bedtime. Beatrice came in and smiled at them; she was captivated by her pretty little niece. Now she reached out and took her into her arms to sing her a nursery rhyme in her sweet soprano, as she sometimes did. Today it was '*Ride a Cock-horse to Banbury Cross*', Beatrice's favourite, and Beth gazed at her as she sang it.

'Edmond loves that song too,' Amy said. 'He once told me he remembered you singing that to him when he was very young.'

The two young women exchanged smiles, in an unusually tender moment.

Soon it was time for Amy to put her daughter to bed. She left Beth to sleep in her cot and went to her bedroom to tidy herself before dinner, thankful she could wear her normal clothes again.

She joined her in-laws in the drawing room. 'Edmond's late back from Cambridge,' she said.

'If they're not here soon I'll tell Cook to serve our meal,' Ma said.

Beatrice was rereading her latest letter from Charles. Her light green dress suited her greenish eyes and glossy chestnut hair.

'How is he?' Ma asked. 'It's a while since he wrote, isn't it?'

'Yes – I was feeling quite neglected. But he says they've been very busy. They've moved on to a different area. He says morale is high in his unit and the trenches are beginning to dry out now the weather is milder.'

Amy suspected that, like most soldiers, Charles was making light of the challenges there when writing to his womenfolk. The newspapers were clear now that the Germans were advancing. When she went into Larchbury she would see people crowding round the Casualty Lists displayed outside the post office.

Voices came from the direction of the entrance hall. 'They're back!' cried Ma. 'I'll tell Cook to serve dinner in ten minutes.'

Edmond came in to greet them, before smartening up for dinner.

'How did it go?' Amy asked a few minutes later as he joined her at the table.

He smiled. 'For a moment the Principal seemed to have quite forgotten who I was,' he said. 'Then he asked me if I was certain I'm well enough to continue as a student, and I assured them I'm much improved, and I'll have you there to support me. Then they agreed I can continue with my second year of studies. There's a shortage of men there now – just ones who've failed their medical for the army or been invalided out like me.'

'You've had a long gap away,' his mother remarked as Cook brought in the tureen of soup.

'It'll be four years – sometimes it seems like a lifetime. But I've got six months to read through my first year studies, ready to take up the course again.'

'I'm so glad you're carrying on,' Amy said.

'What do you suppose you'll do afterwards?' Beatrice asked.

'I'm concentrating on metallurgy.'

'What's that?'

'It concerns metals and their alloys. I'd be happy doing some kind of engineering,' he said. 'I enjoy practical work.' He showed no sign of making any concession to his injuries.

Pa looked at him seriously. 'You'll have to consider your capabilities,' he said. 'You may never be able to do work requiring you to be very active.'

'While I'm studying I can decide,' he said, as bright and animated as he had been when Amy had first known him, and his aim had been to join the British Expeditionary Force.

Cook collected the soup plates and began bringing in dishes of vegetables.

'How have you spent your day?' Edmond asked Amy.

'It's mild enough at last to take Beth outside,' she told him. 'She loves to lie cooing in her pram beneath a tree, watching the branches waving in the breeze.' Their baby was progressing from a new-born to a little person taking an interest in her surroundings.

'We must make arrangements for Beth's christening soon,' Ma said later when they were sitting in the drawing room. 'Sometime in June or July would be best.' She and Pa were delighted with Beth, but Amy suspected Ma would have preferred them to have a boy.

'When we've chosen a date I'll speak to Uncle Arthur about it,' Amy said.

'If only I could fix a wedding day,' Beatrice said wistfully, looking at the silver framed photograph of her fiancé that she kept on top of the bureau. 'I don't imagine Charles will get much notice of when he's coming on leave. But my dress will be finished soon, so I'll be ready.'

Amy had seen her being fitted for her gown, lavishly trimmed with lace.

'I'd like Florence to be a godmother to Beth,' Amy said. 'It would be especially appropriate as she was engaged to Bertie.'

'I suppose she's a good choice,' Ma said. 'Then you can have Beatrice and Peter as the other godparents. I daresay he'll be able to get leave as he's not actually fighting.' Edmond's brother, Peter, was still working at High Command.

Edmond agreed with her choice. Amy had to accept his relatives assuming the roles, though she would have preferred to invite Lavinia to be the other godmother. She might have had difficulty obtaining leave, though.

Soon Edmond admitted to being quite tired and they went upstairs. He looked briefly into the nursery, to see his daughter sleeping contentedly, then he and Amy went to their room.

'We'll need to find somewhere to live in Cambridge,' she said, turning down the damask bedspread. After some two years apart while he had been fighting, at last they were together every night, a properly united married couple. Edmond was even sleeping better now, disturbed less often by bad dreams.

Their bedroom was comfortable but cluttered, for they liked to use it as a sitting room. There were shelves of books, their small sofa, and the carved wooden cabinet that Peter had shipped over from India for their wedding present. The room was a retreat, where they could withdraw from the rest of the family and be alone together. Even so, she longed for them to have their own home.

'We'll take a little house,' he said. 'We'll find one towards the end of the summer, one we can rent, and make sure we have everything there we need.'

'Just a modest place will do.' So long as the three of them were together it was all she asked.

'Yes, and just one servant to help you with the hardest work.'

'Perhaps a maid who calls in twice a week,' she conceded.

As he prepared for bed she considered his other plans. 'I do hope you're right, that eventually you'll be able to take up the kind of profession you always planned.'

'I'm not letting the Huns defeat me! That's how it would seem, allowing one of their shells to deflect me from my path in life,' he asserted, paying little regard to the mutilation of his chest.

'Lots of young men have had to adjust their expectations,' she reminded him as he climbed into bed. 'It's no disgrace.'

'I'm going to aim high and see what I can achieve. But if I'm prevented from pursuing a scientific career I can always help Pa run the forestry business. I know he'd like me to carry it on.'

He leant on one arm, watching her in the lamplight as she shed her clothes and pulled her smocked nightdress over her head. As she joined him in bed he reached out to take her into his arms. His lips came down on hers hungrily and his hands began to move under her garment to explore her bare flesh.

–

One fine afternoon Amy took Beth with her into Larchbury. As usual there were people crowding round the Casualty List displayed outside the post office. Families usually heard quickly by telegram if their next of kin were killed or gravely injured, but people sometimes learned from these lists of more distant relations or school friends who had been lost.

Amy noticed Mother was there; she must have stopped to look at the list when she went to the shops. Amy touched her arm and greeted her.

The Casualty List was long again and Mother was staring at it bleakly. 'Patrick Watson has been killed in action,' she said, a tear trickling down her face. 'He worked on the farm before he joined up.'

Amy put her arm round her mother. 'I know. One of his daughters used to be a pupil in Florence's class.'

'I wonder how the family will manage now, without their father.' Mother seemed to notice Beth for the first time. 'It's lovely to see you two.'

'I was planning to call in and see you.'

'Of course – I'm ready to go back to the house now.'

They had to walk past some of Patrick's family who were there, weeping. Bunches of bluebells had been left by the roadside.

They reached Sebastopol Terrace. 'Do you want to practise your piano exercises?' her mother asked her.

Amy seized the opportunity, as Mother had Aunt Louisa there to sympathise with her about the bad news. She practised on the piano for a while as her mother and aunt strolled around their garden with Beth.

Aunt Louisa came to see her in the parlour. 'Your poor mother,' she said. 'She takes it so badly when someone is killed.'

'I think she relives the day when we heard that Bertie was dead.' The Casualty Lists affected Amy too, but with Edmond and Beth to care for she was not quite so overwhelmed at the sad reminder.

At length she closed the piano lid and went out to the garden to join her mother and aunt. Mother still had Beth in her arms.

'How are you progressing?' Mother asked Amy.

'More slowly than I'd like, especially now I've Beth to care for.'

'Isn't there a good piano at The Beeches?' asked Aunt Louisa, from a deckchair.

'I don't like to inflict my feeble efforts on Mrs Derwent and Beatrice,' Amy admitted.

Mother pursed her lips, annoyed at their intolerant attitude.

Amy gave them the date of Beth's christening at the end of June.

'Wonderful!' exclaimed Aunt Louisa. 'I'll be able to attend now I'm in Larchbury.'

'Uncle Arthur's looking forward to performing the baptism,' Amy told them, sitting down in a deckchair near the flowering lilac. 'He doesn't think James will get leave.' He had sounded anxious that he had not heard from his son that week.

'Have you got a smart dress to wear for the occasion?' Mother asked. 'Shall I make you something?'

'I'm having one made by the Derwents' dressmaker,' she told her, hoping Mother would not be offended.

Discovering that Ma and Beatrice were ordering new outfits she had resolved to look her best. *I'm a Derwent now*, she told herself, *and if I want them to accept me I must aim to meet their standards.*

'Lovely, dear. We'll look forward to seeing you in something extra special.'

–

As Charles had expected, it was not long before he and his men found themselves in the Front Line again. On this particular cloudy day in April he was supervising his unit as they pounded the Germans, who retaliated with terrifying ferocity. This time they were not facing each other across No Man's Land, but on opposite banks of the Lys canal.

As usual there were casualties. Among those carrying off the wounded on stretchers was Orderly Fletcher. As the hours dragged on, Charles tried to think of Beatrice's gentle face. In her latest letter she had told him how proud she was of his bravery in facing the enemy.

Bentley had his binoculars trained on the opposite bank. 'They're bringing up some heavier artillery, Sir,' he reported.

Charles looked grimly towards the narrow stretch of pewter-coloured water and the bank beyond. 'You know what the orders are,' he said. 'We have to hold the Line, whatever happens.'

He was shocked that the land around Ypres, so costly to hold the previous year, had now been seized back by the Germans. So far as he knew, the allied divisions on the Somme were holding on to Amiens, against fierce opposition. In their own area they were fighting to hold

Hazebrouck, on another vital rail line. There had been the recent Order of the Day from Field Marshal Haig, urging them to 'fight on to the end'. The German breakthrough had brought them perilously close to the Channel ports. If the Huns reached the coast – it did not bear thinking about after three and a half years of fighting.

He helped his men to bring up fresh ammunition. All too soon the German attack intensified. Cascades of earth flew up into the air as shells landed nearby. When this operation had started there had been trees on both banks, but now most of them had been obliterated. The noise from both sides of the canal was deafening. There was the whiz of shells passing and the vibrations of them landing. How long could they go on like this?

Something landed nearby and he was thrown to the ground, deafened and rendered barely conscious.

Now his face lay against the damp earth. He struggled to grasp what was happening. The commotion around him was continuing. He tried to pull himself up, but he was dazed and could not manage it. He thought Frank Bentley was there, trying to talk to him. How could he lead his men if he could not focus his thoughts? But something was wrong with his feet, and his right leg. It wasn't just the fall, or some kind of glancing blow: he sensed it was much worse than that. There were spots in front of his eyes and he knew he was losing consciousness again.

–

James heard someone calling for medical help. No-one particularly well-qualified was nearby, and shells were raining down. Trying not to think of the danger, he headed in the direction of the fallen man. Heavens, it was Captain Shenwood. He was unconscious and his right leg looked mangled. Another officer had been pulling him by the armpits further from the fray.

'Carry on, Orderly, please,' the officer said. 'I need to stay with the men.'

James carried on dragging the captain away. He was worried that the officer's wounded leg would be further damaged as he moved him, but it was essential to get him medical help promptly. He shouted for assistance, but everyone was busy or too far away to help. Shenwood was a tall, well-built man and their progress was slow. The ground near the bank of the canal was uneven and shells were still landing around them, even behind them. Shenwood was known as a good leader, always concerned for the welfare of his men. He had to help him, in spite of the risks.

By now he should be used to evacuating the wounded under fire, but today's attack seemed especially frantic. Thanks to all the noise there was still no-one else within earshot.

Shenwood's leg was bleeding heavily and his face was drawn and very pale. When there was a moment's lull James put the captain down as gently as he could. He reached into his kit for a triangular bandage and hastily fashioned a tourniquet around Shenwood's leg. When he touched the officer's forehead it was clammy.

Another shell exploded nearby like a clap of thunder. As James was thrown to the ground he felt loose earth hit his face. He landed heavily, with a pain in his left leg. He looked urgently towards Shenwood; the captain looked no worse.

I've got to get him out of this, James thought, but when he tried to get up he fell down again.

'It's all right, Fletcher, we're here now,' said a distant voice. It was a moment before he recognised his fellow orderly. Two of them had arrived with a stretcher. Carefully they transferred Captain Shenwood on to it, while shells landed not far away.

'Thank goodness you're here,' he said. His own breathing was laboured, as small scraps of earth were lodging in his nostrils. 'Oh, God! The captain's left leg is injured as well,' James said. His boot was damaged and blood was seeping from it, though it looked less alarming than his right leg.

'Hang on, Fletcher! We'll be back for you next,' said his comrade.

'Just see to the officer.'

'You're injured too, and you were unconscious just now.'

As the others carried the captain away, James made another attempt to stand, but was still giddy. He tried to wriggle further from the danger. He took out a cloth from his kit and cleared his nostrils as best he could. He sat on the chilly ground, waiting for the others to return.

The barrage from across the canal continued. He had always hated the interminable war, but now he was horrified at the possibility that the Germans might actually reach the Channel.

–

Charles drifted in and out of consciousness, vaguely aware his legs were injured and that he was being transported to a hospital. When he woke for a while he could not quite gather his wits enough to ask the staff what was going on, but he heard talk of an operation. There was a fierce pain in his legs, particularly the right one, which fought his inclination to sleep.

He thought a night had passed by the time his head was clearer. He was aware of the half dozen beds, probably in a ward set aside for officers. For the moment it was peaceful there, with most men sleepy and only a few staff passing by to observe their progress. He had the feeling it had been frantically busy soon after he arrived.

He felt down inside the bed. There was a dressing on his right leg, that much he could tell.

The light was dim: was it early or late in the day? He thought the light was dwindling. A tall young woman in the uniform of a nurse – a VAD nurse – passed by. It must be Beatrice, come to see him, to help nurse him. No, of course it couldn't be her. Bea wasn't a nurse. The young woman passed by again. Beatrice was tall but she was taller, and her hair was dark under her white cap, not chestnut like Beatrice's.

Now she was heading in his direction. 'How are you, Sir? Are you in pain?'

'My legs...' He sought unsuccessfully for a way of describing the pain which would not sound overdramatic or cowardly.

'You're about due for some more morphia.' She took his temperature and seemed satisfied with the result.

'How bad are my legs?'

'We've dressed your wounds. I'll fetch a doctor to speak to you.'

As she walked away he had the feeling once more that he knew her. She was an acquaintance, someone in his social circle at home.

–

Daylight was fading by the time the doctor arrived. The lights were lit now, though they were not bright.

The pain had subsided a little, thanks to the fresh dose of morphia.

'You're a better colour now, Captain. Good job that orderly applied the tourniquet to your wound: you'd lost a lot of blood.'

'How bad are my legs, Doctor?'

'Very sorry, old man, we had to take off your right foot. It was shot apart.'

He could not mean it. 'You must be thinking of someone else! I can still feel it.'

'That'll be the nerve endings, Captain. I'm afraid we had to amputate it.'

He struggled not to cry out in horror. He had heard of many fine men who had suffered similar mutilations. They almost always reacted courageously, but probably they had found it equally hard to accept.

The doctor hovered, trying to tell him about his treatment, while Charles's brain seemed to be shutting down, unable to comprehend what was happening. He heard a few words: 'prevent infection', 'out of the fray', 'Blighty wound'. He stared bleakly ahead and murmured 'Yes, Doctor', from time to time until the man moved on to the next casualty.

Soon they put out most of the lights. The horror still engulfed him but the morphia was making him doze.

When he awoke the ward was quiet and the night sister was sitting writing notes by lamplight. It must be the middle of the night. Could the doctor's visit have been a dream? No, he was certain it had happened. He tried to fight off despair. He would recover as well as he could and be sent home to Blighty, and to Beatrice. She would understand and support him. But he would be changed, relying on crutches, or an appliance to help him to walk. How dreadful it would be for her.

Then his thoughts returned to his men. Were they still holding that confounded canal?

-

'How are you, Sir?'

Frank Bentley was standing by his bed.

'Better, I believe.' He gave Frank a brief account of his injuries. He must not succumb to anxiety. He had seen his wounds now when they changed the dressings. They had amputated his right foot and had taken off part of the leg as well, almost halfway to the knee. He had stared in disbelief at the ghastly stump.

A day or two later a tall, middle-aged man had come round to check his patients' recovery. He had recognised the distinguished surgeon who he had met socially before the war. 'We were anxious to avoid infection,' Mr Westholme had told him. Even his left foot had been hit: he had lost two toes.

'It's good to hear you're making progress,' Frank said now. 'I've brought you some cigarettes.'

'Thanks, Bentley.' He opened the packet eagerly and they both lit up.

'The men all wish you a speedy recovery.'

'Are they holding the Line?'

'We've hung on along the canal. I even think the enemy bombardment is less fierce now. I gather the German advance is so extended the Huns are having trouble holding the land they've gained.'

'Thank God for that.'

'Our replacements have just arrived.' The men now fighting would fall back for a few days.

'Any fresh casualties?'

Bentley brought him up to date. Of course there had been losses. Two good men had been killed and another injured, though not severely.

'Has anyone told you about Fletcher?' Bentley said.

'What about him?' He was suddenly anxious.

'He got you out of the Front Line when you were hit. He was bloody brave. Shells were landing around him while he applied the tourniquet. He got wounded himself, though not badly. He was suffering from concussion by the time other orderlies arrived.'

'Fletcher got me out of there?' Charles could remember very little of what happened between being hit and finding himself on the hospital ward.

'Yes, Sir.'

'Please call me Charles.'

'Right ho. Fletcher is here in the hospital. He's making good progress, I understand. I'm going to his ward to see him next.'

When his fellow officer left the pain seemed stronger and all his anxieties rushed back to plague him.

Chapter Seven

Larchbury and Flanders, April and May

'I need to see Orderly Fletcher,' Charles told the tall nurse. 'I've heard how heroically he behaved, evacuating me when I was hit and applying the tourniquet. Do you think someone would wheel me to his ward in an invalid chair?'

'Possibly, but I could ask him to see you instead, and make it clear he's welcome on this ward for a visit.'

'Yes – that would be easier. Thank you, Nurse.' He looked at her again. 'I know you socially, don't I?'

'Yes, we've met. I live in Alderbank. I'm Lavinia, Mr Westholme's daughter – you know, he's the surgeon.'

'Of course, I remember now.'

'Father's working out here too. He may well have performed your operation.'

'I believe he did. He was here, checking on my progress. I'm very grateful for his efforts.' They were still examining both his legs regularly, as though anxious they were healing well.

'We all do what we can.'

He remembered suddenly where he had last met the nurse. 'Weren't you at Edmond's wedding to Amy?'

'That's right.'

For another minute they discussed the latest news of Amy and her daughter, and other mutual acquaintances, but she had to hurry away. The nurses were overstretched with casualties as usual.

—

Later that day James Fletcher arrived to see him, limping a little, a bandage visible below the trouser leg of his pyjamas. He was Amy's cousin, Charles recalled.

'How are you, Sir?' the orderly asked.

'Improving,' Charles said, though he was fighting off the fatigue which made him want to sleep in the middle of the day. 'Do sit down. Are you better? You look in reasonable shape.'

James pulled up a chair. The officer who was awake in the next bed looked curiously at him, but would assume the orderly had been invited to visit the officers' ward. 'Yes – I've got a leg wound, not especially serious, and at first they were watching me as I'd been concussed briefly.'

'You were damn brave. I can't remember much about being hit, but I gather I owe you my life. You got me out of the line of fire and stemmed the bleeding.'

'Any orderly would have done the same, Sir.' He had a friendly, open expression but did not have the air of a hero.

'I'm not so sure about that. You took a great risk, with the bombardment continuing. I'm relieved to hear you're making progress.'

'When my leg has healed sufficiently they'll send me to a convalescent hospital for a few weeks, then I'll be back working again.'

'I suppose they'll have heard at home about our injuries now.' Charles was not entirely sure how much time had passed since he was hit.

'Yes – they're bound to write to us, but the letters may take a few days to get through.'

–

'Has Pa gone up to the forest again?' Amy asked Edmond one morning.

'Yes.' He was in the drawing room, drinking coffee and taking a few minutes' break from working in the study on Pa's business paperwork.

'He's spending more and more time up there,' Ma said. 'I'm worried he'll wear himself out.'

'Why can't he leave Walter in charge?' asked Beatrice.

Edmond was silent. He had told Amy once that he suspected his father sometimes joined his workers to do a stint of heavy labour in the forest, worried that otherwise they would not keep up with the demand for timber.

'Have you had a letter from Charles yet?' Ma asked Beatrice. By now the morning mail had arrived.

'No – I haven't had one for a few days. It's unlike him not to write.'

The others exchanged glances. 'I hope he's all right,' Beatrice said. 'One hears such dreadful things.'

Just then they heard voices outside the room and Pa hurried in, his expression strained. His right hand clutched the left one. Amy thought she could see a streak of blood.

'Have you hurt your hand?' she got out of her chair. Edmond stood up too, pale with concern.

'It's nothing – just a splinter,' he told them. 'Ross was making a fuss about it and insisted on bringing me back on the wagon so Amy can clean it up.'

'Let me have a look,' Amy said, gently taking his injured hand. The splinter was easy to see, large and jagged, and blood was still seeping from the wound.

'That must be very painful,' she said. 'Let's go to the kitchen so I can deal with it.' Cook kept a first aid kit there.

'What in the world have you been doing up there?' Ma demanded as they reached the doorway. 'It's not your job to handle the timber.'

'We're behind with an order.' Pa was casually dressed in plus-fours.

Soon he was sitting on the kitchen chair while Cook produced a bottle of iodine and some cotton wool, and Amy manoeuvred some tweezers to catch hold of the exposed end of the large splinter.

'Ouch!' cried Pa. 'Sorry, Amy, I know you're doing your best.'

'I'm trying to pull it out in the opposite direction to the way it went in, to make it as painless as possible,' she said, 'but it's a monster splinter.'

As she made another attempt Edmond came in with a glass of whisky for Pa, which he was happy to drink.

Most of the splinter came out at her second attempt. She cleaned up the wound and examined it. 'I'm afraid there are still a few fragments left,' she said. 'It's important I get those out too.'

At last she had removed all the pieces and turned her attention to disinfecting it with the iodine.

'I know this stings, but the wound will begin to hurt less now I've got the splinter out,' she said.

'I'm very grateful, Amy,' he said as she bandaged it.

'You must take more care,' Edmond said forcibly.

'I can't fall behind on an order,' he said. 'And I'd like some extra supplies to give to a few families in Larchbury who are struggling to make ends meet after they've lost menfolk at the Front. It's still cold at night.'

How committed he was, Amy thought, with a new respect for him. Her own father often told her about children at his school who were facing poverty, and Uncle Arthur sometimes mentioned their problems and encouraged parishioners to be generous.

'You've got a dangerous occupation,' Edmond said. 'I worry you might get hit by a falling tree or have a sawing accident.'

'I think of supplying wood as a patriotic wartime duty.'

From outside came a baby's cry. 'Beth wants feeding,' Amy said. She had left her sleeping in her pram on the veranda now the weather had improved.

'If this nightmare war is ever over I'll ask George to come back as gardener,' Amy heard Pa saying as she hurried out. 'Then maybe Joe might consider working in the forest – and Henry, when he's back.'

–

That afternoon Amy went into the village again, with Beth in her pram, to buy a pair of shoes. She returned as the shops were closing, making the short journey through the quiet streets, still walking slowly and limping a little. Neighbours and old friends stopped to chat to her and admire the baby.

As she turned into the drive of The Beeches a smart motor car was driving away. She did not recognise the middle-aged man at the wheel or the woman in the large hat who accompanied him.

As she approached the house Edmond came out to meet her. She could tell from his stricken face that something was wrong. 'We've had dreadful news,' he told her. 'Charles has been wounded.'

'Oh, Heavens!'

'His parents drove over here to tell Beatrice. She's terribly upset about it, as you can imagine.'

'How badly is he hurt?'

'He's lost his right foot. They hope to save the other leg.'

She felt faint for a moment, struggling to absorb this latest piece of disastrous news.

He helped her bring the pram up the steps as they went in. There was an ominous stillness about the place, as though everyone was tiptoeing and speaking in whispers.

'Where's Beatrice?' she asked, wondering what she could say to her.

'She's gone up to her bedroom. I don't think she'll be down for dinner.'

They went up to their own room. There was a leaden feeling in Amy's stomach again. How could life keep on being so cruel? She had always liked Charles, but she was especially concerned how the news was affecting Edmond.

'It's still going on,' he moaned, sitting down on their bed. His hand went to his chest instinctively, as though to protect his own scars. 'When will all the horrors end?'

She took Beth into the nursery and laid her down in her cot. She went back to their room and took Edmond into her arms. His face was pale and strained.

'Charles is a brave man,' she said. 'He'll make a good recovery and carve out a life for himself, like you're doing.'

He sat staring across the room, in a world of his own. From the nearby nursery she could hear Beth starting to become fretful: she must be hungry. Amy went and fetched her, undid her blouse and sat feeding her. Her closeness with her baby soothed her, and as Edmond looked towards them his face relaxed a little.

Then Mrs Johnson knocked on the door. Amy liked the plump, grey-haired woman, who still worked as a charlady for Amy's parents one day a week and worked as a cleaner at The Beeches some days as well. 'There's a telephone call for you, Mrs Derwent.' She looked a little anxious.

Amy went down to the hall and picked up the receiver from where it was lying by the phone. 'Hello?'

'Hello, Amy…' Uncle Arthur's voice was less calm and reassuring than usual.

'What is it, Uncle?'

'It's James – he's been wounded.'

Amy swayed and caught hold of the telephone table.

'He's got a leg injury. He wrote the letter himself and says he's not in serious danger.'

'Thank Heavens!'

Her uncle explained that he had been injured on duty.

'Poor fellow. I keep telling everyone it's not an easy option, being an orderly. I must write to him.'

Still shaken, she went to tell Edmond this piece of news, reassuring him that her cousin was not in danger. She hoped this assessment of his injuries was accurate.

Dinner was a miserable meal. Later, when they went to bed, Edmond was tossing and turning and Amy could not sleep either. *He's remembering what it was like at the Front*, she thought. She took him in her arms.

'Hold me close, angel,' he said.

As it grew light she woke and he was sleeping. She dared not move for risk of waking him. She lay quietly until Beth's cries of hunger rang out. He stirred and Amy had to get up.

–

Beatrice did not appear until lunchtime. She had shadows under her eyes and was unusually dishevelled. Amy and Edmond told her how shocked they were at Charles's misfortune.

'What will happen to him?' she asked as she took her place with them, turning to Amy for information.

'He'll get the best attention,' Amy said as Cook brought them plaice in parsley sauce. 'They'll have given him emergency help at a casualty clearing station first, then sent him to the nearest hospital where he can get the treatment he needs.'

'Perhaps it'll be the one in Ypres where Edmond was treated,' Ma said.

'It might be,' Amy said, 'but when James last wrote he said they were having to evacuate some of the wounded from that area.' News of the German advance was confusing, but Field Marshall Haig's order to the troops to fight to the end had made it sound alarming.

'They say Charles has lost a foot! He must be in dreadful pain,' Beatrice said, her eyes wide. 'And to think he might never dance again!' She was staring at Amy, as though reminded of her ungainly movements, resulting from her injured ankle, and wondering how badly her fiancé might be affected.

'He'll be brave, and you'll support him,' Edmond said. 'They'll fix him up with some kind of artificial appliance. It will be difficult to adjust, but he'll manage. Have you written to him yet?'

'I simply don't know what to say!' She fiddled with her napkin.

'Just tell him you love him and will stick by him,' Edmond said.

'Yes.' She looked at Amy imploringly. 'They'll have to send him home, won't they? He can't go on fighting if he's badly wounded.'

'Yes, as soon as he's fit to travel they'll send him back, maybe to a hospital in London.'

Beatrice pushed her food round her plate for a few minutes longer, then set aside her knife and fork. After lunch she played a sad lament on the piano, then abandoned it and went back to her room.

–

Florence was shocked when Amy told her of Charles's wounds and that James had been injured. After church Amy and Edmond needed to hurry back, but were able to assure her they had heard that James was making good progress.

The vicar and his wife were talking to their parishioners, so Florence set off home. Her parents were ahead somewhere, but they all walked back as they lived so close to St Stephen's. As Florence walked along briskly she soon caught up with the Fletchers, Amy's parents.

'I'm embarrassed at some of the things I've said about James,' Florence told them. 'It was unkind and ill-

94

informed of me to suggest he'd taken a cowardly option in the war.'

'Lots of people thought the same,' Mrs Fletcher said.

Florence sighed. 'I wish now that I'd become a VAD like Amy and Lavinia,' she confessed. 'I'm here in my comfortable home, doing very little for the men at the Front.'

'You're working in a vital profession,' Mr Fletcher pointed out. Though they taught in different parts of the village school they sometimes caught glimpses of each other coming and going.

'Yes… I try to give what comfort I can to pupils who've lost fathers in the war,' she said. 'There are some very sad cases.'

'I heard about the Watson girls,' Amy's mother said. 'Their family is hard up now so the girls go to the farm to milk the cows before they come to school.'

'They're often tired when they arrive,' said Mr Fletcher.

The younger of the two girls had been in her class when she had started teaching, and Florence knew of the family's struggles.

'The Jones children also lost their father recently,' she told them. 'Harry's in my class. He told me his sister Violet, who is only ten, is virtually running the home, minding the younger children, because her mother has had to go out to work.'

'I call in sometimes to make sure she's coping,' Mrs Fletcher said. 'I can take some cake or leftover meat to help them out.'

'That's kind of you,' Florence said. 'When Mother has something she can spare I pass it on to them, or one of the other families that's struggling. And your sister-in-law, the vicar's wife, makes me keep her informed about children who need help.'

There was plenty to do locally to help the unfortunate, but still sometimes it did not completely engage her.

–

Every morning Charles awoke to the bitter realisation that he was no longer the fit young man who had sauntered through the West End, spent evenings on the dance floor and marched with his troops. That life had been swept away in one brief moment as he defended the Lys canal. He was also desperately anxious that no further infection threatened his legs.

By early May they were allowing him out of bed for part of the day. A nurse or one of the orderlies would wheel him in an invalid chair to the dayroom, where the patients could sit together and share newspapers. The chairs were comfortable and there were a few potted plants. Today the French windows were open, allowing in fresh air from the garden outside. At one end of the room were a gramophone and a piano, and formal photographs of the King in military uniform, and Queen Mary.

'I haven't seen you here for a couple of days,' remarked Captain Turnbull, a thin, lofty officer sitting close by. His foot was injured but Charles had heard the doctors were confident of saving it.

'I had to go back to the operating theatre,' Charles told him. His fears had been realised. The remains of his right leg seemed clear of infection, but the doctors were not satisfied with the way his left leg was healing. They had had to remove some more of his left foot. He was in severe pain again each time the morphia began to wear off.

After being given a dose he would be sleepy for a while, which helped quell his anxiety about the slow healing of his wounds.

Lavinia Westholme came in with her thermometer, moving lithely round the group of men. He waited patiently for his temperature reading, which she said was satisfactory. A raised temperature was often a sign of infection.

'Have you heard from home today?' she asked him. Her waist was trim in her uniform.

'Mother wrote to me again, and one of my sisters.' He was longing to get one of Beatrice's loving letters, but since his injury he had only received quite a brief one. 'Edmond wrote to me, too. He's going back to university in the autumn, determined not to let his war wound hamper him.'

'He and Amy won't make concessions to his injury, if they can help it.' Lavinia moved on, to continue her work. She had a reputation for being brainy but rather opinionated, he remembered, but he was growing to like her.

Around him other officers were dozing or reading newspapers. He had read the latest about the war. He was growing restless, almost wishing he could return to the fray.

He leant across to speak to Captain Turnbull. 'I heard a strange story about you,' he said. 'Is it true you escaped from occupied Belgium at the start of the war?'

'Yes.' A grin spread across his narrow face. 'Back in 1914 I had a particularly eventful few weeks.' Charles gathered he had already been serving in the Regular Army when war broke out.

'I was with one of the first units sent to Flanders,' Turnbull explained. 'I was just a lieutenant then. We were among those the Kaiser described as a "contemptible little army". We were involved in the very first fighting. I was injured around Mons, and I got left behind in the retreat. It wasn't my foot that time: it was a shoulder injury and I was sent to a Belgian hospital near Brussels.'

'Bad luck.'

'I was fortunate, because I was taken to the hospital where Nurse Edith Cavell worked.'

'You mean that nurse they executed in 1915?'

'Yes.'

'Goodness! You actually met her.' Charles remembered that she had been arrested in 1915 and, unwilling to lie, had admitted helping British men, and Belgians sympathetic to the allied cause, to reach neutral Holland. There had been an outcry when she had been sentenced to death, but the Germans had refused to pardon her and she had been executed by a firing squad. In Britain she was regarded as a heroine.

'She was a senior nurse at the hospital, a stern woman of about fifty – we didn't like her at first. But when we were well enough, she arranged for some of us to be smuggled out to join an escape line.'

An orderly brought round mugs of tea.

'Nuns, nurses and brave young couriers all helped us travel. They escorted us on trains and through check-points, and found safe houses for us to stop in briefly. We had false papers. It's only about sixty miles to the Dutch border, but the direct routes were checked more thoroughly.' There was a thoughtful expression in his pale blue eyes. 'There was one young courier chap who posed as a German officer, travelling on the same train. If anyone questioned our identity he would take over the detailed checking of our documents. He had an air of authority, so we always got through.'

'Wasn't he really German?'

'He had a German passport. Let's see ... I can't remember his name, but it was a fairly common German name, I understand. It may not even have been his real name. I woke up after a nightmare once, shaking, wondering if he could be a real German who'd infiltrated the escape line.'

'Could he have been a Dutch or Flemish sympathiser?'

'We got the impression he was from some border area, where there are divided loyalties. Some such place was mentioned, but I forget where it was... Thank goodness we finally crossed the border into neutral Holland and eventually I was able to rejoin my unit.'

The orderly returned for the mugs. Charles enquired, as he did each day, about James Fletcher's progress. He heard that he was still in pain, but his leg was healing well.

Then Turnbull limped over to the piano and played a few tunes. They joined in singing '*It's a Long Way to Tipperary*'.

In his mind Charles went on reviewing Turnbull's account of Nurse Cavell and the escape line. Surely, with courageous actions like that, their side was bound to triumph eventually.

Lavinia and another nurse arrived to take them back to the wards. 'Poor Captain Turnbull,' Lavinia said as she wheeled Charles along the corridor. 'He tries so hard to keep everyone cheerful but his playing is a little amateurish.'

'If I'd been able to move around I'd have offered to play something more classical,' Charles said.

'I believe several of the patients and the staff are musical,' Lavinia told him. 'Some of them have even had instruments sent here from home.'

'You sing, don't you?' he said, remembering her performing at a party long before.

'Yes, I do. You know what, I think we should organise a concert party. I've heard of staff arranging them in other hospitals, and they can be great fun.'

'That would be wonderful – a boost for morale!'

'I'll suggest we hold one,' she said, 'though they might make us wait until there are fewer casualties.'

How long might that be, he wondered.

Chapter Eight

Larchbury, June

One day the dressmaker called at The Beeches with the new clothes she was making for the family. Amy tried on her dress in the pretty floral fabric she had chosen. 'You may take it in a little more,' she told the seamstress, 'for I'm almost back to the size I was before I was expecting.' Otherwise she was delighted with the result.

Ma and Beatrice were content with their outfits, and approved Amy's dress. 'This afternoon we should go to the milliner's,' Ma said.

Amy was a little daunted as they arrived at the smarter of the Larchbury hat shops, with swatches of their fabrics to match. She looked as Beatrice selected a large, wide-brimmed hat lavishly trimmed with artificial flowers, which toned well with her pale yellow dress. She herself reached for a slightly more modest confection in a blue which matched the major colour in her new dress.

Beatrice was surveying her choice critically. For a moment Amy was annoyed, but then she remembered Edmond's sister was renowned for her elegance. 'What do you think?' she asked.

'It's a pretty hat,' she replied in an authoritative tone, 'but you might wear one with a higher crown, to give you a little more height.' She scanned the selection displayed and passed Amy one in a similar colour. 'Try this one.'

Amy placed it carefully on her head and examined the mirror again. She was surprised how flattering it was, somehow balancing the shape of her face. 'You're right, Beatrice! This one is perfect.'

Her sister-in-law smiled, content to have her good taste acknowledged.

It was a mild, sunny day and they had walked into the village. As they strolled back, a young man in uniform was striding along on the other side of the road. He had long shiny boots and a badge with wings on his khaki tunic. He must have been barely old enough to serve.

Mrs Johnson's daughter, Elsie, came out of the nearby grocer's shop and she stopped, her mouth dropping open at the sight of the young man, setting forth bravely like a hero from a legend.

'Doesn't that chap look smart?' Ma said. 'I can't remember who he is.'

'That's Philip, Caroline Brownlee's young brother,' Beatrice told her. Caroline, the daughter of the auctioneer at the local livestock market, was a friend of hers. 'He's training to serve in the Royal Flying Corps. Imagine, going up in an aeroplane!'

'I used to see the flimsy little planes flying overhead when I was in France,' Amy said. 'It must be thrilling to be up there in the sky, but they say there are lots of casualties among the airmen.'

—

Peter reached home just in time to be godfather. As he strode into the drawing room Amy was struck once more by the resemblance between the brothers and could not help recalling how healthy and vigorous Edmond had once been. She banished the thought to the back of her mind, determined to concentrate on the future.

'It's demanding work out there at Headquarters,' Peter told the family as they sat together. 'I've secured my promotion, though.'

'Capital,' said his father.

'We do our best there to support our brave troops.' He always sounded apologetic, as though recognising that his role was not as heroic as serving on the Front Line. 'I've just been moved from handling records and disciplinary matters relating to the army staff. I'm not involved in the strategic planning but I'm one of the team making sure the supplies get through.'

'That's vital work,' Edmond said. 'Make sure the cocoa and dried fruit reach the Front Line so the cooks can make Trench Cake!'

'We try,' his brother said. 'They're so short of eggs we have to send them baking powder and vinegar to make it rise.'

'It boosts morale along the Line when they serve it.'

Peter sighed. 'It's been touch and go lately: we've often had to make fresh plans at the last minute.' He looked fatigued. 'They left it till the day before I was to travel here to confirm they were allowing me the leave.'

When Peter was alone with Edmond and Amy he spoke of returning to India once the war was over, whenever that might be. 'Pa won't be pleased,' he told them, 'but my new rank will give me more status out there and I can ask my girl to marry me. She's kept on writing to me.'

'Is the Front Line secure now?' Edmond asked.

'There was a massive crisis when the Germans began their big push,' Peter said. 'They were driving back our troops, recapturing ground we'd won from them. There was a panic that they might actually win the war.'

'It was that bad?' Edmond exchanged a horrified glance with Amy. 'I was very anxious when I heard Field Marshall Haig's dramatic Order of the Day, but I hoped he was exaggerating the seriousness of the situation.'

'It was every bit as critical as he said,' Peter told them. 'Don't talk about it to anyone else – we need to maintain morale. Now the Americans are arriving in larger numbers we're beginning to turn the tide, otherwise they'd probably have cancelled my leave. There's still a high toll of casualties, though.'

Amy had been shocked to hear of the recent bombardment which had devastated Béthune, the peaceful Flanders town where she and Edmond had enjoyed a break together at Easter the previous year.

As she left to feed Beth, she had the feeling that Edmond was anxious to speak to Peter on his own. They'll be discussing strategy, she thought, or something which is too disturbing or secret for me to hear. But there's a private matter I'd like to discuss with Peter when I get the chance.

–

Edmond accompanied Peter as he went out to the veranda to smoke.

'Everything all right with the forest?' Peter asked.

'Yes – we've been clearing the fire breaks, just in case there's a drought.'

'The ground doesn't look parched.'

'Thunder and lightning could be a problem,' Edmond told him. They had to be prepared in case a fire ever broke out. 'We're short of workers, of course. I help with the paperwork now, but Pa sometimes does physical work up on the plantation. It's a strain for a man his age.'

'I must help him while I'm here.'

'Are you still involved in secret operations?' Edmond asked his brother now they were alone. He had been intrigued, but also horrified, at Christmas, when his brother had confided his secret visit behind enemy lines through a tunnel. None of the others knew about it.

'I haven't made another clandestine trip underground, if that's what you mean.'

'Thank goodness for that! Are you just doing routine work, then?'

'I've got some good informants. A brave young man with German contacts brings me valuable details of what the Huns are up to. If we intercept any written information he can translate it for us.'

'That shouldn't be as hazardous as what you did before.'

'Nothing like. And I'm immensely fortunate compared with the poor chaps in the trenches.'

–

After breakfast next morning Amy found herself alone with Peter. 'We've tried again to pursue your grievance against Captain Fairlawn,' he said, his blue eyes focussed on hers.

She had been impatient to know the latest about her complaint, worried he would escape punishment.

'Oh – I wondered if you'd dropped it,' she said.

'I supported Robert Lambert when he approached the authorities again,' Peter told her gently. 'Fairlawn should be put on a charge for trying to force himself on you. I'm afraid they're not upholding the complaint, partly because they don't want to interrupt Fairlawn's war service.'

'I suppose I guessed that's what would happen.'

'I don't think he'd get away with what he did so easily in peacetime.' He reached for another slice of toast. 'The man's a bounder. I remember him from school: he used to bully the younger boys.'

'His father's a colonel and very influential.'

'That may have been a factor.' He fell silent as Janet brought them fresh coffee.

Amy's fists clenched at the injustice. She remembered her fright the time George had innocently followed her that evening in Larchbury. Wilfrid's attack had had a lasting effect, depriving her of the confidence she had once enjoyed. Apart from Peter and his fellow officer, Robert, she had only told Lavinia of the incident.

'But we've made sure the allegation stays on his record,' Peter said when the maid had left. 'It might deter him from that kind of behaviour. He won't want another complaint.'

–

Carefully Amy put on her fine new hat. 'How beautiful you look!' Edmond exclaimed. She picked up Beth from her cot, adorable in her long white gown, smelling faintly of soap, and smiling at her parents. They joined Pa in the car and set off for the baptism.

The church was almost full as Uncle Arthur presided over the service, his warm voice echoing round the stonework. The weather was better that day and bright streams of sunlight took on the colours of the stained glass as they illuminated the nave. Beth scarcely gurgled as Uncle Arthur made the sign of the cross on her forehead at the most solemn part of the ceremony.

As they came out of the church afterwards, friends and neighbours crowded round to see Elizabeth, as she was officially known, in her long white gown. Around the edge of the skirt Amy had stitched a beautiful panel of Belgian lace that she had made with help from Madame Rousseau.

Uncle Arthur looked weary but thankful that this service had been a joyous one. They had all been relieved recently to hear that James was continuing to recover. But new families were appearing in mourning, and not just from the war. The latest loss had been Margaret Leadbetter, the headmaster's wife, who had been taken ill suddenly. 'It was very shocking, how quickly she died,' Amy's father had told them.

Edmond's father drove most of the family and godparents back to The Beeches, in two trips. Peter walked back, accompanied by Amy's parents and aunt, and Lavinia, who had managed to obtain leave.

Back at The Beeches, a photographer was waiting. Edmond stood beside Amy as she held Beth close, her soft, warm face next to her own. Amy was confident that she looked her best in her elegant new dress and hat. For the photograph of the godparents, Florence held Beth as though she was the most precious bundle, smiling at her in a way that was almost maternal. Amy had seen her friend's dress a few times before, though her hat looked new. Florence paid less attention to her appearance since Bertie had died.

The sky was clouding over but it was just mild enough for the guests to sit outside on the lawn nearest the house, near the bank of pink hydrangeas.

'This is my favourite part of the garden,' Ma said as refreshments were brought round.

Amy took Beth with her as she joined Edmond and mingled with his relatives. She greeted his seventeen-year-old cousin Vicky, who always loved to come to events at The Beeches. Strands of her long auburn hair hung down below her hat, in a pale greeny blue, which matched her close-fitting dress. *How pretty she is now*, Amy thought, *and more stylishly dressed than when she was younger.*

'Your little girl is so sweet!' she cried when she saw Beth. 'May I hold her?'

She took the baby and walked around with her for a while. The summer sunshine had brought her face out in freckles.

'Edmond, you look so much better now!' she told him as she handed Beth back to Amy. 'I hear you're going back to Cambridge soon.'

Vicky's parents seldom visited, as her mother was frail, but this time they had come. *It's high time I got to know them*, Amy thought.

Edmond's aunt approached them slowly. 'Are you really taking up your studies again?' she asked him. 'Is that prudent, after you've been so badly injured?'

'I'm determined to continue,' he asserted.

'Oh, Mother, he must!' Vicky said. 'He's so fortunate, having a place there. I sometimes wish I could study at university, but women hardly ever do, I'm told.'

'A few do obtain places...' Edmond said.

'Really, Victoria, you have strange ideas!' Her grey-haired father glared at her. 'You mustn't damage your chances of marriage by aspiring to appear intellectual.'

Amy felt sorry for Edmond's congenial cousin.

'I don't want to just stay at home, waiting for a suitor!' Vicky persisted. 'Perhaps I'll become a nurse, like Amy.'

'Don't be influenced by her, Victoria.' The girl's father turned his disagreeable gaze in Amy's direction. 'We know about you being sent to jail, young woman!'

Amy cringed. Would the bad reputation never leave her?

'Really, Uncle Eustace!' Edmond cried. 'Amy's highly respected now for her war work – ask anyone here!'

At this moment Edmond's aunt and uncle from the other side of his family were approaching them. She had heard from Edmond that Eustace Harper, Ma's brother, knew the other Derwent relatives, but only from rare family gatherings.

'That's right, Eustace!' Edmond's other uncle asserted now. 'Amy has put the misdemeanour behind her.'

Uncle Eustace threw her one last angry glance before taking his wife's arm and setting off for the other side of the lawn. Vicky drifted off to speak to Florence, who she had met before.

Amy had met Uncle Reginald and his wife briefly on her wedding day, when she had been too overwhelmed with excitement to pay them much attention.

'Everyone is proud of you for the way you're over-coming your setbacks,' Uncle Reginald told Edmond. He looked a little older than Pa, and stouter. He and his wife were the ones who had taken Edmond abroad one summer before the war.

'It's all thanks to Amy,' he replied.

Uncle Reginald turned to her. 'I confess we had a few doubts about you, after that time your marriage was interrupted…'

She felt herself blush.

'…But it sounds as though Edmond made a good choice after all,' he finished, smiling at her.

Vicky continued talking to Florence, and soon Amy was able to join them. Lavinia also settled happily with them, and decided it was her turn now to take Beth gently into her arms. The little girl's fair hair was growing and beginning to curl. She cooed at her new companion in her captivating fashion. 'Already she looks interested in everything going on around her,' Lavinia approved.

'Is Emily still nursing at the same hospital as you?' Amy asked Lavinia.

'No, they've sent her to a place for convalescents.'

Mrs Johnson had brought Elsie along to help serve tea. She was a plump sixteen-year-old with hair almost as fair as Amy's, and a slow way of speaking. She poured them all cups of tea, slopping milk into one of the saucers. Then she handed around the scones.

'Will there be anything else?' she asked Amy.

'We'd like some Dundee cake,' Amy said, knowing Cook had made some of her choicest cakes that morning.

'Listen,' Lavinia said suddenly, 'there's some good news, isn't there? Women are finally getting the vote!'

'Only if they're thirty, and own property,' Florence complained.

'I know, it's not enough, but it's a start,' Lavinia said.

'Remember when we went on our march?' Florence said, grinning. 'That must be about four years ago.' Vicky was listening with rapt attention.

Lavinia winced. 'Poor Amy got into dreadful trouble about that, and it was all my fault.'

'I don't suppose I'll ever completely live it down,' Amy said. She could still recall her feelings on the day she had written slogans in the cricket pavilion, a mixture of excitement and guilt. Today Edmond's uncle had still remembered the serious repercussions of the incident. 'But, in the end, we haven't won the vote by our civil disobedience, but by all the work we've done in the war.'

'That's true,' Lavinia said. 'We've taken occupations once reserved for men, or gone as nurses, and now they can't pretend any longer that we're feeble-minded, frivolous little creatures. I'd like to think that when Beth's grown up she and her friends will have the same rights as men.'

'I haven't done war work,' Florence said, sounding regretful, 'apart from helping refugees and joining the Women's Working Party, in school holidays.'

'Your teaching work is vital,' Lavinia assured her.

'I haven't got any first-hand experience of the war, like you two.'

'I haven't done anything except help in the local Working Party,' Vicky said, looking miserable.

'You're still too young to sign up for war work,' Amy reminded her.

'I've started learning typing,' the girl said. 'Father doesn't approve, of course. But, Amy, I don't even understand what's going on in the war. I'm never certain whether the men are fighting in France or in Flanders.'

'Flanders is part of northern France,' Amy explained. 'Armentières is there, but Amiens and the Somme are further south in France, as you head towards Paris. The province of Flanders extends east into Belgium – Ypres is there.'

Vicky wrinkled her brow in concentration, trying to memorise the information.

Before long Beatrice approached their group. She had been at school with Lavinia, though they were too different to have ever been close friends. Now she was anxious to talk to her. 'My fiancé is out in Flanders, badly injured,' she told her, sitting down on an unoccupied chair.

'That's Captain Shenwood, isn't it?' Lavinia said. She was wearing a familiar outfit, a suit which had been fashionable just before the war. Amy supposed that with her commitments as a VAD she had little opportunity to attend to her wardrobe. 'I'm working at the hospital where they're treating him. He's being very brave.' Amy knew Lavinia had been sent from the hospital near Arras, where she too had once worked, to Ypres, and then, when that hospital had had to be evacuated, on to somewhere near the coast.

'But he's lost part of his leg – how will he manage? He'll need a wooden leg, won't he?' Beatrice asked, drawing her chair closer to Lavinia's.

'They're developing much better artificial limbs now,' Lavinia told her. 'It's an effort for the men to adjust to them, but eventually they become fairly mobile.'

Beatrice's pretty face seemed to freeze as she tried to suppress a shudder. 'How soon do you think they'll send him back?' she pursued.

Lavinia hesitated. 'They'll need to be sure his legs are healing well before they let him travel,' she said. Edmond was listening anxiously. Amy thought Lavinia might be holding back, as though his recovery was not proceeding well.

Beatrice left them before long, anxious to join Harriet, the close friend she had invited for the occasion. 'Come and meet her, Vicky,' she said, enticing her cousin away from their group.

As Elsie passed their table, Amy reminded her to fetch some Dundee cake.

'Have you heard that it was your cousin James who evacuated Charles from the bombardment when he was wounded?' Lavinia asked Amy.

'No – I hadn't heard that.' She remembered hearing about both casualties on the same day. 'Is he at your hospital as well? How's he doing?'

'His leg is healing steadily. He should be ready for a convalescent hospital soon, if they can find a place for him somewhere.'

It sounded as though the situation out there was still very hectic.

Florence was staring at Lavinia. 'Did James actually help during the bombardment?'

'Yes – he put his own life at risk, getting Captain Shenwood away, and that's how he got injured too. Several of the men have told me how brave he was. And he applied a tourniquet, while they were still under fire, because Charles was bleeding heavily.'

Now Florence looked stricken. 'I hadn't grasped that orderlies went into such dangerous situations,' she said.

'Oh yes,' Lavinia said, 'they may have to evacuate men from No Man's Land. Sometimes they come under fire.'

Tears appeared in Florence's hazel eyes. 'If only I'd realised,' she said. 'I wish I hadn't criticised him for not fighting.'

'I hadn't heard about him saving Charles,' Amy said. 'He's been very modest in his letters. I don't think his parents even know.' *I'll tell them later*, she resolved.

Elsie came to their table and topped up their teacups. Amy reminded her once more about the cake.

'What happened to that woman in the village?' Lavinia asked presently.

'Margaret Leadbetter? They think she had the influenza which is going around. Her husband is devastated, especially as she died so suddenly.'

'Had she been in contact with someone else who was ill?'

'At first we didn't think so, but her brother was home from the Front and he'd had cases in his unit. They think troop movements can spread it, don't they?'

Elsie finally brought them slices of Dundee cake. It was deliciously spicy, but Cook had not crammed in as much fruit as she used to before the wartime shortages.

Lavinia passed Beth back to Amy and moved her wicker garden chair a short distance as the sun had come out and was shining in her eyes. Then she sat back and took a sip of her tea from the dainty bone china cup. 'The first cases of the flu were in an army hospital,' she said. 'Most of the men recovered quickly, but since then it seems to have developed into a more virulent form.'

Amy's parents came to their table, with Aunt Louisa. They had previously been talking to Edmond and his family.

Aunt Louisa looked cheery. 'I missed Amy's wedding because Harold had just died,' she said. 'I've so enjoyed this happy occasion.'

'May I take Beth for a little cuddle now?' Amy's mother said.

Amy passed her carefully into her grandmother's arms and she and her contemporaries walked off, carrying the little girl around the upper level of the garden.

The party began breaking up as the afternoon became cooler and more windy. Amy's parents went to say their goodbyes before setting off.

'I'm going to write to James,' Florence told Amy. 'I want to tell him how much I respect him for his bravery.' Soon she left too.

Amy had persuaded Ma to invite Lavinia to stay for dinner, as she only had a few days of leave. When Amy took Beth to the nursery her friend followed.

'Is Charles making a good recovery now?' Amy pressed her.

'He's had a setback,' she confided. 'His other leg isn't healing as they'd hoped. Don't tell Beatrice, for they may yet be able to save most of the foot.'

The familiar dread clutched Amy. 'Don't let's tell Edmond either, just yet. It affected him badly when Charles was wounded.'

She began feeding Beth, sitting in her comfortable rocking chair. 'Poor Florence, she misses Bertie so,' she said. 'I don't know if she'll ever marry now, though she'd make someone a fine wife.'

'There aren't many bachelors left in our age group,' Lavinia said. When Amy had finished the feed she began preparing Beth for bed, with Lavinia helping.

'I've seen a great many young men and helped them in all kinds of intimate ways, as part of my work,' Lavinia went on. 'But that may be the closest I come to any of them.'

'Have you ever cared for anyone?' Amy asked, for her friend seemed subtly changed, softer somehow.

'There is an officer I greatly admire,' Lavinia said, 'but he's not free.' There was a dreamy expression in her large dark eyes.

'Oh… I see.' She was concerned but could not think what to say. She hoped Lavinia would not do anything impetuous she might later regret.

'Try not to worry about Florence and me,' her friend said. 'At least we both have a vocation.'

Chapter Nine

Larchbury and Flanders, July

Amy was soon receiving news of James from Florence as well as Uncle Arthur. 'He's been sent to a different hospital, for convalescence,' Amy's friend told her. It seemed the hospitals were still packed with patients and they had had trouble finding him a place. It sounded as though his leg was healing well.

'When he's better, will he work as an orderly again?' Florence asked.

'It's what he wants.' She and Edmond were sitting with Florence in the garden at The Beeches one Saturday, with Beth beside them in her pram. The nearby bushes of pink roses gave off a sweet perfume but they looked overgrown and untidy without George there to prune them.

It was midsummer and Amy had been urging Joe, the young gardener, to grow plenty of fruit and vegetables in the kitchen garden. She had encouraged him the previous year, once she was back from France. This year the weather was wetter but she aimed to guide him about when to harvest produce in its prime so they could keep the household well supplied. Other foodstuffs were scarce now and some basics like meat and butter were soon to be rationed.

'They're trying to recruit young women to work on the land,' Amy told Florence. 'Elsie, Mrs Johnson's daughter, has started work on a farm.' Apparently the girl was settling to the hard work.

'I thought of doing that in the school holidays,' Florence said. 'Some of the older children at school plan to help with the harvest.'

'I can't imagine you labouring on a farm,' Amy said, looking at her curiously.

'It would be gruelling work,' Edmond agreed.

'My parents are very against it,' Florence said. 'They think it's most unsuitable for someone with my upbringing.' She paused. 'But I've another plan now. I'd like to go out to France to see James. I've got a passport from when I went abroad once with my parents before the war. I can go when school breaks up.'

Edmond's mouth dropped open. 'Go to France?' he exclaimed. 'It's not a holiday destination now, you know! You can't just go there for a jaunt.'

'People visit wounded soldiers, don't they?' Florence said earnestly.

'They usually only go to France if the man is seriously ill,' he told her. 'Then close relatives might visit. When I was wounded I was fortunate that Amy was near enough to get to Ypres to see me. Peter was in France too.'

Amy considered. 'Even Charles's family haven't visited him, though I gather his father is very busy and his mother and sisters wouldn't want to travel without him. It's the same with Uncle Arthur; he and Aunt Sophie haven't managed to visit James.'

There was a determined expression in Florence's hazel eyes. 'All the same, I mean to go. I wrote to Lavinia, and she says if I can get to her hospital, which isn't all that far from the coast, she'll try to get leave and take me on her motorbike to James's hospital.'

'You've really given this some thought,' Amy said. Florence was wearing a pretty floral cotton dress, and Amy tried in vain to visualise her on the back of Lavinia's bike.

Janet arrived with some refreshments and they enjoyed Cook's crisp, freshly baked ginger biscuits.

'France isn't a pleasant place to visit now,' Edmond insisted. 'Please don't go there on a whim.'

'I've missed seeing the war at close quarters, like Amy and Lavinia,' she said. 'I feel I'll understand it better if I go there. The children at my school think it's exciting to go to war – they've little idea how horrible it is, unless someone in their family has been killed. I'd like to be better informed, though the pupils in my class are rather young to grasp what's going on. I may never have children of my own, but my nephews might one day ask me about it.'

'Does Uncle Arthur know you want to go to France to see James?' Amy asked.

'Yes – James's parents wish they could go but they're very much needed here in the parish. They're pleased I'm going.'

Amy imagined Florence wandering around war-torn France. 'Try not to go out on your own after dark,' she said. 'I've heard of someone who received unwanted advances from an officer. Do your parents know what you're planning?'

'I haven't told them yet,' she admitted.

'Dress soberly and try not to draw attention to yourself,' Amy said. 'People may take you for a woman in the VAD, nursing or driving ambulances.'

'And you might want to imply you're James's fiancée, to justify your visit,' Edmond advised her.

After she had left he shook his head. 'What is she thinking of?'

'She's been so miserable since we lost Bertie. It's good to see her enthusiastic about her plans.'

-

It was the end of July when Florence found herself alighting from a ship at Boulogne. She had spoken to some of the other passengers, and learnt that even crossing the Channel was dangerous now: the enemy planted mines there. Besides the risks, she still felt queasy from the choppy night-time crossing by some long, oblique route to avoid the most heavily mined areas.

Here in France the seafront was crowded with men and women in uniform, some of whom had been on her ferry. Most of them were boarding buses or a train on the line that came near the seafront. She remembered the promenade from a pre-war visit: there had been smartly dressed holidaymakers, sauntering along by the sea. She shuddered a little and began to understand Edmond's plea that she should not go to France on a whim. Her parents were very anxious too. With Father too busy to accompany her and Mother unwilling to travel, they had done their best to dissuade her from going. Eventually they had accepted that she was a little too old now for them actually to forbid her to go. How thankful she was for her earnings from teaching, so she need not ask them for money.

What business have I to come here? she wondered now. *Well, James deserves a visit.*

It was a sunny morning but there was a brisk breeze from the sea. Lavinia had sent her instructions for how to reach the hospital where she was working. She approached a woman in nurse's uniform, who pointed out a bus going in the right direction, though it was not due to leave till just before midday. The young woman recommended a cheap café, before rushing off to catch a different bus.

Walking further from the main hubbub, Florence was startled by the noise of an artillery bombardment to the south. She reached the café, tired from getting little sleep. After the voyage she did not want to eat but drank a cup of coffee. Then she climbed on to the bus while it still had spare seats and presently it set off, with hospital staff on board. They passed army vehicles and horse-drawn wagons on the way.

At last they reached a large building which had ambulances outside. There were also lots of huts and tents nearby. With as much confidence as she could muster she went through the main entrance and asked for Lavinia. She was told to take a seat and soon received a message that her friend was not due a break until late afternoon.

Florence went and sat outside on a bench, dozing in the sunshine. The afternoon wore on and she grew more wide awake as the wind became penetrating. Medical staff and orderlies passed by, too busy to show any curiosity about her presence there.

Ahead of her was a tent with its flaps open to admit the fresh air. Inside she could make out wounded soldiers lying in camp beds. She imagined they were lower-ranking soldiers, not officers. Another man was sitting at the opposite end of the tent. Some of the men lay motionless, probably asleep. From the others there was a murmur of chat, and the occasional burst of laughter.

The seated man got up and walked down the tent towards her, then turned and retraced his steps. She noticed he was carrying a rifle. One of the men began talking more loudly and she realised suddenly that they were not speaking English. *Heavens,* she thought, *the wounded men are captured Germans! So these are the evil Huns we've been taught to hate. They don't look any different from the British Tommies.*

'I didn't know what day you were arriving!' Lavinia appeared suddenly and embraced her. Her uniform was clean and tidy and her hairstyle only slightly lopsided under her cap. 'In fact, I wasn't sure you'd even go through with the idea.'

'I felt I should come.'

'I've got a three-hour break so I can take you to the little hotel in the village. It's quite close by. We can get you a room and have a meal together.'

Florence picked up her small overnight bag and accompanied Lavinia out of the hospital grounds and along the narrow road towards the nearby jumble of houses around a stone church. 'It's so windy here,' she complained.

'It's almost always like that near this coast,' Lavinia said. 'It was much worse in the winter. Look at the trees, how they grow at an angle, leaning away from the direction of the sea.'

They booked Florence into the small hotel. She was impressed at Lavinia's mastery of French.

'You speak the language so well!' she said. She had only received a few French lessons in the top class at school, and after her brief visit to the country she was just confident in a few travel-related phrases.

'The locals pronounce it with a strong accent. It takes a while to become used to it.' Then they sat in the small dining room and the elderly waiter told them the limited choice: they could eat mussels or an omelette.

'I'm not very hungry but I should manage an omelette.' Florence's stomach was only just settling from the sea crossing.

'I've managed to get a half day's leave tomorrow and the next day,' Lavinia said, 'but not till the afternoon. I'll take you on the motorbike over to the hospital near Saint-Omer where they've sent James. It'll only take a couple of hours. We'll have to find you somewhere to stay there, too. Then I'll take you back to the coast the day after.'

'Thank you so much. Actually, I'm torn – I want to visit Bertie's grave too. I was wondering, would there be time to see that first?' *How can I visit James without seeing my fiancé's resting place?* she thought. She took a sheet of paper from her bag and told Lavinia its location near Morval.

Her friend examined it. 'That's near the Somme, some distance away to the south, heading towards Paris,' she told her, with a sympathetic smile. 'There's fighting around there, so you almost certainly wouldn't be allowed in the area.'

The familiar sadness swept over Florence.

'Besides, it'll be a temporary grave,' Lavinia told her. 'They'll arrange some proper cemeteries after the war.'

Florence's stomach contracted. There was not even any certainty that the war would end soon.

Lavinia poured her some water. 'At the convalescent hospital there's a nurse called Emily,' she said. 'She's an old friend of Amy's. She can make sure you're all right while you're visiting James.'

Their omelettes arrived, and Lavinia ordered a glass of the local cider, while Florence decided to stick to water.

'You had to leave your old hospital in the spring offensive?' Florence asked.

'Yes. I'd spent the winter working in Ypres. When the Germans advanced, it was chaotic for a few weeks. There was a chance the Huns might catch up with us and we could have been captured. We knew we were heading towards the coast, but they had trouble finding anywhere to accommodate us. Sometimes we had to stay in tents, and it was freezing cold at night.'

'You must have been thankful to settle here.'

'The building used to be a hotel before the war. We still weren't safe. It was bombed and machine-gunned from the air once. They've patched it up since. The Huns were trying to destroy the railway line which runs nearby.'

'That's awful! Were there casualties?'

'No serious ones in our hospital, but at a larger one closer to the tracks some patients and medical staff were killed.'

'I had no idea!' *How can Lavinia describe it in such a matter-of-fact way?* she wondered.

'They may have kept quiet about it in the papers, to maintain morale. You'd better not gossip about it. They haven't attacked us lately. The place where James has been sent is near Saint-Omer, where some of our aeroplanes are based.'

'How's Charles Shenwood now?' Florence asked when she had finished her omelette.

Lavinia's smile faded. 'He's had a setback, I'm afraid. His left foot showed signs of going gangrenous, so they've just had to remove part of that as well.'

Florence shuddered.

Lavinia took out a packet of cigarettes from her bag. 'Do you smoke?' she asked.

Florence shook her head. Lavinia lit a cigarette. 'I don't know if anyone has told Beatrice yet,' she said.

'In the past I've met Lieutenant Shenwood socially at The Beeches. He's charming, but I don't know him very well.'

'He's Captain Shenwood now,' Lavinia told her. 'He's being amazingly brave.'

—

Florence slept badly, her mind often returning to the horrors Lavinia had described. The reality was much worse than she had imagined, though some troops managed to still look cheerful.

She spent the morning strolling along a path by the bank of a river, reasoning that if she kept beside it she should not lose her way. Swallows were wheeling overhead. When she was a little distance from the hospital she found the area peaceful and felt as though she might, after all, be a tourist. Then the bombardment broke out loudly again.

Shall I find lunch somewhere? she debated. *Probably not, before travelling on the motorbike.* In early afternoon she returned to the hospital and was met by Lavinia, who led her to her bike.

'It's been useful for getting away from the hospital in my time off,' her friend told her. 'When we evacuated the hospital at Ypres hurriedly I had to leave the bike behind, and I was worried that would be the last I saw of it. Luckily an orderly who wasn't required to escort any of the injured contrived to ride it out of Ypres for me. It was weeks before we became settled enough in our new positions for him to ride over in his off-duty hours and reunite me with my transport.'

She took Florence's overnight bag and crammed it into her pannier, then looked her up and down. 'I'm glad you're not wearing anything pastel coloured. Climb on to the pillion and hold on tight.'

Florence was travelling in the lightweight grey suit she had bought in her first year as a teacher, aiming for a dignified look. Underneath its jacket she was wearing her favourite pale blue blouse. She had anchored her hat well with a pin, like she did when her father took her out in their motor car, but now she was dubious as she tried to tuck up her skirt and climbed on to the dusty vehicle.

'I hope you weren't expecting high class, comfortable transport,' Lavinia said. 'The roads around here are in poor repair. And with all the storms we've had, some areas are still muddy.' The bike set off with a roar.

Lavinia had not exaggerated about the roads, which had a pitted, uneven surface, with the occasional broken-down wagon. They went beside the river for a while, then between some fields. Progress was slow and Florence began to feel a little sick. The bike swerved fiercely as Lavinia tried to avoid potholes, and landed heavily after crossing humps.

They came up behind a column of soldiers marching along. The men pulled over to nearer the side of the road to let their vehicle pass. They looked dusty and weary. Then they realised the motorcyclists were women and began to wave, cheer or whistle. Florence smiled, for it was all in good humour, and let go with one hand to wave back.

As they continued she tried to ignore the sick feeling. They reached an area of woodland that had been reduced to uneven stumps on both sides of the heavily pitted road. There must have been a bombardment here at some stage of the war. Florence stared at the scene of desolation. There were some broken-down stone cottages as well. Then they passed a field with simple wooden crosses and humps – she gasped at the realisation that war victims had been hastily buried here in shallow graves. There were dozens of them.

Now Florence's stomach started to churn. In a minute she would be sick. 'Stop, Lavinia! Please stop!' she cried. When her friend did not hear her above the noise of the engine she shook her shoulder.

Lavinia drew up at the side of the road. They must be half a mile away from the graves now. 'Are you all right, Florence?'

'No!' She climbed off and hurried to the ditch, where she retched. Her mouth and throat stung as she vomited. She had seldom felt so dejected.

'Here, wash out your mouth and then take a drink.' Lavinia passed her a water bottle.

Florence did as she suggested. 'I've been so foolish!' she said. 'I should never have started this trip. I'm not a good traveller. I've sometimes felt sick even in Father's car.'

'Come and sit down for a while.' Lavinia wheeled the bike a little further along, where there was enough roadside bank for them to sit. 'It's almost dry.'

How kind her friend was, Florence thought. Lavinia, though not always quite tidy, always looked brisk and efficient. Her patience and understanding somehow came as a surprise, but then she was trained as a nurse and used to dealing with sick people.

'I think it was partly seeing the war damage and the graves,' Florence said. Of course she had read the papers and knew that there were many such places, but she had been unprepared for their sudden appearance.

What am I to do now? she wondered. Even if we go back it'll mean a long journey on the bike. It was less windy here and the sun beat down.

'How are you feeling now?' Lavinia encouraged her to take another drink.

'Better now I've been sick.'

'It's not that far to the hospital from here,' Lavinia said. 'Six miles maybe, definitely less than ten. If you're well enough we could go on.'

After another few minutes Florence felt sufficiently better to chance continuing their journey. She settled on to the bike once more, feeling small and frail behind her competent companion.

As if to reassure her that they were approaching Saint-Omer, she saw a biplane flying overhead, then another one that was fairly low as though it had recently taken off. She peered curiously at the flimsy looking contraption, though it was too far away for her to get a good view of the pilot.

They reached the outskirts of a town and Lavinia drove towards a large building with elaborate plaster decoration, and slowed down outside. Along the upper storey was the word *Casino* in bold red letters. Florence stared, open-mouthed, at the place. As Lavinia drove the bike down a turning beside it a woman in nurse's uniform came out of a side door and headed down the street.

Lavinia parked at the back, then alighted and held out a hand to Florence. Looking up she could see a balcony on which some soldiers were sitting in wicker chairs or lying on beds. She looked eagerly for James but without seeing him.

'There's a shortage of hospitals,' Lavinia explained. 'They've needed to adapt other buildings, especially for convalescents.'

They walked towards the doorway. 'I'll have to start back fairly soon,' Lavinia said. 'I'm on duty for part of the evening. If it's all right to see James now I'll just stop to say hello. But I'm worried how you're going to get back tomorrow. If I take you by bike you might be sick again.'

Florence felt helpless once more, and extremely silly for embarking on this excursion. *I should have stayed in Larchbury and tried my hand at haymaking,* she thought.

'What'll I do? Is there a bus or train I could take?' *But I barely speak any French,* she panicked.

She followed her friend into the building. 'I'll ask for Emily,' Lavinia said. 'If she's free we can decide what's best.' She spoke to a blonde woman with an elaborate hairstyle who was sitting at a desk in the lobby. She replied with a strong accent that Florence could barely understand, then got to her feet and went to look for Emily.

'That's Claudette,' Lavinia said. 'She used to work here when it was a casino and now she helps us out.'

Florence stood uncertainly in the lobby, with its smell of carbolic which would not have been there in its heyday. She wanted to go and see James. It occurred to her suddenly that although he had been happy to reply to her letters he might not entirely have forgiven her for her earlier rudeness and unkind taunts. *What if he doesn't even want to see me?* she thought.

Claudette returned with a trim nurse hurrying on short legs to keep up with her. 'Lavinia!' she cried delightedly. Beneath her cap a few strands of dark hair were visible.

'Hello, Emily, how are you?' Lavinia said. 'This is my friend, Florence. She's a close friend of Amy's, too.'

Emily greeted her enthusiastically and demanded news of Amy, Edmond and Beth. She was a charming young woman but Florence was growing impatient.

Lavinia, eager to set off back, told her of their mission.

'Orderly Fletcher should be in the dayroom, where the men go in the afternoon, unless he's out on the balcony.'

'Is he doing well?' Florence asked urgently.

'Yes – he'll be sent back to his duties soon. Follow me up the stairs.'

As they headed for the wide staircase Lavinia mentioned the difficulty of getting Florence back to the coast the following day.

'I'll see what I can do,' Emily said.

They reached the top of the staircase. 'Please don't tell James I've been sick, or that I might have trouble getting back,' Florence begged the others. 'Is there somewhere I can comb my hair?'

Emily took them into a pleasant Ladies' room, with gilt frames around the looking glasses. 'We're fortunate here to find ourselves in stylish accommodation. You should see some of the places where I've worked.'

'I'll try to organise a lift to the station for you tomorrow,' she went on as Florence restored her light brown hair to order. 'Or even a lift back to the coast, if there's any suitable transport.'

'Make sure you send me a message to tell me what you've arranged,' Lavinia told Emily. 'If all else fails I'll come over on the bike for you, Florence.'

Florence wished she could brush the dust from her skirt. 'Thank you both for being so wonderful to me,' she said. *I hope I never need to travel on the bike again*, she thought, *but I'm in no position to be fussy.*

They followed Emily into a large room where several invalids were sitting in wicker chairs. Florence had a brief impression of elaborate décor, but she was looking around for James. Then she heard his voice, unmistakeable, though today he was not reading the lesson in his father's church. He was sitting sideways on to them, with a group of men around a table, playing cards.

As they walked across the room he and most of the other men turned in their direction. He, and those who were not too badly injured, stood up. 'Hello, Lavinia!' he cried cheerily, then 'Florence – is it really you?'

'Yes. Do please sit down.' She rushed over and took James's free hand in hers. 'I'm so relieved that you're making good progress.'

'I'm throwing in these cards,' he told the others, flinging them down. There were heaps of francs on the table, along with a few pennies and shillings and a silver threepenny piece. 'Don't tell Father I spend my time gambling,' he said with a grin.

'I need to get back to the ward,' Emily said, arranging quickly to meet Florence later.

'This is the dayroom, but it used to be the main gaming room, you see,' James explained. Now Florence examined her surroundings more closely she noticed the polished wooden bar at one end of the room, though it was free of bottles, only holding mugs and glasses of water. Behind it some fancy glasswork in a swirling Art Nouveau design hinted at the building's former splendour. 'They've banished the roulette wheels,' he told them, 'but we keep up the tradition with poker.'

He moved away from the other men and took his visitors to chairs around an empty table. He had only a slight limp as he walked. There was a sense of purpose in his movements that reminded her he had changed from the awkward youth of a few years earlier.

An orderly brought them mugs of tea, lukewarm but welcome.

'I need to be going,' Lavinia told them, drinking it down rapidly, 'but I'm relieved to see you much better.'

'How's Captain Shenwood now?' James asked urgently.

She was slow answering. 'He's not recovering as well as we hoped,' she said cautiously. 'I'm sure he'd appreciate a visit if you get the chance.' She took her leave of them.

James looked at Florence. 'It's wonderful to see you,' he said. 'How do you come to be here in France?' His face had changed while he had been serving as an orderly, and it was not just the moustache. He looked more alert now, and she supposed he had spent months facing danger, like the other men.

'I thought I should visit you,' she said. *Will he think me presumptuous or foolish?*

'Did you? You came all this way to see me? It's hardly a holiday resort out here.'

'I know – it's been humbling, travelling near the battlefields. But ever since you were injured, helping Captain Shenwood so bravely, I felt I owed you a huge apology for my criticism of you. I don't know how I could have been such a judgemental prig.'

He smiled. 'Lots of others have said the same about me not joining a fighting unit.'

He asked about her journey, and she told him she had come on Lavinia's bike, omitting the part about being sick.

'The other patients are looking this way,' James said. 'They're envious. They'll want to know who you are. They asked me recently if I had a girl at home and I told them you're an old friend who sometimes writes, but I said there was no-one serious.'

She did not know what to say.

'I daresay you care for me a little, having come all this way.'

She smiled. 'I do care for you, James.'

He took her hand and sat holding it, a contented grin on his face. 'How's Larchbury these days? My parents say life goes on normally and make it sound like a little oasis of peace.'

'It's much the same – no, it's different.' She struggled to explain. 'On the face of it, there's still market day, and there are the same shops, and children attend school just as before. But women have taken men's jobs in many shops, and in the inn.'

'That was already happening before I left.'

'Some women even work on the land now. And there have been so many losses.' It was shocking how many families were in mourning. There had been two more cases of flu, too, one of them fatal. She did not want to upset him. 'We're struggling to keep cheerful. Your father says we must have faith.' She did not dare ask if James thought the war might end soon, for there had been so many over-optimistic pronouncements.

'He sent you a notebook,' she added, taking it out of her bag. In the drama of her visit she had almost forgotten to deliver it.

'That's kind of him – I've nearly finished my present one.'

What's he using them for, she wondered – *writing down instructions he's been given for his work as an orderly?*

After a while staff began helping the patients out of the dayroom. 'It's nearly time for our meal,' he told her. 'I'm afraid they'll want you to leave. I have to abide by the rules – it's not as though I'm dangerously ill. Where will you stay tonight?'

'When Emily comes off duty she's going to take me to the inn.'

'Will you come to see me in the morning?' he asked urgently. 'After eleven is best, when the ward rounds are over.'

'I'll be back tomorrow,' she assured him. When he pressed her further she was vague, not wanting to reveal that she had no idea how she would return to the coast.

He kissed her hand softly and clung to it for a few moments longer. 'I can't tell you how thrilled I am that you came,' he said.

He let go of her hand and she headed for the staircase, light-hearted at having brightened his day. She returned to the lobby to wait for Emily.

Chapter Ten

Flanders, July

Emily took Florence to the inn and, in halting French, arranged for her to take a meal and stay overnight. 'Lavinia gave me a ride once on that motorbike,' Emily said. 'I can see only too well why you wouldn't choose to go on it if you get travel sick.'

'You used to be at the same hospital as Lavinia?'

'Yes, we were near Arras, then at Ypres until they evacuated us. I was at that hospital near the coast with Lavinia, but then they sent me here with Sister Reed. Now, about tomorrow – I'll do my best to find you a lift to the station. If it's difficult to arrange will you be able to stay another night? Have you got enough money?'

'I think so.' Florence was not sure how much she might need to pay to travel by train. Once more she panicked. *Emily and Lavinia are doing vital war work*, she thought. *They shouldn't be expected to deal with the consequences of my impetuous decision to come here.*

–

Next morning Florence made her way back towards the hospital. It was another hot day, with little planes occasionally appearing overhead and the usual sounds of artillery to the south.

Soon she reached the casino. In the dayroom two raucous card games were taking place but James was sitting on his own, reading some kind of magazine. The sun was shining through the Art Nouveau glasswork, creating bright red and blue patterns on the floor.

A broad smile lit up his face when he saw Florence.

'The men have kept asking me how I've attracted such a pretty girl as a visitor,' he told her. She blushed. 'How was your room at the inn?'

'It was fine.' It had been small but clean, and the food, though a little sparse, was well-cooked.

'I sometimes try to imagine what it must have been like here before the war,' he told her. 'I envy Edmond, who was able to travel then. They say Flanders was once a lovely area.'

'It was. I came to France once with my parents and we passed through Flanders on our way south.'

'Many towns in the area have sustained damage now, and much of the countryside is devastated too. In some places there's still a bell tower which is undamaged. They play their carillon every Sunday. Each one has its own tune. It's wonderful to hear one.'

'Amy told me it's bad around Ypres, in Belgium.' The Belgian refugees she knew were anxious about their homeland.

'We had to fall back from that area when the Huns began their spring offensive,' he told her.

She wondered once more how long the war would continue and then how many years it might take to restore Flanders to its previous tranquillity. But she did not want to spend her time with James agonising about the future. She was thankful when an orderly brought around mugs of tea for everyone, interrupting their gloomy conversation.

'What's that you were reading when I came in?' she asked curiously, looking at the magazine which looked scrappily produced.

'Have you heard of *The Wipers Times*?'

'No.'

'The name refers to Ypres, of course. That's where some officers discovered an abandoned printing press and began to produce a newspaper. There haven't been any new editions recently, but some old copies are still circulating.'

'May I see it?'

'Better not – it's, well, a bit indelicate. There's bad language and it's quite crude in places. It's funny, though, and that helps us keep going out here.'

'I understand.' She blushed. On the cover of the magazine was a cartoon of a tall, snooty-looking officer with a bristling moustache. 'That looks like Colonel Fairlawn,' she said.

He laughed. 'You're right.' They both remembered his determination to make Amy face the consequences of writing Suffragette slogans in the cricket pavilion.

A young man limped into the room and sat in a chair nearby. His khaki tunic had a badge with wings.

'I'm sure I've seen that chap in Larchbury,' Florence whispered.

'The airman? That's Philip Brownlee,' James told her. He hailed their friend, who came awkwardly to sit in a chair at their table.

'Philip was injured on a training flight,' James explained.

'I came in to land and the ground rushed up and hit me.' The fair-haired young man, not long out of public school, smiled ruefully.

He can hardly have been abroad for more than a few weeks and already he's wounded, Florence thought.

'I'm nearly well enough to leave here,' Philip told her brightly. 'I'm longing to start flying again. When you get home, tell my parents you've seen me, won't you? Reassure them I'm nearly good as new. And the same, if you should see Alice Shenwood. She's writing to me – I love to get her letters.'

'Alice? Is she Charles's sister?' Florence asked. She had met Charles, at parties at The Beeches, but did not know Alice.

'His younger sister.'

'If I visit Charles in hospital I'll tell him I've seen you,' said James.

A nurse came in and began to check that the men were comfortable. Florence got the impression she was one of the senior staff, probably a sister.

'After you with *The Wipers Times*,' Philip requested.

'By all means. I've nearly finished it.' James turned to Florence. 'The magazine is often critical of the top brass. They tried to close it down, but there was an outcry. Since the offensive has stopped them producing it they try to confiscate old copies, but we won't let them, because it keeps up our spirits.'

The sister appeared suddenly at her side, peering from behind her glasses. 'And who might you be?' she demanded of Florence.

'I've come to visit Orderly Fletcher,' she replied as calmly as she could.

'I wasn't aware anyone was planning to visit him. He's not seriously ill. Are you one of his family?'

'I'm just a friend,' she faltered.

'Florence Clifford is a close friend of my cousin, Amy Derwent,' James explained with a confident air. 'I'm thankful to see her, Sister Reed.'

'Amy Derwent, who used to work at the hospital near Arras?'

'Yes, that's her.' She wondered whether to mention Beth, but suspected the sister had little time to chat.

'She was almost as headstrong as Nurse Westholme,' Sister Reed remarked. 'But she was a devoted nurse.' She looked Florence up and down and seemed to conclude that she was respectable. 'Well, Miss Clifford, make sure you don't disrupt our work here, for we're all frantically busy.'

'I promise I won't cause any trouble.'

'And don't encourage any friends to make unannounced visits here. This isn't a holiday resort.'

'No, Sister. I'll make that clear when I get home.'

As Sister Reed hurried away James gave back their mugs to an orderly. 'The doctor examined me this morning,' he told Florence. 'He says I'm fit to start work again, so I'll get my marching orders soon. It's as well you came this week.'

She felt dizzy at the idea of him going back into the fray. 'Must you return already?'

'Don't look so shocked. I want to get back to doing my duty.' He smiled at her and took her hand.

Philip picked up *The Wipers Times*. Florence wished him well as he got up to go out to the balcony with it.

'He's a brave young chap,' James said.

'Where do you think they'll send you when you're fit?' Florence asked.

'I may be posted down towards the fighting along the Somme,' James said, 'but it's quite likely I'll be helping out in hospitals well away from the battles.'

'Let's hope so.'

'We're allowed to dispense drugs and perform lots of tasks that don't need advanced medical skills, like recording details of the men as they arrive at hospital. Sometimes I chat to a badly wounded man, maybe help him write to his family. The men deserve support like that but the medical staff find it hard to spare the time.'

'That's so worthwhile.'

He looked confused. 'My idea of being an orderly hasn't entirely allowed me to uphold my principles. I'm not actually fighting, but I'm helping other men to recover, and then they're sent back to fight.'

She drew her breath. 'Surely you don't regret helping them?'

'No, that would be very wrong. Sometimes I still wonder if I should have refused to serve at all but once I was here I knew I had to help the wounded. And it's hard to explain to them how I feel. If I tell soldiers they shouldn't be here it sounds as though I'm belittling all the courage they show under fire.'

She began to understand his principles. She wanted to know what he planned to do when the war ended, but that day being so elusive, she did not ask.

Emily bustled into the room. 'Hello, Florence. I've found some transport for you. There's an ambulance going to the coast, with space for you to travel on board, but you'll need to leave in half an hour.'

'Oh – I hoped I'd have longer.'

'I don't know when there'll be another chance. There aren't any other ambulances scheduled to take men that way today.'

James squeezed her hand. 'I'll be sorry to see you leave, but you'd better grab the transport.'

She arranged to meet Emily downstairs when it was nearly time to go.

'You'll go on writing, won't you?' he said, turning his grey eyes on her pleadingly.

'Yes, of course. And make sure you reply promptly!'

'I love getting your letters, and Amy's, and ones from my parents, of course.'

They fell quiet as it was nearly time for her to leave. How uncertain the future still was. As she stood up to go he got up and followed her out to the top of the staircase.

'Do be sure not to take unnecessary risks,' she begged. 'And let me know when you're coming home on leave.' She did not want to depart.

'I will.' He took her arm. 'May I kiss you goodbye?'

She raised her face to his and he kissed her gently. She lingered for a few moments, until another soldier left the dayroom and whistled at the sight of them.

'Stay in touch!' he called after her as she dragged herself away. As she went down the large staircase it occurred to her that she had been appalled at the idea that he might be serving near the Front again. Only a few months before, she had been urging him to do his duty there. And as for that kiss – she had thought she would never kiss a man again after losing Bertie, but now she had, and felt elated.

–

Emily was waiting in the lobby. 'The ambulance isn't quite ready yet,' she said. 'Come with me quickly to the dining room and I'll get a sandwich for you.'

Once there Florence could only nibble at the food, anxious not to risk further sickness. She drank another mug of army tea, wishy washy as usual. Then she went and collected her overnight bag from where she had left it with Claudette.

'I managed to phone Lavinia's hospital and leave a message that you've found transport,' Emily said. 'You'll be travelling with some Americans.' They went out to the back of the casino and headed for a waiting ambulance.

'Americans?' She had never met anyone from the United States.

'They're fighting further east, but one of their casualties ended up here, so they've come to collect him.'

She led Florence to the vehicle, which had the words *American Field Service* along the side. Orderlies were transferring a casualty into the back. An officer was standing at the front, smoking. He looked relaxed and vigorous, the way British young men had looked in 1914 as they enlisted, imagining the war was a huge adventure not to be missed. 'Warrant Officer Fawcett? This is Florence Clifford, who needs to travel to the coast.'

The officer put out his cigarette and shook her hand. 'Pleased to meet you.' He was tall and wearing a khaki uniform hardly different from those worn by the British. What a strong accent he had!

A nurse appeared from around the back. 'Sister Jenkins?' Emily said. 'This is my friend, Florence. Take good care of her.'

'We sure will.' Her accent was almost as hard to understand. She was plump and middle-aged, which reassured Florence, who for a moment had imagined she might have to travel in an ambulance full of men.

'Florence occasionally gets travel sick – may she go in front with the driver?'

'Very well.'

'Are you going to Boulogne?' she asked the sister.

'We'll drop Private Staines and the other casualties there, then go on to Le Havre to collect some fresh medical men arriving on a troopship.' She went to check that the new patient was settled in the back.

'Let's go,' she told the others a minute later.

'Give my love to Amy,' said Emily.

Florence hugged her and thanked her for her help. Warrant Officer Fawcett helped her up into the front of the vehicle, and Sister Jenkins climbed up next to her. The officer cranked the engine. When he took his place in the driving seat they were packed quite tightly. He started the ambulance, turned it carefully and drove along the side of the casino and into the main road. He began to gather speed and soon they had left the town behind.

'Our men are fighting along the Marne,' the sister told her. 'But Private Staines got badly injured in a road accident on his way there and his unit had to leave him behind. He's been in a British hospital until recently, then spent a fortnight here convalescing.'

The driver looked around. 'You all right, Miss Florence?'

The state of the road still bothered her. 'I don't feel the bumps quite so much as on my friend's motorbike,' she said. How she would hate to feel sick perched here between the driver and the sister.

Before long they turned on to another road. They were taking a different route from the one Lavinia had used, travelling across a wooded area. The road was generally in a better state than the previous one, and the ambulance less prone to juddering over humps than the bike had been. It was another hot afternoon.

After about an hour she was only feeling faintly sick. She was relieved when they stopped by the roadside and the sister went to the back to check the welfare of the men and pour them drinks of water. The driver got out, helped Florence down and passed her a mug of water. He offered her a cigarette, which she refused, before lighting one himself. She followed him into a patch of shade beneath the trees.

'Where do you live, Miss Clifford?' he asked her.

'In Sussex. Our village is nearly forty miles from London.' She felt a little awkward, standing there beside the confident young officer, who had sandy hair below his cap. *I'd better be polite,* she thought. *His ambulance crew are getting me back to the coast, and sparing me another trip on Lavinia's contraption.* 'Where are you from?' she asked.

'New England – a town called Concord.'

She had no idea where that was. 'Your uniform is quite like ours,' she commented.

'Yes, but you'll find we have very little variation between the different ranks. I'm just a Warrant Officer, but my uniform is almost the same as the commissioned officers wear.'

'How long have you been over here?'

'Only a couple of months. It was thrilling to have the opportunity to travel to Europe.'

She fidgeted, irritated at his blithe manner. She supposed he and his unit were yet to find themselves in the Front Line. 'You've already sustained some wounded,' she pointed out. She considered telling him about Bertie's death and Edmond's injury.

'Yes. We're not here for fun, I know that,' he said more soberly.

The sister summoned them back to the ambulance and soon they were on their way again. There was more traffic on the road now. Her sick feeling was beginning to intensify but she thought the air was fresher here, as though they were approaching the sea. The woodland was giving way to more open countryside with trees that were leaning from the intensity of the prevailing wind.

They passed a signpost indicating Boulogne and caught up with some other vehicles. Soon they were in a queue dawdling towards the coast. They inched forward for almost an hour before reaching the busy port as the shadows were beginning to lengthen.

'I guess this is where we leave you,' said the sister, as they drew up.

'Thank you so much for letting me travel with you,' she said.

Warrant Officer Fawcett helped her down. 'Will you be able to get a ship tonight?' he asked.

'I hope so,' she said. 'Thank you for your help, Warrant Officer Fawcett.'

'Call me Caleb. How would it be if you wrote to me?' He turned his light blue eyes on hers with an intense look.

'I already write to a great friend who's an orderly,' she told him gently.

'Just a few lines – to cheer a soldier who's far from home.'

'I suppose so.'

He wrote down the name of his unit and where they were based on the Marne. 'What's the name of that village in Sussex where you live?'

'Larchbury.'

'Larch – like the name of the tree?'

'Yes.' She did not want to encourage him.

He took her hand. 'It's been a pleasure meeting you, Florence.'

'I hope the war isn't hard on you and your unit, Caleb.' Accepting her overnight bag from him, she took her leave.

She set off towards the promenade hoping to secure a place on a ship.

At least when she got home she could tell Amy, and James's parents, that he was nearly well and in good spirits.

Chapter Eleven

France, August

They sent James to serve in a hospital north of Abbeville, where casualties from the fighting around Amiens were being sent. He was anxious to hear that Florence had reached home safely, and before long was reassured by Amy in a letter. One from Florence soon followed and it seemed she was indeed beginning to return his affection. How thrilled he still was at the memory of her trim figure walking into their dayroom at the casino. He had never imagined she would come to see him. To be there she had undertaken a long journey, including the hazard of crossing the Channel. Later she had also endured being interrogated by Sister Reed.

As she had chatted and passed on news of home he had sat admiring her light brown wavy hair and dainty hands. She had looked happy to see him, and had allowed him to kiss her soft lips: he loved reliving the memory. Even so, he did not think her face had dimpled in the merry way it used to when she had been engaged to Bertie. But all of them had changed since those days. He replied to her letter and asked her to send her photograph.

He was uncertain whether Charles would still be at their original hospital, or at a place for convalescents, or, with good fortune, back in Blighty. He made enquiries and found out he was still in the same ward as before. One day when he had forty-eight hours' leave he set off north to see Charles, alarmed that Lavinia had implied he was not making a good recovery. He booked a room at the modest inn, then walked to the nearby hospital.

'Good to see you, James,' Charles said from his bed. He managed a smile that was a shade unconvincing.

'How are you now, Sir?'

'Please call me Charles.' He levered himself up to a sitting position. 'I needed another operation. The other damn foot was showing signs of gangrene.' He reached for a cigarette and offered James one. They both lit up.

'Very sorry to hear that, Charles.'

'They're trying to cosset me here, to give the remains of this foot the best chance of healing. I had a stupid setback two days ago and it was all my fault.' He took a deep puff of his cigarette. 'The major was visiting the wards. I was sitting in a chair at the time – they were usually getting me up at least once during the day. When the major came in I tried to stand to salute him – what an idiot! But my legs feel as though I still have both feet: it's the nerves, still active. I fell over, as you can imagine, and they had to haul me up again and give me a thorough examination to see how much damage I'd done.'

James was used to hearing alarming stories like his. 'Little harm done, I hope?'

'Only minor bleeding. They cleaned me up and confined me to bed for a few days.'

'I've brought you a copy of *The Wipers Times*.'

'Splendid!' He reached for it and glanced at the front page. 'This is one I haven't seen… So, you're back serving in a hospital again.'

'Yes.' He told Charles about his latest posting. In some ways he was relieved to be helping the injured once more. At present he was working some distance from the Front Line, but he might yet find himself posted to a more dangerous position. 'Have you heard, Charles, we've sent the Huns into retreat around Amiens now!' There had been a spectacular British advance one day recently which had been hailed as a victory at last.

His smile was genuine now. 'Yes, that's capital. Everyone's been talking about it. If only we can keep them in retreat.'

There had been many previous 'significant break-throughs', most of which had come to nothing.

'Have you heard any plans to send you to Blighty?' James asked.

'They were talking of it, just before my latest accident. I expect they'll send me soon.' He looked thoughtful. 'Beatrice, my fiancée, knows I've been injured badly, of course. I haven't told her yet how much my second foot is damaged. I don't think my parents have told her.' He stubbed out his cigarette and lit another one. 'She still writes me encouraging letters, but she's got to accept that I'm handicapped now.'

'Yes, of course.' Beatrice was a lovely young woman but from what he had heard from Amy, she could be demanding.

'Captain Shenwood? Might I have a quick word, Sir?' An orderly had come in, a jolly looking fellow, probably in his mid-thirties.

'Orderly Cole – how are the arrangements going for the concert?' Charles asked. 'We're holding it in the dayroom tomorrow afternoon,' he told James. 'I hope you can come and see it.'

'I'd like to, if it doesn't go on too late. I mustn't miss my train back,' he said eagerly. 'We had a first rate concert party at my hospital last winter. Another one was planned for Easter time, but by then the German offensive was at its height, so it was cancelled. They held one a week ago at my new hospital, but I had to miss it as they needed some of us to stay on duty.'

'Bad luck!' said Charles.

'In the end I heard some of the singers – they came up to the ward after the concert. They performed a few songs to cheer up the dangerously ill men who hadn't been able to attend.'

'It must have brightened their day.'

'I'll say. One of them unexpectedly pulled through.'

'There's nearly a full programme now.' Orderly Cole flourished a list of performers.

'Thank goodness – we've had to postpone it more than once,' Charles told James. 'Captain Turnbull was keen to play for us, but he got sent on. There were some Scottish soldiers nearby for a while, who would have played bagpipes for us, then they got sent nearer the Front.'

'Nurse Westholme has promised to sing for us,' Cole told him, 'and one of the doctors plays the violin and has his instrument here in France. We've roped in a few musicians from the village, and some of we orderlies will sing a little and put on a sketch or two.'

'First rate work, Cole.' Charles was enthusiastic now.

'Thing is, Sir, we could do with some good piano playing, and I understand you're gifted in that area.'

'They weren't sure they'd even allow me down to attend after my latest problem,' Charles said, 'but I'm planning to see the show, with or without permission. I can't imagine playing from an invalid chair. I'll attempt a performance if at all possible.'

'We'd really appreciate that, Sir.' Orderly Cole scribbled something on his programme. He looked across at James.

'How about you? Are you musical at all?'

'I'm afraid not.' His father had hoped he might learn to play the organ but he had lacked musical talent.

Cole looked disappointed.

'I recite a bit, if that's any use. I often read the lesson in Father's church, and I used to perform Shakespeare at school.'

'That would be very welcome,' Cole told him. 'Even the men in the ranks enjoy hearing Shakespeare or poetry at these events. Henry the fifth's speech before Agincourt is very popular.'

James cringed. 'I'd prefer not to read anything warlike.'

'Very well – is there any other speech you remember which the men might like?'

'I know a few – I'll choose something from one of the comedies. But it'll need to be near the start of your programme to make sure I'm not late leaving.'

'Right ho.'

What was that speech in *Henry IV, Part One*, about honour only going to soldiers who had died? The Bard had conveyed cynical views of battles, though he had been writing in the sixteenth century. If only he dared perform that speech – but no, it really wouldn't do.

Perhaps he could give the speech from *As you Like It* beginning *'All the world's a stage'*. Then he remembered Jaques' speech included mention of a soldier, as though that was an essential part of a man's life.

'Listen, Cole, this show won't be bawdy, will it?' Charles said. 'There are bound to be nurses attending.'

'That's understood, Sir. We haven't even got a female impersonator this time – I couldn't find anyone prepared to dress up.'

'I don't want to hear anything at all about *"Mademoiselle from Armentières."'*

'No, Sir – that song's strictly for the trenches.'

–

Extra rows of chairs had been brought into the dayroom and there were fresh vases of bright orange dahlias. Lavinia was officially off duty. She had received a letter from Florence that day, thanking her for her help in travelling. It was a relief to know she had got back safely. In her friend's letter she had detected an element of pride that she had contrived to visit Flanders. Compared with Amy and herself Florence had spent a relatively sedate war, though doing valuable work as a schoolteacher. Now she had asserted herself and proved to her somewhat protective parents that she could escape pre-war concepts of ladylike behaviour.

She stood, smiling, as injured men were helped into the dayroom, some of them on crutches or in invalid chairs. They settled as comfortably as possible, facing the royal portraits at one end of the warm, sunny room. The show would take place around the piano.

What shall I do about Charles? she wondered. Officially he was not on the list of men well enough to attend. She was disappointed that Matron here was so strict, as Captain Shenwood had encouraged them all to take part in the show. With a few minutes left before the opening chorus she considered helping him down from his ward. Then she saw James Fletcher wheeling him into the room in an invalid chair, a blanket over his injured legs. The other officers and men fell silent and then there were a few cheers that he had arrived.

'I'm not sure you should be here,' Lavinia said. Matron might be angry but she could not find the resolution to send him back.

'Nothing will stop me seeing the concert,' he said firmly. He smiled at her. 'How lovely to see you out of uniform,' he said. She had put on her blue crêpe de chine dress, the one smart garment she had brought to France.

James positioned the invalid chair beside the others in the space to one side of the room. A doctor and a sister were looking in Charles's direction dubiously as Orderly Cole played a few introductory bars on the piano. Lavinia could sense the patients' anticipation.

Charles should be congratulated on his timing, Lavinia thought. *By arriving at the last minute, without assistance from any staff working at this hospital, he's presented them with a fait accompli and little opportunity for argument.* Her own anticipation was intensified by the knowledge that he was there to enjoy the show. *But I'll check he doesn't look overtired*, she thought. *Any sign of a problem and I'll get him back on his ward straight away.*

The show began with a rousing chorus from *HMS Pinafore*, with the choir, mostly orderlies, dressed in their tunics turned inside out to the blue side. Charles was pale again after his recent setbacks. His dark curly hair was tidy but his face more haggard than in the old days when he had charmed her and the other girls at social events.

Next Doctor Shaw played a violin piece by Paganini. Charles looked relaxed, leaning back in his chair to enjoy the music.

Then James was invited to the front to recite. He had remained short of ideas for a suitable piece and had finally resorted to the speech from *As you Like It*. He had a good voice, projecting well and conveying the theme meaningfully. The audience sat quietly, enjoying the words. As they clapped afterwards he smiled and returned to his place.

After a humorous sketch performed by the orderlies, everyone joined in the song '*Belgium Put the Kibosh on the Kaiser*', a rousing number before the interval. The concert was proving to be of a patchy standard, but patients and nurses were smiling and laughing. The French doors were open and the sweet smell of honeysuckle wafted in from the garden.

Charles smiled at Lavinia, who was standing nearby at the end of a row of patients. 'It's turning out well,' he said.

The orderlies were bringing around mugs of tea and some bowls of small, sweet strawberries which had been supplied by a French family with large grounds who lived nearby.

'They're very variable, these concerts,' Lavinia said. They were just happy to secure any reasonable form of entertainment. The men were uncritical, glad to be diverted.

'I was fortunate in seeing a good one in the winter,' James said. He was still standing beside Charles's chair. 'They'd managed to get hold of some real entertainers from before the war.'

'There's a Suffragette called Lena Ashwell who organises them,' Lavinia told them. 'She's worked as an actress, and she managed to persuade the authorities to send volunteer performers over here. I met her once at a concert party back in 1916. There was a lot of prejudice against them to start with but she said they could wade through mud and sleep in barns the same as anyone else. I wish we'd managed to get her group to come here.'

'Soon after I came out I heard Ivor Novello perform *Keep the Home Fires Burning*', not long after he'd written it,' said Charles. 'The men were very struck with it.'

The concert began again with some local musicians performing, with Orderly Cole accompanying them on the piano. A patient in an invalid chair had a choking fit and Lavinia rushed to him with a glass of water. She helped a nurse on duty to prop him more comfortably with cushions.

After another sketch, the elderly concertina players from the local band entertained them with a couple of folk tunes, showing more enthusiasm than musical skill. Then they were joined by a pretty dark-haired singer who performed *Madelon*' and *Sous les Ponts de Paris*', which were well received, some of the men humming along to the tunes. At the end the valiant little group were applauded.

Then it was Lavinia's turn to sing. She had chosen an operatic song, '*Je veux vivre*' from Gounod's *Romeo and Juliet*. She had taken singing lessons when younger and had often been persuaded to sing at parties. She felt her voice soaring confidently as she performed it in French. As the short piece closed the men burst into applause and she thought she heard Charles calling out 'Brava!'

'Have you a second song for us?' asked Orderly Cole.

'Oh – I didn't bring any other music…'

'Please sing something, Nurse Westholme. I'm almost through the performers now. Do you know a folk song you could sing unaccompanied?'

She allowed herself to be persuaded, and sang '*She Moved Through the Fair*'. This too was well received.

'Your turn now,' she told Charles. James wheeled him to the front and she helped him manoeuvre Charles on to the piano stool.

He assured her he was comfortable there and began to play while she remained nearby. The notes of Erik Satie wafted through the room, calm, relaxing, though Lavinia felt she had heard it played better. *This must all be a strain for him*, she thought.

Afterwards the men clapped and she and James congratulated him. James looked at his watch. 'I hate to leave, but I simply have to catch my train back,' he told them. The station was a mile away. 'At least I managed to hear both of you perform.'

'We're nearly at the end of the programme,' Cole told James as he left. 'Thank you for your contribution.'

'I wish I'd played better,' Charles said to Cole. 'I've spent too long without practice, and being on medication doesn't help.'

'Nonsense, you played it very well, Sir,' Cole assured him. 'How about a second piece?'

'I'm not up to it at the moment.'

'How about a duet? I've got Mozart's Turkish March here, arranged for four hands. It's relatively easy.'

Charles wavered. 'Have you ever played this, Lavinia? Didn't I hear you once at a party, playing it with a friend?'

'Oh – yes, I believe I did. But Orderly Cole will play it much better.'

'I'll only play it if you'll join me,' Charles insisted, with a coaxing smile she could not refuse.

Cole positioned the music in front of them, and they agreed that Lavinia should play the *primo* part and Charles the *secundo*. Cole brought a chair across, which was not at a good height, but she sat next to Charles, determined to encourage him. Cole announced the encore. For a moment she panicked, worried that they had had no opportunity to practise together, but it was too late to escape performing. Cole brought down his arm as a signal to start them together.

Lavinia launched into the piece with what confidence she could muster, and soon Charles was playing in an assured fashion. She was hardly breathing as she concentrated to avoid any mishap when the score brought their hands close together. She began to relax as they progressed through the piece. With his damaged legs he could not reach the pedals and she had to use them, especially for the loud conclusion. Now she was thrilled to have the opportunity to perform with him.

As the applause broke out he turned to her, beaming. 'I could never have done that without you,' he said, kissing her hand gallantly.

Orderly Cole helped him back into the invalid chair and returned him to his place to one side of the audience.

Doctor Shaw came across. 'I must congratulate you, Shenwood,' he said, 'though strictly you should have stayed quietly in bed.'

Orderly Cole led the audience in '*Roses of Picardy*' to end the concert. Then he sounded the opening bars of the national anthem. Lavinia reached over towards Charles, anxious he should not attempt to stand, but Doctor Shaw had already reached him with the same goal. Everyone who was able to stand got up respectfully.

The men began to disperse, some of them needing help to return to their wards. 'We must get you back in bed,' Lavinia said to Charles urgently. Orderly Cole had the same idea and began steering his invalid chair as Lavinia accompanied them, opening doors. Charles was humming the conclusion to the Turkish March.

It's been a tremendous afternoon, she thought. *But soon Charles will be off back to Blighty, and to Beatrice. How I'll miss him when he's gone.*

Chapter Twelve

Larchbury and Cambridge, September

'You can leave Beth with us for the weekend when you visit Cambridge,' Mother suggested one afternoon when Amy was visiting Sebastopol Terrace.

'Are you sure she won't be too much work for you?' She looked at her lively daughter crawling across the carpet.

'We'd simply love to look after her, now you've weaned her.' Mother's hair was whiter now; her ageing was more noticeable since they had lost Bertie.

'How's Aunt Louisa getting on, back in London?' Amy's aunt had been nervous of returning to her west London home for a while, before becoming convinced that the air raids were a horror of the past.

'She seems very content in her letters. Now she's made the move she's seeing her London friends and settling back.'

Amy was relieved, though she often shuddered at the memory of the terrifying night in February when they had experienced the raid which had killed Katherine.

'Will there be the usual fête at The Beeches?' Mother asked, for the Derwents traditionally held a charity fête in their grounds at the end of summer.

'At first they weren't going to hold it this year.' Young men were abroad or fallen, and many families were disrupted or in mourning as the result of the war. 'It was Edmond who persuaded his parents that it would help raise morale, and bring in money for the war effort. We decided we'd invite the school children to take part, and maybe the Scouts.'

While she was speaking Father came in, looking weary from weeding the garden. It was the last day of his summer holidays. 'What are the children supposed to do for the fête?' he asked her, slumping down into an easy chair. Mother poured him a cup of tea from the pot she had made a few minutes earlier. 'I met the headmaster yesterday and heard about it.'

'Singing folk songs would be fine, or something patriotic,' she said.

'Right. We must start practising. We haven't long to prepare.' He considered. 'There's lots of garden produce in September. Villagers can bring in their spare fruit and vegetables to sell cheaply to raise funds.'

Soon he was talking about the school again. 'I hope young Florence will settle to teaching again after exploring France,' he said. Amy's parents had been intrigued to hear of Florence's trip there. They understood why she had not been able to visit Bertie's grave. It seemed she had cheered up James by visiting him, and the pair were exchanging letters regularly.

'I'm sure she'll soon get back into her routine,' Amy said, though she had noticed a difference in her friend since her audacious trip. She seemed more confident and less apt to sit quietly at home with her parents.

Amy could not resist talking about their house. 'I'm longing to see it,' she told them. Edmond had found it on a visit to Cambridge with his father, and the coming weekend they were taking her to approve it before completing the arrangements.

Father looked at her in a serious fashion, his grey eyes probing hers. 'Will Edmond have enough money to support the three of you at Cambridge?' he asked.

'Yes, of course!'

'Look, darling, we know he means well,' Mother said, drinking the last of her cup of tea, 'and you're used to hard work, but with Beth to care for and a husband who's not fully fit you should have a maid to help.'

'We mean to get one, at least for a couple of days a week,' she reassured them.

'I'm going to give you both a sum of money to help you set up home,' Father said.

'Oh – that's so sweet of you – but you should keep it for when you retire.' She was moved by their generosity.

'We want you to have the money,' Mother said. It was clear they had discussed the matter. 'Look, to be honest, darling, we put money aside in case Bertie needed help in buying a house one day…'

'Oh, I see…' She often thought of her brother, and he was never far from her mind when she visited her parents.

'We can't bring Bertie back, but we'd be delighted for you and Edmond to make good use of the money.'

'If that's what you want it'll be wonderful,' she said, thankful as ever for their constant support. Beth was examining the fire irons enthusiastically, and Amy picked her up and placed her on her lap.

'Edmond will be very grateful, too,' she told them. 'At first we thought it would be hard to live well with only his army pension, but his father's giving him an allowance, and he has a small inheritance from his grandfather. It turns out we'll be well provided for after all!'

Outside the shadows were beginning to lengthen. 'I'd better start back,' Amy said.

'Let me come with you and help push the pram,' Father said, getting up.

He still looks tired, Amy thought. 'There's no need, honestly.'

–

It was still mild outside as she set off back towards The Beeches. A few villagers were wandering home, including the two red-headed Watson girls, looking weary as they wandered down the road on their way back from working on a nearby farm. Besides milking the cows they had been helping with the harvest. Their faces lit up as they stopped to peer into the pram at Beth, sleeping contentedly.

'Your skin is less burnt now,' Amy told the younger girl.

'Yes, Miss – er, Mrs Derwent. It's not been so hot lately. And my arms got better when I put that cream on them.'

'Thank you for giving it to us,' the older one said.

They were only twelve and ten, and Amy wished they had not needed to work all through their summer holidays to help keep the family fed. She waved to them as they continued towards their cottage.

She turned off towards The Beeches. It was the hardest part of her journey, where the lane began to rise. Her bad ankle still hampered her progress. She paused to admire the view of the sheaves of corn in a field, in the reddish glow of the sun.

Soon the path forked. To the left it rose steeply towards the forest, just outside the Derwents' land, while Amy needed to take the right fork towards the drive to the house. A young couple were approaching down the hill from the forest. The girl was Elsie, bright-eyed as she walked along beside a young soldier. Now, who was that private? Amy had the feeling she knew him. Ah, yes, of course, it was Henry Smith, one of the family who had been gardeners at The Beeches. Henry was the middle one, between George and Joe in age. He was slimmer than George, with a merry, freckled face. He greeted Amy, asking after Edmond, before continuing towards Larchbury. He had his arm around Elsie, whose fair hair glowed in the sunshine. Amy took the turning for The Beeches.

Becoming tired, she slowed for a moment and looked around. The couple were entwined in an embrace, exchanging kisses. Amy went on her way, a little uneasy. Elsie did not strike her as a sensible girl and she hoped she was not allowing the soldier too many liberties, even if he would soon be returning to the Front at the end of his leave.

–

'This will make a fine home while you're at university,' Amy told Edmond that weekend. Pa had driven them to Cambridge. The little terraced house Edmond proposed renting was built of red brick with ivy climbing up one side of the façade.

'It's near enough to Edmond's College for him to walk there easily,' Pa approved.

'With three bedrooms we can use the smallest for the nursery and still have a spare room for visitors,' she said, glad she would be able to invite her parents. It would be good to welcome Florence for a weekend too.

She looked out of a front bedroom window into the quiet street as a young man cycled past. 'This is a lovely town,' she said, 'but I suppose it gets much busier in term time.'

'It can get hectic,' Edmond told her, grinning, 'but some parts are so ancient they seldom lose their dignified atmosphere.'

They went back downstairs, to the sitting room, empty apart from three upright chairs, for the agreement was that they would supply most of their own furniture. The rooms were smaller than in her parents' home, but would surely be large enough for their basic needs. 'So the landlord is leaving the curtains and carpets?' Amy checked.

'Yes,' Edmond said. 'Thank goodness we needn't spend time searching for fabrics and rugs.'

She knew they were short of time to complete all the arrangements, and tried to suppress her dislike of the dark, heavy curtains.

He seemed to read her thoughts. 'Unless there's anything you particularly want to replace,' he told her kindly.

'I'll consider making some fresh curtains once we're settled,' she said.

They spent the rest of the early autumn Saturday in visiting a store and choosing a few basic items of furniture. 'Let's buy a new cot for the house here, and keep the present one at The Beeches,' Edmond said. 'Then Beth will have somewhere to sleep when we visit my family.'

At length they returned wearily to the hotel where they were booked to stay overnight, and continued making plans over dinner that evening. They discussed with Pa which of the furniture from their room at The Beeches would be suitable for their house and would need to be brought from Larchbury, along with clothes and their favourite books and gramophone records.

Next morning they wandered down to the river to enjoy the mild weather. She liked Edmond to take a short walk each day; but even now he tired easily and needed to sit on a bench for a while before they went back. Her own walking was still laboured too.

'It's over a year now since I was wounded,' he told her. 'I'm far less breathless than I used to be.'

'Yes, I can see you're improving,' she said. She hoped he would not find life at university too demanding. It would be tempting for him to participate fully in the activities, but she must not allow him to become exhausted.

Along the banks willows trailed their branches towards the water. The few students there before the start of term were eagerly plunging poles into the Cam as they surged along in punts.

'One day when I'm a little fitter I'm taking you out in a punt,' Edmond promised her. It looked a delightful way to spend the day.

Meanwhile there remained important questions to discuss. 'We must advertise for a maid,' Edmond said. 'I've taken down the address for a local paper and I'll send them an advertisement to publish.'

'We couldn't have managed without all your help,' Amy told Pa as they began the journey back. 'We're so grateful for all the driving you've done, and the allowance you're giving us.'

'Your generation are the unfortunate ones who've had to endure this terrible conflict,' Pa said. 'All I've done is look after the forest. The very least I can do for you two is help you make a fresh start now.'

Amy nestled up to Edmond contentedly. At last they would have their own home. Their room at The Beeches was comfortable, if cluttered, but under that roof she was always aware of critical gazes from Ma and Beatrice, who still seemed to regard her as a disappointment.

As they approached London they stopped for lunch at an inn.

'So it's still science you're studying,' Pa asked Edmond, when the waitress had taken their orders, 'but what's this particular branch you're interested in, metallurgy, is it?'

'It's the study of metals,' Edmond said. 'It's a subject that interested me when I first went to Cambridge, before the war. But now, lately, I've heard they're doing pioneering work on lightweight artificial limbs, for the war-wounded.' He still wrote to some of his friends who were fighting and met local serving men when they came on leave.

'It sounds as though Charles will be needing an artificial limb,' Amy said.

'Exactly. It's made me realise how valuable the work can be.'

'It does sound worthwhile,' Pa said.

'At the start of the war, there were only clumsy artificial limbs, unless men could afford to buy their own higher quality ones,' Edmond told him.

'That's right,' Amy said. 'Someone Father knows, whose son is in the school, preferred to use crutches than the awkward artificial limb they offered him.'

'There's the new hospital at Roehampton, in south London, now,' Edmond said. 'They're planning a lot of research and development there. I aim to work there after university.'

'I'm proud of you for having such a fine ambition,' Amy said. *If only he stays fit enough to follow his chosen career*, she thought.

–

It was late afternoon when they arrived back at Larchbury and collected Beth from Sebastopol Terrace. As they motored up the drive to The Beeches Amy recognised a familiar figure walking ahead of them. 'It's James!' she said, delightedly.

'Are you fully recovered now?' she asked as she got out of the car.

'Yes, I'm back at work. I've been escorting some wounded back on the ship and train,' he told them. 'One of the nurses who came with the group is your friend, Lavinia… I've got leave till Wednesday morning.'

'I'm so glad you and Florence are close now,' Amy said.

'She sent me a cake last week,' he said brightly. 'It's tremendous, getting gifts from home.'

Amy was glad, remembering earlier days when she had sent cakes to Edmond and Bertie.

'How's the offensive progressing?' Edmond asked. Each day he scanned the paper and he and Amy were encouraged by the consistent advance that seemed to be taking place. There were reports of chaotic scenes in German cities now.

'We've moved a long way further east,' James said.

'Can you join us for dinner?' asked Mr Derwent. 'I'm sure Cook will have plenty for a guest.'

'That's very kind but I promised my parents I'd be home for dinner,' he told them as they went into the hallway. 'And I'm hoping to see Florence too. I've news for Beatrice, though. One of the officers who arrived back was Captain Shenwood.'

'How is he?' Edmond asked.

'He's had a few setbacks with his recovery,' James told them.

Amy was frightened by his words, remembering the gangrenous wounds she had seen while nursing.

They could hear the mellow notes of the piano as Beatrice played a piece of light music by Sullivan. They all followed the sound into the drawing room. Mrs Derwent sent for tea and cake.

Beatrice had met James before but he was not the kind of impressive young man who she might welcome enthusiastically. She only showed an interest in his arrival when he mentioned Charles.

'So he's back at last!' she exclaimed, packing up her sheets of music. 'But he's in a hospital, you say.'

James gave them details of where he was being treated in London. 'I think he'll be staying there for a few weeks,' he told them.

'And then he'll be discharged, and we can get married?'

'They might want to send him to a hospital for conva-lescents first.' James seemed to be considering his words carefully. 'Captain Shenwood's wounds have not healed as well as they first hoped.'

Edmond was looking stricken now.

'What do you mean?' Beatrice demanded. 'Is his other leg affected too?'

'I believe it is.'

She chewed her lip, clearly concerned at the disquieting news. 'How dreadful. How badly will he be handicapped?' she asked. The room had gone quiet.

'I think you should discuss that with Captain Shenwood and the doctors. Give him a little while to settle in after the journey, though.'

'Yes, I must go and see him!' she said. 'Can you take me to London one day soon, Pa?'

—

Edmond and Amy spent the next few days preparing for their move: there was much to organise. As they packed books into a tea-chest Beth was crawling around the floor again and occasionally seizing a chair leg and trying to pull herself up. 'She'll be walking before long,' Amy said one morning.

Presently they went out for a stroll around the grounds with Beth in her pram. The sunshine was driving away the last of the early mist.

When they returned to the house, raised voices were coming from the kitchen. Amy headed towards the commotion. 'Is everything all right?' she asked.

'No, far from it,' her mother-in-law said from a kitchen chair. Her eyebrows rose towards her hairline. 'Janet's just told me this is her last day.'

'I'm very sorry, Mrs Derwent, but I did give my notice two weeks ago. You have it in my written letter.' The maid looked respectful but determined.

'Quite so, but I've been unable to find a replacement.' They had already lost Mary, their kitchen maid, when she had taken a job at the inn, replacing a man who had joined up.

'I have to go and help with my sister's family,' Janet said steadily. Amy had heard her say a few days earlier that her sister was very ill with tuberculosis. 'The neighbours have been helping so far, but they have their own families to attend to. I'll have to leave today, as I arranged.' She looked at Amy. 'They're my family,' she said.

'Yes, I understand,' Amy said. Copper pans gleamed on the range.

'You're placing me in a very difficult position,' her mistress said, standing up, hands on hips. 'Where am I supposed to find another maid suddenly in wartime?' She turned to Amy. 'Do you think Mrs Johnson would come here every day?'

'I don't think so. She has her own house to run. But she might manage an extra day or two, at least for a short while to allow you to find a replacement. There's Elsie, too. Now the harvesting is nearly finished they might spare her from her work on the land.'

'That scatter-brained creature?' Besides her farm work she had been coming to The Beeches once a week. 'When she was here earlier this week she couldn't stop yawning. She can barely cope with doing the laundry once a week and peeling vegetables,' Ma said. 'I wouldn't trust her with anything else.'

'Perhaps I can help a bit, till we move,' Amy said.

'That wouldn't be suitable at all,' her mother-in-law told her.

'I might just manage some of the lightest duties,' she said. 'Remember Edmond and I won't complain if there's a little dust, or we need to make our own bed. We've been in France and we're used to making do in difficult circumstances.'

'One must try to maintain standards,' asserted Ma.

–

The journey back to London tending to all their sick charges had been tiring for Lavinia. She had found time to chat to James and noticed the spring in his step at the prospect of seeing Florence again.

'Will you get much time here before you return?' he had asked her.

'Only a couple of days, I think.' She could not be certain, for there was talk that the London hospitals were short of nurses and requesting help from any who could be spared from work overseas. She would like to keep in contact with Charles. They had grown closer while they were preparing the concert, and he was still grateful for her joining him in their piano duet. Not long after their performance a fragrant bouquet of white roses had arrived for her; she heard he had asked Orderly Cole to arrange for them to be sent.

It had seemed like fate that she had been one of the staff detailed to travel back with Charles and some other invalids from Flanders. There was a shortage of ships and they had had to wait for two days in a hospital near the coast. In her very limited free time she had liked to sit with him in the dayroom.

However, by her second day in London she had been given her orders to return to her hospital near the French coast, on the Thursday. She went home to see her mother, but returned on Wednesday to visit Charles in his London hospital. Of course she could never be more than a friend to him, but she was anxious to check he was settling well.

'Lavinia! How good to see you,' he said, smiling. He was sitting in a chair by his bed, with a blanket over his legs, and looked a little pale. His body must still be adjusting to his severe injuries.

'How are you feeling? The journey was taxing.'

'I'm getting better gradually. You nurses have been so supportive, you especially.'

'It's our job.'

'I've heard from Beatrice!' His face lightened. 'She's coming to London to see me.'

'That's excellent news.' Her words were less than sincere, but his fiancée, pretty and elegant, was the one he longed to see, and the one who had inspired him in the worst of his suffering.

'When do you return to France?' he asked.

'Tomorrow.'

'All the best, Lavinia.'

—

Amy gathered that James visited Florence soon after his arrival, and then met her when she finished her teaching on the Monday and Tuesday. Pa drove her and Edmond to see him off to France again on Wednesday morning.

Further down the platform Elsie was embracing Henry Smith, whose leave was also ending.

'Those two have been seen together a lot,' Florence remarked. She had obtained permission to take the morning off and clung to James's arm until the train arrived.

–

The following Saturday they held the fête at The Beeches. The involvement of the schoolchildren had ensured it was well supported.

'Don't some of them look healthy and tanned, after their summer working on the farms,' Florence said. 'At last there was some fine weather in August.' She was walking around the stalls with Amy, and taking turns at carrying Beth.

Amy told her about the Watson girls getting sunburn, but agreed that the outdoor activity had suited some of the children.

A group of the younger ones, some from Florence's class, began singing a folk song.

'I'm spending the day with my parents after church tomorrow,' Amy told her.

'I haven't forgotten – it'll be the second anniversary of Bertie's death, won't it? May I join you there?'

'Of course – we thought you'd want to come.'

'I haven't forgotten Bertie, you know. I never will.' Florence's eyes filled with tears.

'You won't, and neither will I.'

Florence wiped her eyes. She seemed to find it difficult to go on. 'Does it seem fickle to you that I'm interested in James now?' she asked.

'Of course not. That's what Bertie would want for you. My parents think the same.'

Presently they joined Edmond, who was sitting with his parents in a wicker chair on the upper lawn as Cook served them tea and seedcake.

Beatrice rushed up suddenly. 'I can't stay at Harriet's when I go to London,' she told them anxiously. 'When I telephoned their house the butler told me the family are all away on holiday.'

'Never mind, darling – I'll book us rooms in a hotel,' Pa told her.

'I'm going to the hospital to see Charles on Monday,' she explained to Florence.

'I do hope he's making a good recovery.'

'If you decide to stay longer I can arrange it,' Pa assured Beatrice.

'I might get the chance to shop for some more of my trousseau,' she said brightly.

Edmond passed the seedcake to his sister and her mother poured her some tea.

'If only the war ends soon,' Beatrice said. 'How I'd love to go to France for our honeymoon!'

'It was delightful in Nice when we made that trip before the war,' her mother agreed.

'Yes – and Charles told me he's visited Paris. How simply wonderful it would be to go there!'

'France is very changed from the way it was before the war,' Florence told her.

'But it's northern France that's suffered all the bombardments, surely,' Beatrice said.

'Peter visited Paris when he had leave,' her mother reminded her.

'So did Charles – that's where he bought me that lovely shawl. You see? It would be perfect.'

Edmond had been looking at her curiously. 'It might be months before Charles is fit enough to travel!' he said forcibly.

Amy had been thinking the same.

Beatrice looked put out. 'Then we'll just have to wait, I suppose,' she said.

'Better be prepared for that, darling,' said her father.

'I'll visit him often and keep him cheerful.'

There was a sudden burst of sound from bugles, as the Scouts prepared for their parade. Ma put her hands over her ears as they began marching along the lower lawn below, their uniforms smart and their feet in step.

Chapter Thirteen

Beatrice wrinkled her nose at the smell of disinfectant as she and her father walked along the hospital corridors. Pa had driven them to London and booked them into a comfortable West End hotel where they had stayed before. Now it was Monday morning and he had driven them to the hospital. On the way she had been turning over her plans for her marriage. At present Charles lived with his family in their large house near Alderbank, but he had spoken of buying his own house after the war; he had inherited some money from his grandfather. How she would love choosing the furnishings! And they would enjoy entertaining friends, for they deserved some fun after all the dismal years.

Nurses, in their drab, unflattering uniform, bustled past as they followed the signs to Charles's ward.

The place looked vaguely familiar. 'Is this the hospital where Edmond came when they sent him back from France?' she asked her father.

'Yes. I expect Charles is in one of the wards for officers.'

When they found it, there were four beds in his small ward, three of them occupied. At first she looked blankly from one injured man to another.

'Beatrice! How wonderful! I've been longing to see you.'

She had failed to recognise him for a moment, sitting up in bed. His face looked pale and haggard compared with the handsome captain she so loved.

'Darling!' she cried, rushing towards him. 'Are you really getting better? It's been so long since I last saw you.'

Her father took Charles's hand and shook it enthusiastically. Beatrice took off her leather gloves and let Charles seize her hand. She sat down in the chair beside his bed and unbuttoned her jacket with her free hand.

'You've scarcely been out of my thoughts,' he told her, fixing his dark eyes on hers. 'All the time I've been stuck in hospital I've lived to see you again.'

She was glad she was wearing her best suit and her hat with the ostrich feathers. Her heart leapt at the realisation of how much he cared for her. All the same, seeing him still in hospital so long after his injury that spring was disturbing. 'Do you still need to stay in bed?' she asked.

A nurse was helping one of the other patients, who had a bandage around his forehead, get up and sit in a nearby chair. The man looked at Beatrice admiringly.

'They allow me to get up for part of each day,' Charles assured her. 'Listen, Beatrice, has anyone told you about my second operation? My wounds didn't heal as well as they hoped.'

'You had a second operation?'

'We haven't heard about that,' her father said. 'How dreadful for you.'

Charles clutched her hand, where the diamonds in her engagement ring sparkled brightly. 'I need to explain to you the extent of my injuries,' he said, looking at her intently.

Her father looked from one to the other of them. 'I'll leave you two to talk,' he said. 'I'll be waiting outside.'

Panic gripped her, for Charles seemed to be preparing her for bad news.

'I heard you lost your right foot and part of your leg,' she said faintly, trying not to think too hard about how he was changed from the dashing officer she had agreed to marry less than a year earlier.

'That's right. They hoped my left leg would heal well, but then I'm afraid I had a setback. I expect you've heard how infections can break out before a wound has a chance to fully heal. They had to take off part of my left foot as well.'

The room seemed to spin round. 'Oh, no – that's awful! How will you get around? I suppose you'll need wooden legs, or artificial limbs of some kind – Edmond and Amy told me better products are becoming available…'

'That's right. Trust me, I'll get as mobile as I can, but I won't be the healthy officer you used to know, who could walk well and dance.'

She struggled for words to say.

'But remember how well Edmond has recovered,' he told her. 'He's my inspiration. With Amy at his side he's making a new life for himself. He told me he was determined to study and have a career – anything less would seem like allowing the Germans to defeat him.'

'Yes, of course.'

The patient sitting beside his bed seemed engrossed in a book, while the third occupant of the ward was fast asleep.

'I can travel around by car, though I expect I'll need a chauffeur. For short distances I'm happy on my horse. Before the war I began to study to be a solicitor and I plan to continue with that.'

'I can see you're being very brave.'

He was looking at her intently again. 'You must understand my wounds are unsightly,' he said. 'In time they'll look less raw, and they won't show when I'm kitted out with artificial appliances and fully dressed, but as my wife you'll have to see them.'

She gasped. How could life be so cruel?

'So I'm afraid you'll need to face that, if you're to marry me,' he told her solemnly. 'It's fair to say that I'm no longer the man you agreed to marry last Christmas. If you decide you want to break off the engagement I'll understand. I'll give you your liberty if that's what you'd prefer.'

'Oh – no – I still want to marry you,' she found herself saying automatically. Ever since they had become engaged she had looked forward to the thrilling day when he would become her husband. Her wedding gown was ordered and the guest list only needed to be finally agreed. How could she set aside that dream?

'Think about it,' he insisted. 'I've got to receive treatment for a few more months, including being fitted with appliances and practising getting around with them. We shouldn't get married until after that, so it will be some time next year. But if you decide you'd rather marry a healthy man I'll release you from the engagement without any bad feelings.'

'No,' she said softly, 'of course I'll stick by you.' This appalling war had lasted four years now and she had heard about disfigurements. This was what people did in these circumstances, wasn't it?

–

'What's the matter, Beatrice: you look awful,' Pa asked her as they left. 'What's the position with Charles? Has he needed surgery on his other leg?'

'Yes.' She faltered as she told him the details. 'In fact, he offered to release me from the engagement.'

They got back into the car. 'I'm sorry, Bea, that's dreadful news. But I'm sure you'll stick by him and help him make a new life. He'll be brave and resourceful like Edmond and everyone will admire him.'

'To think he'll never be able to dance again!' she cried. 'Imagine how hard it will be for him to wander along a seaside promenade on a fine day.' As she pictured him sitting forlornly in a corner of a room, hampered if he wished to move elsewhere, she could not help reflecting on all the things they had planned to do together and how much their future was changed.

As they reached the hotel she was subdued. She changed into an evening dress before they went down to dinner. She did not feel like eating much.

The restaurant had flowers and soft lighting from candelabra. It was not as full as sometimes and many of the men were in uniform. A few of them looked at her admiringly as she took her place with Pa and ordered consommé followed by chicken.

He began asking her about Charles's future prospects and she told him what she remembered of his plans to be fitted with artificial limbs. A tall man in an officer's uniform was sitting alone at a nearby table and smiled as she met his glance. *Have I met him before somewhere,* she wondered. *Yes, I know him socially, I'm certain now.*

She finished most of the consommé and picked at her chicken and sipped a little wine. Her mind was still reeling with Charles's news. She told Pa she would not eat anything else but did not mind if he wanted a dessert. He ordered cheese and a glass of port, besides coffee for them both.

The tall man finished his meal, got up and headed in their direction. 'Mr Derwent – Beatrice – how lovely to see you!' he said confidently.

As he shook hands with them she remembered he was Captain Wilfrid Fairlawn, the colonel's son.

'I'm here on leave for a few days,' he told her. He was broad shouldered and towered over them.

She had not seen him since around about the start of the war, she thought. In fact she believed they had spoken at the fête in September 1914, when he had accompanied his father on the recruiting campaign.

'I'm planning to make good use of my time in London,' he went on. 'I might see *The Maid of the Mountains*, or *Chu Chin Chow*. I've missed the theatre so much while I've been in Flanders.'

Pa was gulping down his cheese and port, and any minute now he would suggest returning to their rooms, realising she was in no mood for social niceties.

A waiter approached their table. 'Mr Derwent, Sir? There's a telephone call for you.'

He hesitated, then got up to take the call. 'Please excuse me,' he said. 'I don't suppose I'll be long,' he told Beatrice.

She looked at the officer, smart in his uniform. 'I believe you were already in the army when the war began,' she said.

He sat down in the chair her father had vacated. 'That's right. I've been through the whole campaign – well, almost – and I've been promoted to Major.'

'Congratulations!' If she had not been so downcast at Charles's news she would have noticed his impressive rank. 'Your father must be proud of you. You seem to have escaped being badly injured,' she said, wondering at his good fortune.

'I got a bullet through my shoulder on the Somme,' he told her. 'Luckily it wasn't a severe wound. It was just enough to keep me out of the fighting for the rest of the year. Apart from that I've been very fortunate.'

'You have.' There could not be many men who had survived the whole war so far relatively unscathed.

'I say, Beatrice, would you come to the theatre with me one night this week?'

'I can't possibly!' she exclaimed. 'Don't you know I'm engaged to Charles Shenwood?'

'Beatrice, please forgive me.' He looked at her hand. 'I'm sure I should have known, but I'm afraid I'd forgotten. I should have noticed your lovely ring… Let's see, Shenwood was badly injured, wasn't he? Is he recovering well?'

'It's a slow process,' she managed. If only Pa would come back.

'Would you write to me at the Front, Beatrice? It would brighten my days.'

She considered. 'I don't think that would be appropriate.' All the same, it was flattering that he was interested in her.

'It's so wonderful to have news from home.' He scribbled his details on a piece of paper and thrust it into her hand. She sat awkwardly for a moment, then put it hurriedly into her bag as she saw Pa returning. Wilfrid stood up to make way for him.

'That was your mother,' Pa said. 'She was anxious for news of Charles. Well now, Captain Fairlawn—'

'Wilfrid is a major now,' she said.

'Excuse me, Major Fairlawn – would you excuse us if we retire now? It's been quite a hectic day.'

–

Beatrice tossed and turned all night, trying to accept the new situation.

'Are you all right, darling?' Pa asked as she joined him for breakfast. 'You look wretched.'

'I couldn't sleep.' The hotel was well supplied, in spite of the war. Waiters were rushing around bringing guests eggs and bacon, or kippers. 'I don't feel much like breakfast – I'll just have some toast.'

'Very well. I expect you're planning to see Charles again? Try to keep cheerful for him.'

She fiddled with her napkin. 'Pa, I've decided, I simply can't marry him. I'm going to call it off.'

He stared at her from the other side of the table. 'Don't be foolish, Beatrice. You can't let him down now!'

'I can't face marrying him, Pa. Please don't try to make me.'

There was a stern expression in his blue eyes. 'Come, now, Beatrice – I'd expect better of you. Think of how you care for him. Stay with him, help him recover. Adjust to the new circumstances – plenty of other women do.'

As she delayed her reply his expression grew more angry. It was much worse than the way he looked at her if she explained that she had spent her allowance and needed more money.

The waiter set a dish of kippers in front of him, but he left it untouched.

'Listen, Pa, Charles accepts that he's no longer the man I said I'd marry.' Her voice trembled as she explained. 'He's willing to release me from the engagement. He actually urged me to consider breaking it off.'

'Please don't do anything hasty. Go to see him again, but be sympathetic. Think how he's suffered…'

'I'm not going to visit him again.' She felt certain it was the only way ahead.

'You mean you intend to just drop him?' His voice had risen.

The smell of his fish was making her feel nauseous. 'I thought I'd write him a letter. You can deliver it, if you like.'

He shook his head. 'Beatrice, I can't force you to marry Charles, but please consider carefully before you end the engagement. We could stay here a few more days – Ross and Walter can look after the forest.'

'No – there's no point. I've made up my mind.' The more he argued the more determined she became.

'I want you to spend some time thinking about the implications, and try to find the strength to support him.'

How could she stop him pestering her to set aside her resolution? 'I'll think about it some more for the rest of this morning,' she said. 'I won't change my mind, though.'

She went to her room and fiddled with the perfume bottle, powder compact and other trinkets on the dressing table, reviewing her decision, but could see nothing else to be done. *A life spent tending an invalid, remembering the bright dreams I once had — how could I bear it?* she thought. *The sooner the better, there's no point in prolonging the situation.* She stared out of the window at the multi-storeyed houses along the sunlit street. *I meant to do some shopping*, she thought, *though I won't be needing a trousseau now. But while I'm in London I should use the opportunity to visit some good shops.*

She put on her coat and hat without telling her father, and asked a man in reception to call her a cab. Her heart beat a little faster at the sight of fashionably dressed women in the street. Visiting town was part of the life she loved, shopping, visiting West End theatres, strolling through the parks, and eating in restaurants, especially ones where there was dancing. She was longing to be part of it again, with Charles by her side. *Except now it can't happen*, she thought. *He'd be too handicapped by his injuries.*

Swarming carts and cars and omnibuses impeded her progress to Harrods. The store was not as flourishing as it had been before the war, and the selection of gowns was not as tempting as it had once been. She looked around the departments unenthusiastically, still sick at heart. If only Charles was still the captivating man he had once been, instead of a pitiful invalid.

She could not settle to her task and left the store with a velvet scarf her only purchase. On her way back by cab she leant back against the slightly dingy upholstery, turning over in her mind what she should write in her letter to Charles.

–

Amy and Edmond left the veranda as the late afternoon grew cooler. She gave Beth her meal, prepared by Cook, and put her to bed.

Amy joined Edmond and Mrs Derwent in the drawing room, where a fragrant bowl of pink roses adorned the side table.

Almost immediately they heard Beatrice and her father arriving home.

'You're in good time for dinner,' Mrs Derwent approved as they joined them.

The new arrivals both looked tense.

'What's the matter?' Edmond demanded. 'How's Charles?'

Beatrice sniffed and fiddled with her hair. She sat down on the edge of the sofa.

'He's lost his right leg halfway to the knee, and part of his left foot,' Mr Derwent said bleakly.

'Oh, Heavens!' said his wife. 'You told me on the phone last night that he'd needed another operation, but I hadn't grasped the extent of his disabilities.'

'Poor Charles.' Edmond's face was frozen with dismay. 'At first they hoped his left leg would hardly be affected.'

Amy's mind dwelt on some of the severe leg injuries she had seen, and the men who had endured repeated operations to try to halt the advance of gangrene.

'If he's otherwise fit he'll be resolute enough to learn to walk with artificial limbs,' Edmond went on.

Beatrice and her father remained silent and Amy detected an uneasy atmosphere between them.

'I shall not be marrying Charles now,' Beatrice announced. She took off her gloves and Amy noticed the diamond ring was missing from her finger.

'What?' Edmond cried angrily.

'When I went to see him in the hospital he explained the extent of his injuries,' Beatrice said. 'He said that he was no longer the man I'd agreed to marry and offered to release me from my engagement.' She looked down, avoiding their gaze.

Edmond stiffened. 'Charles is the most noble of men,' he said forcefully, 'but if you ever really loved him you would stick by him now and help him make the best of his life.'

'My dreams have been ruined as well as his,' Beatrice said.

'Thank God Amy has stuck beside me!' Edmond said. 'I'm sure her support has hastened my recovery.'

'It's very different for you,' Beatrice retorted. 'For one thing, you were already married when you got wounded. I haven't taken my vows. And besides, Amy is a trained nurse. She's used to tending the wounded. I'm not sure I could bear to even see Charles's injuries.'

'Why do these terrible things keep happening?' asked her mother, wringing her hands.

Beatrice looked around at them, finding little sympathy. 'I'm going to my room,' she said, picking up her gloves. 'Ma, would you ask Cook to bring me a light supper there?' Her usual elegant comportment was scarcely diminished as she walked out.

Mr Derwent shrugged and sat down. 'Yesterday, when Beatrice saw Charles, and heard about his injuries, she said at first that she'd stick by him. She was very upset, though. By this morning she'd decided she couldn't go through with the marriage. I tried very hard to persuade her otherwise. She wrote Charles a letter and I had the unhappy task of delivering it. Charles looked devastated but was very understanding. I'd have been proud to have him as a son-in-law.'

Soon dinner was ready. They ate their meal, mainly in silence. Edmond reminded them of a young woman living nearby who had faced a similar dilemma when her fiancé was badly wounded and who had gone ahead with the wedding, determined to stick by him.

'Beatrice may receive some censure for this,' Pa said.

Edmond and Amy went to their room soon afterwards. Amy had seldom seen him so angry. While she sat on the sofa he paced up and down.

'Perhaps it's better that Beatrice realises her limitations now,' she ventured, 'rather than marrying Charles and them both being unhappy afterwards.'

There was a tortured look on Edmond's face. 'Charles was wounded while doing his duty,' he said forcibly. 'If he had decided he'd prefer not to fight he'd have faced a court martial for cowardice. Now my pathetic sister can't see she has any kind of obligation to support him.'

'You think she should marry him from a sense of duty?' Amy asked, unusually questioning his opinion.

'I suppose, when you put it like that, it's a great deal to ask.' He sat down on the bed, his head in his hands. She went and put her arms around him. She remembered Katherine, long before her tragic death, when they had first worked together at the London hospital. Her friend had come from a privileged background and had found the work extremely gruelling to start with, but had summoned the resources to fulfil a valuable role in the hospital. *But Beatrice isn't Katherine*, she thought.

'I keep wondering if you would have a better life, married to a man who's whole.' The words seemed to be dragged from Edmond.

'Don't say that! You know I could never imagine being married to anyone else. You make me happier than I could ever have dreamt!'

Chapter Fourteen

London and Larchbury, September to October

Charles was sitting in a chair beside his bed, with a blanket over his ravaged legs, when Edmond arrived. 'The doctors here have done what they can for me now,' he said, managing to summon a smile. 'They're talking of sending me to a hospital for convalescents, only they're short of places.' At least that meant they had finally stopped any further risk of gangrene.

'I imagine you're still in a lot of pain,' Edmond said.

'Less than at first. I'm managing to come off the morphia gradually. We wounded have to challenge fate, don't we, and live as best we can. You've been my inspiration.'

'I don't think I can ever forgive Beatrice for abandoning you.' Edmond's voice was harsh.

Charles could hardly sleep since her father had brought him her letter. He had been thrilled when she had visited him, almost more beautiful than he remembered, and at first she had still seemed prepared to welcome him as her future life companion. When she had left, one of the other officers in the room had congratulated him on his good fortune. But of course, Beatrice deserved a healthy husband.

'You mustn't blame her. Releasing her was the only decent thing I could do,' Charles said. 'She's from a good family, gently brought up and ladylike. She's never faced anything disturbing like war wounds. Most young women from her background would be the same, unless they've taken an active part in the war.' He did not want Edmond to realise how broken he felt inside and blame his sister. 'Let me give you her letters and photos to return to her. I've got some at my parents' house as well, which I'll send on later.'

Edmond took the package from him grimly.

'Thanks, Edmond. How are you now? Did you come to London by train?'

'I told Pa I could manage to travel alone, but he insisted on driving me up here. We'll stay in our usual hotel and go back tomorrow.'

Compared with the thin, often breathless, man Charles had seen at Christmas, Edmond looked almost fit again, but it was not clear how much he would continue to be affected by the damage to his lung. 'Are you off back to Cambridge soon?' Charles asked.

Edmond's eyes lit up. 'Yes – the weekend after this coming one we're setting off, the three of us. Amy's thrilled that we'll have our own home at last.' He told Charles about the little house they had found.

Charles related good news from France, for on the eve of his return to London the advance eastwards had been progressing well. Edmond stayed talking for over an hour but then noticed that Charles looked tired, and took his leave.

Charles closed his eyes, no longer obliged to look resigned to the loss of Beatrice. During his worst moments in the French hospital he had looked forward to choosing a home with her. How comfortable they would make it, he had thought, and what a delight it would be to see his beautiful wife installed there, and hear her accomplished playing of the piano. He longed to think of their tender moments together, which would surely be possible in spite of his injuries. Sometimes when he awoke now he imagined for a few moments that they were still planning their marriage, then he would remember the visit from Mr Derwent and the sudden dashing of his dreams.

His bleak mood oppressed him again. Once, when he had considered all he had lost, he had found himself wishing James Fletcher had not been there to rescue him, and he had bled to death on the bank of the Lys canal. Since then he had managed to quell his very darkest emotions. He was determined not to allow his injuries to crush him, but now he could only rely on his own resources.

–

Edmond was still anxious about Charles. He visited him again the following day and left him whisky, cigarettes and a John Buchan novel to read. He promised to be in touch regularly, especially in his university vacations.

It was just over a week now till he and Amy moved. They had already engaged a maid to come to their house twice a week when they had moved in. Grace, the middle-aged woman, had good references.

When he reached The Beeches, Amy greeted him happily, anxious for news of Charles. She looked a little pale.

'Are you tired, darling?' he asked her.

'A bit. I've been making lists of things to take and doing some more packing.' He knew Beth needed a good deal of her attention, too.

Beatrice accepted the bundle of letters and photographs that Charles had returned. For a moment he thought he noticed a glimmer of unease in her manner. Then she said she was relieved that he was being brave, but she did not waver from her decision to end her engagement. She was restless and ready to complain of the blow fate had dealt her.

His mother was out of sorts, partly on account of Beatrice and partly from her domestic problems. After dinner Amy began mending some clothes, including one of Ma's dresses.

'Dearest, you shouldn't have to do that,' Edmond told her.

'Nonsense, I'm used to mending.'

His mother refrained from commenting, probably reasoning that her dress would otherwise go neglected.

—

A few evenings later, Edmond spent time alone with his father, drinking port and discussing recent newspaper accounts of the war. The Germans were finally joining peace negotiations.

Soon they went to the drawing room to join the others. 'Where's Amy?' he asked. 'Is she taking an early night?'

'I believe she's ironing in the kitchen,' his mother told him.

'You shouldn't let her do that!' his father exclaimed. 'This morning I found her cleaning the silverware.'

'Mrs Johnson wasn't here today,' his wife said.

'This has got to stop,' Edmond said angrily. He went to the kitchen and found Amy diligently ironing a blouse.

'You look worn out,' he said. 'Stop doing that and come and sit down.'

'I'll just finish this garment,' she said.

When they joined the others his father shared his concern. 'You're not a servant,' Pa told her firmly. 'We'll manage somehow till we can find a new maid.'

'I do feel weary,' she admitted.

'Are you all right, darling?' Edmond asked her.

'I think I might have a cold coming. My throat feels sore.'

They went to bed and soon she was sleeping peacefully. By the following day she was sneezing, and that night her stuffed up nose seemed to be keeping her awake.

The next day was Wednesday. They got up and began to dress, then she broke off to sneeze a few times and sat down on the bed.

'Are you getting worse?' Edmond asked.

'I think I'm running a temperature,' she said.

He laid his hand on her forehead, which seemed hot. He had a sudden feeling of dread.

'I'd better go back to bed,' she said. 'Can you get Beth ready?'

'I will in a minute,' he said, fully dressed now, 'but first I'm calling Doctor Stanhope.'

He rushed downstairs to the telephone. The influenza epidemic was continuing in an alarming manner and it was often fatal. There had been a few more cases in their area. When he had called the doctor, he took Amy a cup of tea and got Beth out of her cot. 'Dada,' she said contentedly.

When she was dressed he took her through to Amy.

'Hello, sweetie,' she said, blowing a kiss to Beth. 'Better keep her away from me, darling, I don't want her catching my germs.'

Beth began crawling around the floor. Edmond sat on the bed next to Amy, anxious for the doctor to arrive.

Amy blew her nose a few times.

'How are you feeling now, darling?' he asked her.

'I haven't any energy,' she told him.

Cook arrived with a breakfast tray, but Amy had little appetite. Edmond spooned food into Beth's mouth and ate his own breakfast. He was just pouring a second cup of tea for Amy when Doctor Stanhope arrived. He was somewhat stooped and moved slowly, but Larchbury relied on him working while younger doctors served in France.

'It looks as though you have quite a bad cold,' he told Amy. By now her nostrils were red. He took her pulse and her temperature and listened to her chest with his stethoscope.

'Are you quite certain it's just a cold?' Edmond said.

'It's not the flu, if that's worrying you,' he said. 'Her temperature would be higher.'

'I could have told you it's just a feverish cold,' Amy said. 'Oh, dear, I don't know if I'll be well enough for the move on Saturday.'

'You must take it easy for the next week,' the doctor told her. 'No exertions.'

'I'll stay here with you till you're completely better,' Edmond told her when the doctor had left.

'No, you mustn't miss the start of your term!' she cried, suddenly wide awake. 'I absolutely insist you go on Saturday. I won't be there to help you, but Grace will come to clean and you can go to a restaurant for some of your meals. I'll join you as soon as I can. Perhaps Grace can come for a day or two extra, and prepare some meals for you.'

'If I'm here I can look after Beth for you.'

'My mother will gladly have her to stay with them. Perhaps you should take her there this morning, so she doesn't run the risk of catching my cold.'

Gradually she persuaded him he must set out for Cambridge at the weekend on his own. The resumption of his studies would be very different from what he had planned.

—

For the next two days Amy got up for an hour or two to help Edmond complete his packing and decide which of their joint possessions to have delivered to their house. Her mother telephoned daily around noon from the nearest public phone to assure her that Beth was well. Amy could talk to her daughter down the phone line, though it was mystifying for the little girl.

'I've been making arrangements,' Pa told them later as they sat in the drawing room. 'I've asked Chambers to clean the silver regularly.'

'Good idea,' Ma said. 'It's a reasonable task for a butler.'

'He understands how we're placed and he's proving very helpful. He said that if Mrs Johnson cleans the drawing room and dining room on her days here, and the main bedrooms, he'll sweep the other rooms for us, except the nursery, perhaps.'

'That will certainly help,' she told him.

'It's only till we can get another maid. Chambers is ageing now and I should be decreasing his tasks.'

'Amy mustn't be burdened with extra tasks,' Edmond said. 'And besides, she'll be joining me in Cambridge.'

How fortunate they are, having the butler's loyalty and goodwill, Amy thought.

Early on Saturday Chambers helped Pa load the remainder of Edmond's belongings into the car. The furniture would be delivered separately.

'Make sure Edmond doesn't do any heavy work!' Amy begged Pa as they prepared to set off for Cambridge. 'He hasn't got the stamina to heave tables and chairs around, or packing cases.'

'Absolutely. He's not strong enough.' Mr Derwent promised to make sure the men unpacked everything and distributed it around the house. He would stay overnight before returning.

Amy and Edmond embraced before he left. 'I'll join you as soon as I can,' she promised. He got in the car and she waved as Pa drove off. How bereft she felt suddenly.

–

'How you must miss Edmond,' Florence said when she phoned Amy the following day.

'Yes, but I'm a little better today and I hope we'll go to Cambridge soon.' Amy's voice sounded husky from her cold. 'Have you heard from James since he went back?'

'Yes, we correspond regularly.' As she said this, Florence's sister, Sarah, who was visiting for the day, passed through the hall and glanced at her curiously.

Florence longed for James's letters now, anxious about him in a way she had not been until she had realised it was his principles making him determined not to fight. When he had become injured she had begun to understand how dangerous his duties could be.

Lately she had heard some gossip about Beatrice. 'I say, Amy, is it true Beatrice has broken off her engagement to Charles?'

'I'm afraid she has.' Amy sounded dismayed. 'We were shocked at her decision.'

'Poor Charles.' She could not find anything pleasant to say in mitigation of Amy's sister-in-law's behaviour. 'I'll tell James, when I write, and Lavinia, though they might have heard the news already.'

'It's kind of you to phone,' Amy said. 'I was getting bored here without Edmond or Beth.'

'Hurry up and get well!'

'Yes – I want to fetch Beth home as soon as possible.'

I never told Amy about the other recipient of one of my letters, Florence thought, as she replaced the receiver. She had written a letter to Warrant Officer Fawcett, the confident young American who had driven her back to the coast at the end of her visit to France, remembering his plea for her to write to a soldier far from home. Her letter was brief but amiable, and she had not headed it with her address, so he would not be able to reply. It would be unfair to encourage him. She gathered from the newspapers that the Americans were advancing against the Germans in the Marne area.

Florence joined her mother and Sarah.

'Are you writing to James, the vicar's son?' her sister asked, staring at her as she sat down.

'Yes…' If only the others in her family could begin to understand his merits. 'He's doing valuable work as a medical orderly, and even got injured himself while attending to Captain Shenwood.'

'I've heard about your trip to France to see him,' Sarah said in a disapproving tone. 'But James refused to fight!'

'This war should never have been started,' Florence said. 'You're very fortunate that your Geoffrey wasn't called up to fight.'

Sarah's husband had been forty at the start of the war, and the shop he ran was well established. Eventually conscription had started, but at first only single men had to sign up. By the time they included married men he had just passed his forty-second birthday and so need not fight.

'He thinks the same as me, that it was shabby of James not to join a fighting unit,' Sarah said, choosing to ignore that some men of her husband's age had volunteered to serve.

'Well he should know better!' said Florence.

'Now then, Florence, that will do.' Her mother took Sarah's view as usual. She was weary of them both looking at her in that critical manner.

She rose to her feet and hurried out of the parlour, up to her room, and sat down in her easy chair. On her small table she had arranged a bunch of roses in her glass vase. Bertie's photo was still displayed there, and now she had a small one of James as well. She took refuge in her room more often these days, weary of the company of her family.

Will they ever accept James? she wondered. They had tried to ignore her Suffragette views as well. *James and I are both determined to act according to our values*, she thought.

Maybe one day the others will understand, but even if they don't respect our beliefs, they'll never make us change them.

It had been nearly a week since she had heard from him. Some nights she found it hard to sleep. She was back in the situation of waiting impatiently for mail, anxious what might become of him. It was like the days when she had been engaged to Bertie. Although her brain had told her that Bertie was risking his life, she had on one level felt that the happy-go-lucky young man was indestructible. The fighting on the Somme had shown her the extent of her mistake.

The last two years had brought her many reminders of the fragility of life on the Western Front. She remembered Amy saying that she could not look ahead while Edmond had been in France, for the future had seemed like a landscape shrouded in thick fog. Florence could not console herself with the fact that James was a medical orderly, or that recent reports suggested there might soon be victory. Men on bicycles still delivered horrifying telegrams and there was no solace to be had.

-

Besides her mother and Florence, Amy was soon getting phone calls from Edmond. He had to use a call box as he did not have a telephone installed.

'I'm a lot better now,' she told him on the Tuesday, wondering if she could join him at the weekend. 'Is Grace looking after you?'

'Yes, she's managing well. She's coming for three days a week at the moment, and she's making me some meals.'

Amy was relieved. 'How's it going at College?'

'Give me a chance – I've only just started back! But I'm finding it stimulating. At last I can put the battlefields behind me and concentrate on my studies.' He paused. 'But come as soon as you can, dearest, I miss you so much.'

'You know nothing will keep me away longer than necessary!' In the long nights she would worry about him, and the emptiness of his side of the bed was hard to bear.

Chapter Fifteen

Larchbury, October

On the Wednesday her mother-in-law asked Amy if she was well enough to go with her to the Working Party in the village hall.

'Not today, I'm afraid. I should go and collect Beth from Mother's house.' She was longing to have her back. Every day she missed Beth's affectionate presence, besides yearning for Edmond.

'That's a pity. Bea won't be going so I shall have to attend by myself.' Beatrice had been unable to avoid hearing gossip about her treatment of Charles. She considered the critical remarks were undeserved.

That afternoon Mr Derwent drove his wife and Amy into the middle of Larchbury, leaving his wife at the village hall before going on to Sebastopol Terrace.

'Mamma!' Beth cried in delight as Amy picked her up.

'I've missed you so much, sweetie!' Amy said, kissing her.

'She's getting a bit snuffly now,' her mother said. 'It can't be your cold, after all this time. I wonder if she picked up an infection when I took her with me to the shops yesterday? Do you think I should have kept her at home?'

Amy felt Beth's forehead, which was no warmer than normal, and wiped her nose with a clean handkerchief. 'It was best to take her out for some air, I think.'

She wrapped up her daughter well. 'Are you going to the Working Party?' she asked Mother.

'It's rather late to go there now – I'll give it a miss today.' She was moving slowly, the way she did when she was tired. *She finds Beth hard work*, Amy thought, *even if she's too kind to admit it*.

Beth came back with them to The Beeches and Amy spent the rest of the afternoon playing with her, making up for lost time.

Over the next two days the little girl developed a cough.

'It's nothing serious,' Amy told Edmond when he phoned, 'but I don't think we should travel to Cambridge until she's better. It's a long way and there's a cold wind.' She wished Pa had a more modern car, instead of an open one.

'I suppose I'll have to manage without you a little longer,' he said, sounding forlorn.

'How are you settling?'

'There's a chap called Horace on my course,' he said, more brightly. 'He's the younger brother of someone I knew when I was here before. He was excused conscription because of his eyesight. He's living in a rented room nearby and he's got a telephone. He says I can give you his number, then in an emergency you can contact him and he can pass on the message, instead of you having to wait for me to ring.'

'That's a wonderful idea.' She wrote down the number he gave her. They went on talking until he ran out of pennies for the telephone.

–

The following morning as they were eating breakfast Beatrice received a letter from France. 'Is that from someone I know?' her mother could not resist asking.

Beatrice used a knife to open it, a satisfied smile appearing on her face.

'It's from Major Wilfrid Fairlawn,' she said.

Amy stopped spooning food to Beth as a jolt of dismay ran through her. With difficulty she managed to avoid commenting. No-one else at the table knew of her appalling experience in Ypres, when Wilfrid had assaulted her.

'He was staying at our hotel when we were in London,' Pa said, shooting Beatrice a questioning look, as though critical that, having broken off her engagement so recently, she was already corresponding with another officer.

'He begged me to write to him,' Beatrice said. 'You know how soldiers long to receive letters.'

'They're a very distinguished family,' Ma approved.

Amy abandoned the rest of her breakfast and took Beth off to the nursery, still climbing the stairs awkwardly. By what horrific failure of judgement had Beatrice given up Charles, only to pursue her acquaintance with Wilfrid? At least the man was in France now, lacking the opportunity to spend time with her.

The morning was quite mild, so Amy took Beth out in her pram, wandering along the paths in the grounds for a while and urging young Joe to pick some of the remaining apples in the kitchen garden. As she walked slowly back to the house she resolved to speak to Beatrice: it would be unfair to leave her in ignorance of Wilfrid's behaviour. She pushed the pram up the slope to the sunny veranda, left Beth there, and went in search of her sister-in-law.

Once inside the house she could hear Beatrice's confident piano playing. She joined her in the drawing room, thankful she was on her own.

'May I have a word?' she asked at the end of the piece.

'What do you want?' Beatrice frowned at the interruption. She was elegant as ever in a lacy blouse and dark skirt which emphasized her tiny waist.

'It's about Wilfrid Fairlawn.' *Heavens*, she thought, *this isn't going to be easy*.

'What about him?'

'I just thought you should know that in Flanders he has a very bad reputation. I understand he's liable to make unwanted advances to nurses.'

Her delicately arched eyebrows shot up. 'You must be mistaken. I don't know where you've heard such a thing. How dare you blacken his name!'

'Listen, Beatrice, I'm not trying to persuade you to marry Charles. You may write to whoever you like, and marry whoever you like, and I wish you well, but I strongly advise you to keep Captain Fairlawn at a distance.'

'He's Major Fairlawn now, didn't you know?' she snapped.

'Yes, I remember now, Major Fairlawn. I know he's got an impressive war record.'

'You don't even know his rank! I've known Wilfrid since we were both children, though I lost touch while he was away fighting. He's from a very good family and has had an outstanding military career, like his father.' Her eyes widened. 'Ah yes, I understand now what all this is about. Colonel Fairlawn was the one who wanted you sent to jail, wasn't he, after that disgraceful incident when you and your Suffragette friends damaged the cricket pavilion. I can see how embarrassing it might be for you if we continue to socialise with the family.'

Amy gasped. She could see now that her warning about Wilfrid might give that impression. 'No, you're wrong. Of course it would be awkward if I had to meet Colonel Fairlawn, and it would be my own fault, but it's his son I'm telling you about. I thought it was only right to warn you.'

Beatrice's greenish eyes were blazing now. 'Just who do you think you are?' she sneered. 'You're just a schoolteacher's daughter and you've never moved in our social circle, at least not till you became involved with Edmond. We've always moved among families with a good status. How dare you think you're entitled to attack them on the basis of some gossip you've heard among your nursing friends – probably from some foolish girl who's led him on.'

Amy struggled to keep calm. She wanted to tell Beatrice how unjustly she was describing Wilfrid's victim. She dug her fingernails into the palms of her hands to avoid making some kind of incoherent outburst. That would make her sister-in-law even less likely to believe her. 'I assure you that a woman I know well was assaulted by him,' she explained as patiently as she could, 'although she'd made it very clear to him that his advances were unwelcome.'

'I'm simply not going to listen to any more of this,' Beatrice said, packing up her music sheets and slamming down the piano lid. 'You've ruined my morning.'

'I meant well, Beatrice.'

'You've never liked me. You don't want me to be happy. I'll never allow you to influence the company I keep.' She swept out of the room.

She says I've never liked her, Amy thought, *but the complete reverse is true. I've always wanted to be closer to her but she generally keeps me at a distance. But I'm partly to blame because of that stupid incident at the cricket pavilion, and being sent to prison for it. I'll never live that down and it's poisoned my relationship with Beatrice.*

–

Two days later Beatrice went to London, to Amy's relief. She would spend some days with Harriet, her old school friend. By now Beth's cough was getting better, though she was sometimes fretful from teething. Amy was hoping once more to join Edmond soon.

Then one morning Pa came down to breakfast looking agitated and asking Amy to take a look at his wife. 'She's ill,' he told her. 'She looks quite dreadful.'

Mrs Johnson was there that morning and Amy left Beth with her while she went to her in-laws' bedroom, with its faint aroma of Ma's favourite perfume. Mrs Derwent was breathing rapidly and there was a sunken look around her eyes. Amy touched her forehead and it was alarmingly hot. 'Send for Doctor Stanhope,' she told Pa. 'Ask him to come at once in case it's the flu.'

She fetched a warm drink for the invalid. Ma seemed scarcely aware of what was happening. Amy sponged her forehead.

The doctor arrived soon afterwards. He looked at Ma and examined her.

'You were right to call me. It's almost certainly the Spanish influenza.'

Horrified, Amy sat down in the nearest chair.

'I haven't heard of any fresh cases around here,' Pa said, suddenly pale.

'I've seen one earlier this morning.' It seemed that a woman who had been at the Working Party had developed the flu. She might have caught it from a relative who was on leave from France.

'Can you get my wife a hospital place?' Pa asked.

'The hospital in Wealdham is overflowing,' Doctor Stanhope said. He looked weary. 'There are a lot of cases there.'

'I could nurse her,' Amy said. 'I've been a VAD. I know how to nurse infectious patients.'

'That might be safer than moving Mrs Derwent,' the doctor said. 'I'll send a mask for you to wear, Amy, and some aspirin. Try to get her to take warm drinks. I'll call in every day.'

'Yes, Doctor.'

'Some people have given patients more aspirin than the recommended dose.' He looked at her solemnly. 'Don't do that – it can give rise to side effects that make the situation worse.'

'I'll stick to the correct dose.'

Mr Derwent saw the doctor out, then returned to his bedroom. His features drooped with concern. 'Please do everything you can to save her, Amy!'

'I'll do my best.' It was natural to her to nurse the patient, but now she recognised what a challenge it might be. 'We must take the utmost care not to spread the infection,' she told him urgently. 'I should be the only one to nurse her.' She tried to plan what to do. 'Can you phone my uncle Arthur to tell him what's happened? He's on the phone. He can tell my mother and ask if she can take Beth again, to get her away from here.'

'Yes, I'll do that.'

'You should sleep in another room till Ma's better.'

'I'll move into Peter's room.'

'Do you think Beatrice can stay longer with her friends?'

'I'll phone them and ask,' he said. He seemed to draw some comfort from following her careful instructions.

She began sponging the sick woman's face and hands once more. How hot she felt!

'When Edmond phones this evening I'll tell him she's sick,' she told Pa. 'I'll try not to make him worry.'

'I'll write him a letter.'

'No, don't – if you happen to be infectious you could pass the illness on to Edmond, via the writing paper. Remember his lung is impaired. He simply mustn't catch the flu.'

Amy settled her patient as best she could. For the moment the room was warm enough.

The doctor returned with aspirins and a mask. Soon Mrs Johnson told Amy her mother had arrived. Beth stared at Amy who was wearing a face mask and some old cotton gloves as she packed her tiny clothes and other belongings.

Amy would have loved to pick up her daughter and kiss her, but she was anxious she might already be infectious. She allowed her mother to gather up the little girl. 'I don't want Mrs Johnson working for you and for us while there's sickness here,' she said.

'I believe I should stay here and help you,' Mrs Johnson said. The expression on her round face was concerned but reassuringly competent. 'Is there a room where I can sleep?'

'There's the one Janet used to have.' Amy was grateful for Mrs Johnson's loyalty but concerned for her mother. 'I'm leaving you with extra work and no maid,' she said wretchedly.

'Don't you worry. Just make sure you don't take any risks yourself.' Mother spoke calmly, but Amy could sense her concern.

'I'm afraid Beth may be fretful sometimes as she's teething.'

'It's all right, dear, I can manage. Remember I raised you and Bertie.'

Mrs Johnson suggested a neighbour who might oblige Amy's parents with a few hours' work.

When her mother and Beth had left, tears began to run down Amy's face. She was separated once again from those she loved best.

–

By midday Amy had made arrangements for the servants to keep their distance from the sick room. If she rang the bell Mrs Johnson would come to see what was required and bring it up, leaving it outside the door. Amy would keep her contact with the others to the minimum.

When she was not tending her mother-in-law she sat trying to remember what she had read about the disease, and what Lavinia had told her. The chief danger was that the illness would lead to pneumonia or septicaemia. A patient could turn blue in the face and then death would soon follow.

Pa looked in.

'She's much the same,' Amy told him.

'Is there anything I can bring you?'

'May I read the newspaper, when you've finished with it?' she asked. It would relieve the tedium. 'Afterwards I'll need to burn it, to avoid passing on the infection.'

Presently he brought it to her. She looked through it, noting that the news of peace negotiations was encouraging, but she could not concentrate. Nursing her mother-in-law reminded her of her war work, and young men they had not been able to save.

The room was large and expensively furnished, though Amy found the drapery unnecessarily flounced and ruched. She looked out of the window at a faint view of the trees shedding their leaves, visible through the afternoon mist. It reminded her of the dense mist that she had seen after Bertie's death, and the old feeling of being lost, without a signpost. It had haunted her in the days soon after Edmond had been wounded, when she had been terrified she might lose him. Now they were facing a fresh crisis.

Mrs Johnson brought her some logs to make up the fire and then later left her dinner outside the room.

Soon afterwards Edmond phoned and she was called down to speak to him. His father had already told him that Ma was ill.

'How is she really?' he demanded.

'She's about the same as this morning,' she told him. 'Her temperature is still very high, and she's listless, but I don't think she's any worse. I'll stay in her room overnight so I'm aware of any change.'

'Take care, dearest.'

'I will.'

She did not want to end the conversation and he seemed equally reluctant. 'Promise me, darling, promise me you'll make sure you don't get ill.'

'I promise.'

He rang off and she disinfected the phone with some carbolic she had placed beside it, before going back to the sick room. She was being as careful as she could but there was still a risk she might catch the disease, and they said it was more often fatal in younger adults. *I mustn't catch it*, she thought. *Edmond needs me and so does Beth.*

She had not felt so frightened since Edmond had been wounded.

Chapter Sixteen

London, October

'Have you heard how your mother is today?' Beatrice's friend Harriet asked, dawdling to the breakfast table.

'Yes – I've already rung her.' Beatrice had been anxious for news. 'Pa says she's definitely no worse, perhaps a little better.' She turned to Harriet's parents. 'It's so sweet of you to let me stay longer.'

'You're always welcome to visit,' Harriet's mother said. She was a kindly woman, still attractive in her smart clothes, and content to spend her days running their homes and playing her part in a Working Party, providing comforts for the troops, as Beatrice did with her mother.

She had known Harriet Patterson since her school days. She was a striking young woman with black hair. The family had a lovely home near Wealdham, but they also had an elegant Georgian house in a terrace in west London, where they generally stayed during the cooler months, though they had kept away at the height of the Zeppelin raids. Happily there had not been any raids for months now.

Beatrice was glad to escape the unpleasant gossip in Larchbury. Harriet had been understanding about her broken engagement, for though she had liked Charles and been shocked to hear the extent of his injuries, she had said she would probably have done the same in the circumstances.

Mr Patterson was tall and serious looking, with grey hair becoming thin on top. He was smart in his business suit and soon left the breakfast table to go to his London office.

Shortly afterwards there was a telephone call for Harriet. The maid brought some fresh toast and Beatrice took another slice to complete her breakfast.

How lovely to be away from The Beeches for a while longer, she thought, *at least now I know Ma's no worse*. Her illness had lasted around a week already. This had been a trying year, with Edmond's poor health – though he was much improved – and the horror of Charles's injuries. Little Beth was sweet, but Amy carried her around the house with her instead of confining her to the nursery with a nanny. The child would begin to cry if she became hungry or wanted to be put down to crawl, exploring the room. Then there was the lack of servants.

'That was Zadie on the phone,' Harriet told them, returning to the table. Zadie Fairlawn was a young woman they had known at school.

'Is she still joining us for dinner tonight?' asked Mrs Patterson.

'Yes, but guess what? Her brother Wilfrid is on leave. May he join us too?'

'Of course – I'll tell Cook there'll be another guest.'

'Wilfrid?' exclaimed Beatrice. 'Is he on leave again?' He had not told her in his recent letter that he was expecting to return so soon. Normally leave was hard to obtain, as Edmond had found when he had served in Flanders.

'I believe he was allowed to come back because his mother is ill.' Harriet flung down her napkin. 'What shall we do this morning? Shall we go shopping?'

They put on their outdoor clothes while they were waiting for a cab. One of the manservants had been sent to engage one, and few were available these days. When one eventually arrived they went out into the fresh morning. The trees along the street were turning golden.

Beatrice passed the day in pleasant anticipation. How thrilling it was that she was here in London just as Wilfrid returned! Mrs Patterson happily allowed her maid to attend to Beatrice's hair that evening, and the young woman arranged it in attractive large curls. She put on her pale blue evening dress, which was smart but not too showy for dinner in a friend's home. She felt warm, in spite of her bare arms, for a generous fire was blazing.

Before long Zadie and Wilfrid arrived. As they came into the drawing room Mr Patterson was greeting Wilfrid enthusiastically and enquiring about the progress of the war.

He assured his host that the troops were continuing to advance. 'Beatrice!' he exclaimed, his eyes lighting up, 'This is an unexpected pleasure! How lovely to see you again!'

She smiled back, her heart leaping. They all went into the dining room, where they seated him next to her. He was in uniform as usual.

'I was surprised to find you back on leave so soon,' she said.

'Happily surprised, I hope.'

'Naturally.'

Zadie and the Pattersons were looking curiously in their direction. 'Beatrice has been writing to me in France,' he told them. 'It's so wonderful to receive letters from her.'

Their cook came in and began serving the soup. There was an array of sparkling glasses, and a vase of late-flowering roses in the centre of the table, though she felt their arrangement was a little haphazard.

'I gather you came on leave because your mother is ill,' Beatrice said to Wilfrid. 'I do so hope she hasn't got the Spanish flu.'

'At first we were afraid it might be that,' Wilfrid told her. 'Father wanted to dash home, but he couldn't be spared from France. At least they allowed me to come.'

'As it turned out, her illness isn't the Spanish flu, but a less severe form of the disease,' Zadie said.

'Oh, what a relief for you! My own mother is ill with the Spanish flu now,' Beatrice told them.

Wilfrid and his sister exclaimed with concern.

'That's why they wanted me to stay away from the house,' she told them. 'I'm happy to say Ma seems to be holding her own.'

Soon they were served the saddle of lamb, without a fish course, as meals were less lavish now. The wine flowed and the little group became more light-hearted.

'How long do you expect to stay on leave?' Beatrice asked Wilfrid.

'For a week or so, I hope, now we have the Huns in full retreat,' he told her. 'Next week I want to attend a fellow officer's wedding.' He leant towards her and lowered his voice. 'I must say, Beatrice, you're looking very lovely tonight!'

She smiled as she allowed the butler to refill her glass. There was just a faint thought stirring in the back of her mind, nagging a little. What was that elusive memory? Yes, of course, it was Amy's ridiculous claim that Wilfrid made unwelcome advances to women. But she did not believe a word of that. Amy was, at best, deluded by some idiotic female who had led the major to imagine she welcomed his intimate attentions, and then changed her mind. She had heard of a few women behaving like that. There was absolutely no need to pay attention to Amy's allegations.

After the meal the men were quick to join them in the drawing room, where Beatrice was happy to play a Chopin nocturne. She felt that Wilfrid was watching her, and when she finished he was lavish with his applause.

By the time Harriet and Zadie had taken their turns to perform, without reaching her standard, Mrs Patterson was beginning to yawn.

'It's been a delightful evening,' Wilfrid said, 'and what a bevy of beauty I've found here! Might I take you young ladies out for a meal tomorrow evening? Are you free, Beatrice and Harriet? And how about you, Zadie?'

'I'm meeting a friend tomorrow, Wilfrid, dear,' said his sister. Beatrice and Harriet accepted his invitation.

'It's extremely kind of you,' Beatrice told him.

'I must make the most of my leave while I have the chance.'

–

How well my visit's turning out, Beatrice thought. After her morning phone call to her father, when she had been reassured that Ma's temperature was falling a little, she spent the day reading magazines and chatting with Harriet about their old school friends. Harriet mentioned Lavinia Westholme, asking if she was still nursing in Flanders.

'I believe so,' Beatrice said, changing the subject as soon as she could, for she thought Lavinia had nursed Charles.

At last it was time to get ready for their evening out. 'Are you going to wear your new green dress?' Harriet asked.

'I think I will.' Pale green had always suited Beatrice's colouring. It was cut a little lower than her other evening gowns, but no lower than the ones Harriet wore. The maid arranged her chestnut hair attractively again and fastened her dainty platinum necklace for her.

Promptly at seven o'clock the tall major arrived with a taxicab. 'This is the best I could find,' he said. 'The vehicle must be almost as old as its driver.' Few new taxis had been produced during the war, and young drivers had been called up to fight.

Wilfrid sat opposite them in the back. 'How lovely you both look,' he said, though Beatrice was sure she was the chief object of his interest.

The cab dropped them at a smart restaurant near Piccadilly, where he had made a reservation. Heads turned as they walked in, and she was glad once more that she had made an effort with her appearance. As for Wilfrid, he was not as handsome as Charles, for his eyes were pale and rather small, while his nose was large and lips fleshy. He was an imposing figure, though, especially in uniform, thanks to his height and broad shoulders.

They sat down in the dining room, and a waiter brought them menus. 'It's not too bad here,' Wilfrid said. 'They manage to get ducks and partridges.'

Beatrice scarcely noticed the meal or the wine, content to find herself at a stylish restaurant in the West End, with agreeable companions. There was a hum of genteel conversation and a middle-aged lady pianist was playing music by Debussy. Around her most of the young men wore uniform, and the other clientele were well-dressed.

Wilfrid was attentive, asking her about her mother's progress, and how Edmond was recovering. Amy was not mentioned. *What an embarrassment my sister-in-law is*, Beatrice thought. *Wilfrid almost certainly knows she's been in jail.*

As they ordered desserts Beatrice congratulated him on his taste in restaurants.

'Do you think the war will really be over soon?' she asked him. 'How lovely it'll be to get back to normal, with the men back home, so we can enjoy parties and dances again!'

Wilfrid agreed with her. Harriet was looking a little strained, and Beatrice realised she had been somewhat monopolising Wilfrid's attention. But it was not her fault if he happened to prefer her company.

Harriet stood up suddenly. 'I believe that's Gilbert Barnet over there!' she cried. 'I didn't know he was on leave. He's a great friend.'

She waved to the man in captain's uniform and he recognised her and came to their table.

'Harriet!' he exclaimed. 'It's been ages since I've seen you.'

He was of medium height and a little plump, but had a jolly manner. Harriet made introductions and he hovered beside their table.

'I've only just come on leave,' he told them. 'I'm here with my brother tonight, as he's recovering from a war wound and about to be sent back. Mother and Father were asking me when I'd be getting in touch with you, and I was thinking of phoning.'

Harriet was clearly flattered by his attention, and followed him across to his table to greet his brother.

Wilfrid was smiling across the table at Beatrice, and refilling her glass. 'I was planning to visit the theatre to see *The Maid of the Mountains*,' he told her. 'Would you like to come with me tomorrow, if I can get tickets?'

'I'd absolutely love to,' she said, thrilled that her social life seemed to be gathering pace.

The next minute Harriet and Gilbert returned. 'Gilbert is eager for me to go back with him and his brother,' Harriet said. 'Then I can say hello to his parents, who are staying in town with a relative for a few days. Would you mind awfully if I left you two? You'll take Beatrice back to my home in a cab, won't you, Wilfrid?'

'Certainly. You go ahead with your plans.'

'Thank you so much for bringing us here,' Harriet said. 'It's been a delightful evening.' Then she went to join her friends.

'At last I have you to myself!' Wilfrid said, with a mischievous smile. 'I am right, aren't I, that you're no longer engaged to Charles Shenwood?'

'No, not any more.'

'I thought that was what I'd heard.'

She confided briefly how Charles had offered to release her from the engagement. 'I hope you don't think it was unkind of me to accept his offer,' she said, anxious at the censure she had experienced from some quarters. Sometimes she even felt guilty for not marrying Charles and devoting her life to caring for him.

'I'd never presume to comment on a young lady's decisions in matters of the heart,' he assured her.

They sat chatting happily for a while longer, but most of the other diners had left and the pianist was packing up her sheet music.

'I'd better ask them to get us a cab,' Wilfrid said. He helped her into her soft velvet cloak. As they waited in the lobby she thought what a fine couple they made.

In this part of London it was less difficult to find a cab. He sat beside her in the back and took her hand as the driver set off. *What a delicious evening this is turning out to be*, she thought. *Maybe he'll put his arm around me, and when he drops me at the Pattersons' he might venture a respectful goodnight kiss.*

She was conscious that she had drunk slightly more wine than usual, and that he smelled quite strongly of drink. She thought it must be a mistake when he let go her hand and began running his fingers along her skirt, against her leg.

'I say, Wilfrid, would you stop that, please.'

'Darling Beatrice, it's been such a wonderful evening. You can't blame me for being enchanted with you.'

His hand was wandering to her bosom now. *Why's he behaving so badly?* she thought, struggling to put more distance between them. She suspected he had already had a few drinks before calling for them that evening.

'Beatrice – I love you so much!' Now his lips were finding hers, and there was nothing respectful about the hungry way he kissed her.

She pulled away from him desperately. 'Stop this at once!' she cried, growing alarmed. His tall, broad-shouldered physique struck her for the first time as threatening.

'We needn't end the evening like this,' he said, slightly slurred, and gripping her arm. 'We can go somewhere to be private and…'

'How dare you!'

'I'm sure that's what you really want…'

'Stop! Please stop the cab!' she called out. She had to call again before the driver heard her and pulled over to the side of the road.

'Everything all right, Madam?' he asked.

'No! I'm getting out.'

He opened the door for her and held out a hand to help her on to the pavement. 'Are you sure, Madam? Will you be all right here?'

'Yes,' she said, trembling at how Wilfrid had treated her. He was staring at her angrily from inside the cab as she stood at the side of the road. As the driver closed the door and drove off her shock was turning to outrage at what had happened. Why hadn't the driver said something to Wilfrid, thrown him out of the cab and taken her back? She supposed if you wore a major's uniform a lot could be excused.

A light drizzle was beginning to fall, and here she was, in an unfamiliar part of London. At least she was still in the West End, and people were becoming slack about the blackout now air raids were no longer expected. A little further along the street was a modest hotel, and as she walked towards it a taxicab was approaching.

She hurried towards the cab, which was stopping outside the hotel. 'I'm sorry, Madam, this cab is booked,' said the driver.

'Oh, please!' Tears of frustration were beginning to run down her face.

A middle-aged man was heading for the taxi. 'Thank you, driver,' he said. 'Please allow the young lady to take the cab. I can wait for another one.'

'Very good, Sir.' The driver opened the door for her and she gave him the Pattersons' address.

'Thank you so much!' she said to her rescuer. He raised his hat to her as she stepped into the cab.

As it set off she sank back into her seat, fighting back her tears. She could still taste Wilfrid's alcohol-laden lips and remember the pressure of his hand as he explored her body. Amy had warned her about him, she remembered now. But it had all seemed so unlikely that she had not been able to credit it. How could he treat her like that? It was extremely insulting that he might think she would succumb to such an approach.

The journey back seemed to be taking a long while, but eventually she began to recognise streets near the Pattersons' house. She felt in her bag for her purse. Now she was suddenly worried how much the journey would cost. Pa had sent her allowance, but although she had cashed the postal order she had not transferred any of the sovereigns to her dainty evening bag.

The driver helped her out and asked for four shillings. She looked in her bag and found only a half crown. How positively ghastly this evening was becoming. There was nothing for it but to ring at the doorbell and ask the Pattersons for money, and they would be curious about what had gone wrong.

Just then another cab came around the corner, and to her relief she saw Gilbert helping Harriet out.

'Hello, Beatrice!' Harriet cried. 'Is anything wrong?'

'Yes! Listen, have you got any money? I haven't got quite enough to pay for my cab.' She was shaking with embarrassment. You were meant to tip the fellows, too, she remembered.

'Let me take care of this,' Gilbert said. In no time he had paid her cabbie and the man had driven off.

'Goodnight, Gilbert. It's been a lovely evening,' Harriet said as Gilbert kissed her hand.

'I'll phone you tomorrow,' he said, before getting back into his own cab.

Beatrice was still shaking as she followed Harriet up the steps to the house.

'Whatever's the matter, Bea? Why didn't Wilfrid bring you back?'

'I don't want to talk about it. Please just let me go to bed.' Once inside she rushed up the stairs to her room and collapsed on to the bed as her tears flowed.

–

Beatrice hardly slept that night, horrified that the evening which had begun with such promise had ended disastrously. She needed to provide some kind of explanation for Harriet and probably for Mr and Mrs Patterson. She could not bear to tell them how Wilfrid had assaulted her: it would mean recounting her experiences. All the same, he deserved to be shunned by decent women and punished for his behaviour.

Next morning she composed herself as best she could and joined the others at the breakfast table, a little late. They all stared at her. It was clear that Harriet had mentioned that something had gone amiss the previous evening.

The maid offered her the fruit bowl and she nibbled some grapes.

'Are you all right, Bea?' Harriet asked.

'Yes, thank you.' She paused, unsure how to continue. 'I was obliged to leave Major Fairlawn last night. His behaviour was most insulting.' The others were staring at her. 'He behaved improperly in the taxicab – he kept touching me.'

'Oh, what nonsense!' cried Mrs Patterson. 'They're a distinguished family. We've known them for years. He'd never behave in such a way. If he touched you inappropriately it must have been entirely by accident.'

'I assure you it wasn't.' The maid brought Beatrice some porridge and she took tiny spoonfuls. She was about to tell the others that she had heard a previous complaint about Wilfrid's behaviour, but stopped in confusion. If they knew she had heard a complaint they would want to know why she had gone with him alone in a cab.

Mr Patterson was glaring at her and Harriet looking curious.

'I don't want to hear any more about this,' Mrs Patterson said.

Beatrice had seldom felt so wretched. She turned down the offer of scrambled eggs with mushrooms and excused herself from the table.

'One moment, Beatrice,' said Mr Patterson. 'Would you come to my study, please.'

She followed him. His manner was unsympathetic.

The room was gloomy, lined with wooden panelling, and unheated as he would be spending the day away at his office.

'Take a seat, please.'

She sat down at the desk. He sat down opposite and fixed a cold stare on her.

'Now let's try to get to the bottom of this matter,' he said impatiently. 'Did you do anything last night which Major Fairlawn could have regarded as encouraging impropriety? If you did, I assure you I will be discreet.'

'No!' she cried. 'I did nothing of the kind. I imagined he would accompany me back here in a respectful manner.' She tried to marshal her thoughts. 'I've never been treated in such a way in all my life.'

Harriet's father was standing now, red in the face. 'That's enough, Beatrice. Let me make myself clear. Whatever kind of misunderstanding you may have had with the major, you are not to make this kind of lurid accusation. The Fairlawns are held in high esteem, and both father and son have had outstanding military careers.'

'I know that,' she said, trying to hold back her tears. 'But Wilfrid should still not be allowed to molest women,' she said feebly.

'That will do. Get out of my study, and if you make any kind of trouble for the Fairlawns you will not be welcome here again.'

She hurried out of the room as her tears began to flow again. She rushed upstairs and sat down on her bed. *How am I to get through the day?* she wondered.

There was a knock at her door. 'May I come in?' asked Harriet. She was neat and collected in a fine woollen dress, her hair tastefully arranged.

'Yes.' *Will she understand?* Beatrice wondered.

'What really happened last night?' Harriet asked, her hazel eyes probing Beatrice's face as she went to sit beside her on the bed. 'Did you lead Wilfrid on in some way? If you did I promise I won't tell anyone.'

'I didn't do anything to encourage his behaviour... Have you ever heard any other woman complain about him?'

'No – but then he's mostly been abroad during the war. I think you'll have to stop accusing him of impropriety, Bea – no-one will believe you.'

'Why won't they?' she demanded, pounding the pillow. 'Why does everyone imagine I'd make up something like that?'

A maid knocked on the door. 'Are you there, Miss Patterson? Captain Barnet is on the phone for you.'

Harriet rushed out, looking rather relieved at ending the awkward conversation.

Beatrice strode up and down, wringing her hands. Then she began pulling blouses and gowns from the wardrobe and undergarments from the drawers and heaping them up on the bed. She piled clothes back into her suitcases, less carefully than usual. She looked around and remembered her other pairs of shoes and crammed them in, pushing them towards the bottom. Then there was her hairbrush, and jewellery to wrap in tissue paper. She was too distraught to send for the maid. After a while she went down to the hall, and found to her relief that Harriet was no longer on the phone.

Normally she asked before using it, out of politeness, but this morning she simply began the call. As long as Ma was well enough she would go home straight away. If not she would need to find a different friend to stay with for a while.

Chapter Seventeen

Larchbury, October

The days had dragged past, without Amy getting much sleep. She would deliberately stay up late so she could check on Ma around midnight and sponge her to cool her down. Pa looked washed out too, as though concern was keeping him awake. The doctor had called in each day and seemed satisfied that Mrs Derwent was no worse.

One morning Amy's mother phoned from the public telephone to say that Beth was well. 'How lively she is now!' she remarked. 'She's crawling around the room so quickly, and keeps trying to pull herself to her feet. She'll be walking soon.'

In the evening Florence phoned Amy to check Ma was no worse. 'It must be dreadfully worrying for you,' she said.

'I'm missing Beth so much,' Amy said. 'I'm wondering if she'll take her first steps while she's away from home. And thank you for helping with her. It's such a relief, because I don't want Mother to be exhausted.' Florence had called at Sebastopol Terrace at the weekend to take Beth out in her pram.

'It's a joy to see her,' Florence said. 'I'm planning to call there tomorrow after school, and if the late afternoon is warm enough I'll take her out again.'

The following morning Amy received a letter from Lavinia. Her friend had come back, escorting wounded soldiers again, and now she had been required to remain at a London hospital as they were very short of nurses. It would be good to see her again, but once her mother-in-law was better Amy should move to Cambridge, so there might not be the opportunity.

It was hours before Edmond would phone. He had wanted to come home to see them at the weekend but she had had to insist that he stayed away for fear of infection. She tried to imagine what he might be doing at College, and how he was settling in their little house. She wondered how it looked, now their furniture was installed.

She went once more to look at her patient. Ma was sleeping quite peacefully, and when Amy laid her hand lightly on her forehead it was less hot. She had thought earlier that the fever might be subsiding.

When Doctor Stanhope called he confirmed her impression that her mother-in-law was beginning to recover. Mr Derwent broke into a broad smile.

'Amy, you're a wonder!' he told her when the doctor had left. 'I don't know how we'd have managed without you. When she's better I'll make sure she knows how devotedly you nursed her.'

'When she's more wide awake I'll ask Cook for some porridge for her,' Amy said. 'Then later we might try a little chicken broth.'

–

Soon it was clear her patient was recovering and that neither Amy nor Pa had caught the disease. Ma looked thin and wasted when they helped her dress and brought

231

her downstairs. Then Amy set about disinfecting her in-laws' bedroom thoroughly, as she had been taught.

'You look exhausted,' Pa told her afterwards. She needed to catch up on her sleep. 'I'm doing my best to find another maid,' he went on.

Next day Amy was able to bring Beth home at last. What a joyful reunion it was for both of them!

Then Pa went to the station to collect Beatrice who had returned suddenly from London. She seemed in a particularly bad mood, perhaps as she had been obliged to take a train, for Pa had not wanted to leave his wife for long enough to travel to London to collect her.

'Ma looks dreadful,' she said, after visiting her room and seeing her pallor and sunken cheeks.

'It'll take a while for her to recover fully,' Amy told her. 'I'm encouraging her to get up in the afternoons.'

Mrs Johnson made up the fire in the drawing room and that afternoon they waited for Ma to join them, Beatrice still out of sorts.

'I want to talk to you about something,' she said suddenly to Amy. 'Would you come up to my room so we can talk privately?'

'Yes,' she replied, surprised, and limped up the stairs behind Beatrice. Beth was in the nursery, taking her afternoon nap.

Amy followed Beatrice into her large bedroom. She had never been there before, and looked around at its blue ruched curtains and stylish Art Nouveau pictures. There was a sweet aroma of perfume and face powder. On the bed lay Beatrice's suitcases, one half unpacked.

'Oh, Heavens! I thought Mrs Johnson would have put away my clothes by now!'

'It's not one of her days today.'

Beatrice sat down on a well-upholstered chair and indicated another one for Amy.

'Is something the matter?' Amy asked.

'It's about Major Fairlawn,' she said. She wrung her hands, and took a while to continue. 'Harriet and I went to a restaurant with him last night, and then Harriet met a friend and I had to go back with Wilfrid in a taxi and – well, he assaulted me – there really isn't any other way to describe his behaviour.'

Amy gasped. 'How awful for you. I'm dreadfully sorry.'

Tears began to run down Beatrice's face as she gave an account of how he had treated her. Amy felt the blood leaving her own face as she remembered the way Wilfrid had grabbed her that night in Ypres. She bit her lip. She was not ready to confide that experience to Beatrice. She had not even told Edmond about it, as he had been so gravely ill at that time.

Beatrice was wiping her eyes. Amy went and put her arm around her sister-in-law's shoulders in a rare moment of closeness.

'It was awful,' Beatrice went on. 'Harriet and her family didn't believe me when I told them what had happened. You don't think I encouraged him, do you, Amy?'

'No. The man's a monster. In Flanders he's becoming notorious, but because he's valuable to the war effort no-one will take any action against him.'

Beatrice was screwing up her handkerchief. 'I don't know what to do about it. He deserves to be punished.'

'Ask your father, Beatrice. It's best not to mention the incident to your mother, while she's still not very well, but Pa will know what to do. He might complain to the War Office, or the police.' She was still stooping beside Beatrice's chair.

'Oh, no, I simply can't tell him what happened. Suppose he believes it's my fault too!'

'I'm sure he wouldn't think that.'

Beatrice ran her hands through her hair, spoiling its neat arrangement. 'But I'd have to tell everyone all the details of what happened! I couldn't bear telling Pa about it, let alone officials who don't know me. How can I prove I never encouraged him? No-one else saw what he did.'

'It's a hideous situation,' Amy agreed, getting up awkwardly and going back to her chair. 'Only you can decide if you want to try to bring a charge. There's no certainty any action will be taken, though I suppose the allegations against him are mounting up.'

'I simply can't face telling anyone,' she said dully.

'I understand how you feel. The trouble is, if a woman is afraid to challenge him he's liable to go on pestering others.'

Beatrice sniffed.

From the nearby nursery Amy could hear Beth calling for her. 'I'd better get Beth's tea,' she told Beatrice. Cook would purée some vegetables for her. 'And you'd better see if Ma has got up yet. Listen, Beatrice, talk to me about what happened again if you feel you need to confide in someone. I won't tell anyone, but if you decide to take any action I'll come with you.'

'Thank you.'

For a moment Amy was anxious. She had already complained unsuccessfully against the man and was not sure her support would impress the authorities.

'Amy...'

She stopped in the doorway.

Beatrice hesitated. 'I'm sorry if I was rude to you before. I simply didn't believe you about Major Fairlawn.'

'I understand.' *It's the first time she's ever apologised to me for anything*, Amy thought.

-

Ma was listless when she joined them in the drawing room later. Beatrice was concerned to start with but soon became restless. When they went into the dining room for their evening meal Ma ate a few small mouthfuls of the plaice that Cook had prepared especially for her, and then returned to her bed.

'Beatrice, would you do something to help cheer up your mother?' Amy said next morning.

'What do you want?'

'There's that vase of chrysanthemums I picked – some of them are fading. Could you fetch some fresh ones from the garden, while it's bright out there, and arrange them nicely? You'll do it much better than I could.'

She looked critically at Amy's effort. 'I'm sure I can do better than that,' she said, and soon there was a fresh array of flowers, tastefully arranged.

After lunch Ma came down, huddled in a shawl, and lounged on the sofa.

Pa still handled the paperwork for his business but generally allowed Ross or Walter to oversee the forest work now, for he was anxious to help his wife recover. He sat down beside her. 'How would it be if we went away to a hotel by the sea, while you're convalescing?' he asked her.

'I shouldn't like it at this time of year,' Ma said firmly. 'I remember when we went to Bournemouth in late autumn that time, how bleak it was on the coast.'

Beth was crawling around, uttering half-learnt words. 'That child never stops,' Mrs Derwent complained. 'I can't seem to settle, having her in the room.'

'I'll take her upstairs,' Amy said, picking her up. 'Beatrice, I'm sure Ma would love to hear you play something on the piano. We've missed your music while you've been away.'

As she went upstairs she could hear Beatrice launching into a familiar sonata. She wondered how soon she and Beth could join Edmond in Cambridge.

–

Next morning Beatrice received a letter and looked disturbed as she read it.

'I'll take coffee in my room,' she told Cook, as she came in with a tray. 'Would you join me, Amy?'

'Yes, of course.' Beth was playing on the floor so Amy picked her up. She hung on to the banister while she carefully carried her daughter.

Once in Beatrice's boudoir Cook served them coffee and biscuits before leaving them alone. Beatrice had arranged some more chrysanthemums in a vase in her room. Amy helped Beth sip some cordial Cook had brought for her, before putting her on the carpet to play again.

Amy took a gulp of the coffee. 'Is everything all right, Beatrice?'

'I've had a letter from Wilfrid.' She had brought the envelope with her, and took out the letter once more.

'He's trying to apologise for what happened the other night... I simply don't know what to think.'

'Apologise?' Amy asked, bewildered.

'He says he may have drunk a little too much and is sorry if he behaved inappropriately in the taxi.'

'Do you think he means it?' Amy asked, unwilling to trust him.

'I'm not sure.' Beatrice raised her eyebrows. 'His apology is completely inadequate for the way he handled me. I don't think I'll even reply.'

'You're doing the right thing.'

'There was just one point that made me think. Where is it? Ah yes, just here. He says "Perhaps you don't realise what a strain it is serving at the Front, and how it affects us. It's very hard to adapt to polite society when we return." Do you think that's true, Amy? Does it excuse him at all, being traumatised by the war?'

'I don't believe that's an acceptable excuse,' she said firmly. 'Other men manage to return without becoming brutes. And I can remember Edmond, and Peter too, saying Wilfrid was a bully at school.'

'You're right. Nothing excuses his behaviour.'

'Practically all men conduct themselves decently.'

'That's true. There was a gentleman who gave up his taxi for me that night. And when I didn't have enough money for the cab, Harriet was arriving back with Gilbert and he settled the payment for me.' She considered for a moment. 'Wilfrid wants to see me again but I'd be frightened to be in his company.'

'Don't even consider it.'

Beth was becoming restless and Beatrice looked a little relieved when Amy picked up her daughter and left her on her own.

Later that afternoon a splendid bouquet of pink lilies was delivered for Beatrice. Ma was downstairs and admired them as Mrs Johnson brought them in.

'Who are they from?' she asked.

Beatrice examined the card. 'Major Fairlawn,' she said, with an anxious glance to Amy.

'How magnificent!' said her mother. 'You've certainly made an impression on him, Beatrice. Mrs Johnson, can you bring us a suitable vase?'

'Actually, Ma, I'm not keen on lilies,' Beatrice ventured.

'But they're superb! And at this time of year they must be costly ones from a hothouse.'

'It's the smell I don't like. They're very pungent. Let's put them outside in the hall.'

When Mrs Johnson brought a vase of water she plonked them in it without ceremony and asked for them to be removed from the drawing room.

–

After dinner Amy approached her father-in-law to discuss joining Edmond in Cambridge.

'Could you bear to stay a little longer?' he begged, puffing on his cigar. He had remained in the dining room after Ma had left, so he could smoke. Some doctors suggested that an atmosphere laden with smoke from cigarettes or cigars could delay an invalid's recovery. 'You're the one who knows how to nurse a patient recovering from a severe illness. You're the best person to decide what food to give her to tempt her appetite.'

Pa loved his wife but he was not practised at bathing her or tending to her hair, and she could not imagine Beatrice patiently helping her.

'She's very run-down,' he went on. 'You probably think she's had few worries during the war, compared with what you and Edmond have been through, but she has struggled. She's had to manage with fewer staff and food shortages. Then she was desperately worried about Edmond's injuries. Now she's anxious about Beatrice and whether she'll ever find a suitable husband. And there have been unpleasant remarks made in Larchbury by people who think Bea should have stuck by her fiancé. It's all combined to wear her down, before she fell ill with the flu.'

She tried to understand her mother-in-law's problems. 'Edmond needs me too,' she told him.

'He tells me Grace is looking after him and he's enthusiastic about his university work.'

'No-one is with him at night. He sometimes sleeps poorly and has bad dreams. His experiences at the Front still prey on his mind.'

He looked at her, now anxious himself. Previously she had not sought to burden him with her worries, but now it was essential he was aware of the problem.

'Suppose I went to visit him at the weekend?' she suggested. 'He'd love to see Beth, too. Then I could come back here for another week or so.'

'How would you get there?'

She realised he would not want to drive her there and spend the weekend away from his frail wife.

'If you drive me to the station I can take the train. I'll need to change in London but I can take a cab between stations.' As soon as she had said it she felt uneasy. In Ypres she had not managed to travel a few hundred yards on her own without being molested. It shocked her how that incident had changed her outlook and made her question her desire for independence. *Nonsense*, she thought, *this time I'll be travelling by daylight, through well-populated areas. I simply mustn't change how I behave because of that beast Wilfrid Fairlawn.*

'I doubt very much if you could manage it with Beth,' Pa said.

She was impatient to visit their house. 'Wait – I know what I'll do! I'll ask my parents if they'll come with me,' she proposed. 'There's room for both of them in our spare room. Oh, if only they're able to come. I've asked a lot from them lately.'

Chapter Eighteen

Now I'm back in London, I simply must see Charles, Lavinia thought. Letters from Amy and Florence had told her that Beatrice had ended their engagement. How could she do such a thing? He was still the same decent, courageous man, in spite of his injuries. Beatrice was not only being selfish and cruel, but one day she might realise what she had lost and regret her action.

He'll still be heartbroken, Lavinia thought, *but I can at least visit and try to divert him for a while*. She put on her best winter coat with the fur collar, took a bus to his hospital and sought out the ward.

Charles was sitting beside his bed with a blanket over his legs. Nearby one of the other officers was sitting, and between them was a small table. They were engrossed in a game of chess. Apart from them there was only one patient, who was asleep.

As she approached, Charles looked up. 'Lavinia!' he exclaimed. For a moment he looked as though he would try to get up.

'Charles!' she cried urgently, but he remembered just in time to stay seated. The other officer, who had a bandage over one eye, stood up until she asked him to sit down again. Charles introduced her to Lieutenant Warner and they shook hands. 'I'll leave you two to talk,' the lieutenant said. 'We can finish the game later.' He climbed into his bed and reached for a book.

Lavinia took off her hat and gloves and unbuttoned her coat. She sat down beside Charles's bed.

'It's lovely to see you,' he said, taking her hand. She was thankful that he was less pale than before, though he did not look as blithe as when he had been expecting Beatrice's visit.

'And you,' she said.

She told him about her new posting to a London hospital. *His face is just as handsome as before he was wounded*, she thought. 'How are you now?'

'I'm ready to go to a convalescent hospital, only they're short of places.'

She was still hot in the ward, so she took off her coat and folded it over a spare chair. 'I'm so glad you're getting better.'

There was something else she needed to say. 'I heard that Beatrice had broken off the engagement.' She wanted to give him the opportunity to talk about it if he could bear to do so. 'I was quite shocked.'

He smiled ruefully. 'I've no rancour against her,' he said. 'She deserved to be offered her freedom in the circumstances.'

With difficulty Lavinia restrained herself from further comment on the matter. 'Do your family manage to visit often?' she asked.

'They've been very kind, coming up from Sussex at least once a week,' he told her. 'My sister, Isobel, is staying with an aunt in Holloway so she can call in regularly.'

Lavinia remembered Isobel from school. She was a pretty girl, a year younger than she was.

'Have you seen Amy?' he asked her. 'I've had one letter from Edmond when he'd just started again at Cambridge. He sounded thrilled to be back there. Has Amy been able to join him yet?'

Lavinia explained about Mrs Derwent's illness. 'Fortunately it sounds as though she's on the mend now.'

'I love to hear news from friends, especially Edmond and Amy.'

She sat and chatted about their acquaintances for a while longer, Charles not showing any urgent desire to return to his game.

A brisk young nurse came in to take the temperatures of her patients. She nudged the sleeping officer until he woke up enough to co-operate.

'This is Lavinia,' Charles told the newcomer. 'She's a nurse who looked after me in Flanders, besides being a friend.' Lavinia was flattered that he regarded her in this way. He was still holding her hand.

'I've never made it over there,' said the nurse, examining the reading on the thermometer.

'Lavinia was famous for driving around Flanders on her motorbike,' Charles told her with a mischievous grin.

'I'd love to hear about your experiences,' the nurse said as she took Charles's temperature, 'but I can't stop now – there's too much I've got to do.'

Lavinia was enjoying seeing Charles but wondered if it was time to leave.

'We did have fun at the concert party, didn't we?' he said, as the young nurse completed her round of the patients and left.

'Oh, yes! Helping to arrange it, and then taking part…'

'And playing our famous duet! We must do it again some time.'

'I'd love to,' she said, without having any idea when such an event might take place. 'I suppose I'd better be going – I mustn't tire you.'

'You will come again, won't you? If you can spare the time, of course.'

'Yes – I promise.'

–

That Friday Edmond sat by the window of the Cambridge house, waiting for the cab to arrive. He understood his father-in-law had permission to leave the school at lunchtime so they were not too late reaching Cambridge. It was growing dark when at last – there they were! He watched Amy's father helping her and Beth out of the cab, followed by Amy's mother. Scarcely aware of his surroundings he found himself at the front door, embracing Amy. *At last she's with me*, he thought. *And Beth – how she's grown.*

'I'll take the luggage in,' Amy's father told him sternly as he reached for a case.

Edmond welcomed them inside and helped Amy off with her coat. She took off her hat, revealing her lovely hair, coiled on top of her head. She brought him up to date on his mother's progress.

The day was already memorable, and now his spirits rose further, for at last Ma seemed to be out of danger. 'You've nursed her back to health!' he told Amy, wondering if Ma understood how much she owed to her.

'Grace has left us a meal,' he told them next. 'I'll heat up the soup, now you're here, and there's a chicken and leek pie to follow.'

Downstairs there was a tiny dining room as well as the parlour. As they arranged the meal on the table Amy's mother was congratulating them on their comfortable little home.

'How was your journey?' he asked as they all sat around the table. He stirred Beth's soup to cool it and began spooning it into her little rosy mouth, glad of the chance to care for her again.

'Better than I expected,' Amy said. 'People rushed to give a hand when they saw we had a baby with us. They helped with the pram and some of the luggage.'

'Beth looks as though she's falling asleep,' he said as her eyelashes drooped on to her plump cheeks.

'I must get her ready for bed as soon as she's had a little mashed-up food,' Amy said.

Edmond turned to her mother. 'I'm very grateful to you for looking after Beth when Ma was sick,' he said.

'It was a joy having her with us,' she said. Amy had told him once on the phone that her grandchild was giving her a sense of purpose after the tragedy of losing Bertie.

'Mother's got a new plan for the future,' Amy told him now.

'There are several new orphans in Larchbury,' Mrs Fletcher told him. 'Besides the usual illnesses, men have been lost in the war and some people, mainly women, have died of the flu. They're talking of extending the orphanage and looking for volunteers to help run it. I thought I might apply. Amy thinks it's a good idea.'

'You should: you're just the kind of person they need,' he told her.

'Tell us how your studies are going, Edmond,' Amy's father said.

He told him a little about his lectures. Mr Fletcher had been his tutor for a while; he was competent in most subjects but not well educated in scientific matters, and understood little of laboratory work, though he was eager to hear what Edmond was doing.

'I'm determined to put my studies to good use when I leave, by working on the development of artificial limbs,' he told his father-in-law. 'War heroes like Charles deserve the very best modern devices.'

Amy had already shown herself eager to support his plans, and now Mr Fletcher nodded approval.

'I expect you find your studies demanding,' Amy's mother said.

'I work hard at College and sometimes I need to study in the evening,' Edmond said, conscious of the pile of textbooks cluttering the top of their small sideboard. 'Grace tries to keep me in order but I don't have much time to tidy up.'

'I daresay you still tire easily,' Mrs Fletcher pursued.

Do I look as tired as I feel? he wondered. He had to admit she was right.

'Don't you spend time with your fellow students?' Amy asked.

'An occasional evening in the public house with Horace,' he told her with a grin. 'He's a friendly young chap.'

After the meal Amy put Beth to bed in the nursery. 'I hope she settles there,' she said. 'I've brought her favourite toy rabbit so she has something familiar.'

When they crept up a few minutes later to peep in at the infant she was sleeping peacefully. He caught hold of Amy on the landing, and embraced her more passionately than before, feeling the softness and warmth of her body, aware of her faint perfume. 'How I've missed you!' he said.

Mrs Fletcher had valiantly done the washing up and she and her husband retired quickly to the guestroom, leaving him alone with Amy.

'I was so desperately worried you'd catch the flu,' he told her. 'I worried more about you than about Ma.'

They were soon settling in their bedroom. 'At last you're here,' he said, drawing her into his arms as she joined him in the bed.

'I should have come weeks ago,' she agreed, nestling against him.

'Let's make up for lost time,' he said, his lips eagerly finding hers.

–

Amy awoke, still drowsy, as it was getting light. Beside her Edmond began to stir.

'Do you sleep all right now?' she asked him. She had not been aware of him waking in the night.

'I still have nightmares sometimes,' he admitted. 'Usually I'm tired when I go to bed, but later I may wake up after a bad dream and it can take a while for the dread to leave me. Or I wake up unnecessarily early, remembering what it was like in the trenches, or how I struggled to breathe when I was first wounded. But last night I slept soundly. Having you here is such a comfort.' He still looked thin.

She held him close. 'I'll move here properly just as soon as I can,' she said. He looked as though he was continuing to recover, but she yearned to be with him every day, making sure he did not exert himself more than was wise.

She looked around her. 'I like this room,' she told him, for although it was small its floral curtains and bedspread were cheerful.

They heard Beth calling out from the next room. 'She won't know where she is,' Amy said, and rushed to comfort her.

It was chilly, so they agreed to stay in for most of the day. 'But we'll take you to a café for lunch,' Amy's father said. 'We could go out for a meal in the evening too, but it might be rather late for Beth.'

'There's some leftover pie from yesterday,' his wife said and they all agreed that would do for the evening.

They went with Father to look around the little garden at the back. A few Michaelmas daisies were flowering in its overgrown beds.

'I haven't had a chance to work on it,' Edmond said.

'Don't do any such thing!' Amy told him. 'You're not fit enough.' Father began pulling out a few weeds, while she picked some of the flowers.

She took them indoors and placed them in a jug. 'We need a vase or two,' she told Edmond as she set the jug down on the dining table. They went to join Mother and Beth in the parlour, which held the sofa from their room at The Beeches, and two easy chairs. She was impatient to make a few improvements. A little palm in a china bowl would add a pleasant touch. If only they could have a piano, but she would have to do without for now.

On the mantelpiece Edmond had placed his photo of her, the one he had taken with him to Flanders. It was framed now but she could still make out its rough, damaged edge.

They set out just before eleven and dawdled down to the river. The day had grown a little warmer and her parents enjoyed the view of the Colleges across the Cam.

'I'm enjoying the trip,' Mother told them. They had hardly spent any time away from Larchbury since before the war.

From there they went to a modest restaurant that Edmond recommended. Young children were welcome there. 'This is fine,' Amy said as she ordered, 'but tomorrow I'm going to cook us all a meal.'

'There's no need, darling, we can go out again.'

'It's high time I cooked you a proper Sunday lunch,' she insisted. 'Do you realise I've never been able to do that in nearly three years of married life, not once? I've often planned what I'd cook, but I've never even used the china we were given when we got married.'

'It's been waiting for nearly three and a half years,' he grinned, remembering what had gone wrong on their first wedding day.

After they had finished their lunch, Amy put Beth in her pram and took her to the shops. Mother willingly helped her choose food for the next day. She was content calling at the butcher's, and buying vegetables from a barrow boy.

'This is all fine,' her mother said, 'but you've been working hard at The Beeches and you're not to exhaust yourself.'

'I want to do it for Edmond.'

'Let me help you prepare it, that's all.'

–

The following morning she settled in the kitchen, trying out their pots and pans. Though space was limited she and Mother worked well side by side. Not long after midday there was a savoury smell of roast meat. Mother made the gravy while Amy concentrated on the mint sauce. She was still new to the layout of the kitchen and lunch was a little later than she had planned.

The dining room was only just large enough to accommodate them all. 'You shouldn't have gone to all this trouble,' Edmond said as she set a dish of lamb in front of him, served on a Royal Albert Crown china plate with a gold rim, part of their dinner service.

'I like cooking. I used to help Mother with Sunday lunch most weekends,' she reminded him. At last she was fulfilling her proper role.

'I miss you so much when we're apart,' she told Edmond as they prepared to return to Larchbury. 'I wish I needn't return to The Beeches, but I've promised to look after Ma for a little longer.'

–

There was an air of anticipation, two Mondays later, for there was a rumour the Armistice would be announced.

All through Ma's illness the peace negotiations had dragged on.

Beatrice lounged in an armchair, reading a fashion magazine, with other issues on the table beside her. Mrs Derwent had a better colour now and was recovering her spirits. Amy was hoping to make the move to Cambridge at the weekend.

'Peter's due home on leave soon,' Mrs Derwent said. 'If the war's really over they might let him stay for two or three weeks. They should be agreeable if he tells them I've been ill.'

She turned and smiled at Amy. 'And I keep meaning to tell you how grateful I am for all you've done to help me get better.'

'I'm relieved to see you so much fitter,' Amy said. Perhaps at last her mother-in-law was beginning to accept her.

How would the Armistice news reach them, if it was really over? It would be announced officially in London, Amy supposed, and then people on the telephone would pass on the news: it should spread very fast.

Beth was playing with her bricks. Soon she would try her next attempt at walking, Amy suspected.

Mrs Derwent picked up one of the magazines. 'Oh, dear, I seem to have left my spectacles upstairs,' she said.

Beatrice made no move, except to turn her page. Amy set down the tablecloth she was mending and got up to go to her in-laws' room. Her walking was still a little awkward.

'I'll go!' Beatrice offered suddenly.

'Thank you, dear,' Mrs Derwent said. Soon her daughter returned with the spectacles and she reached for the magazine.

'Listen!' cried Beatrice, 'I believe I can hear church bells!'

Amy held her breath. Sure enough, she thought she could hear ringing from St Stephen's. She opened the window a crack, though the day was chilly, and there was no mistaking the merry peal. 'It must be the Armistice!' she cried.

Spontaneously the others rose to their feet and the three women embraced.

'At last it's all over,' said Beatrice. 'Our lives will begin to return to normal!'

But it can never be the same, Amy thought. 'It's too late for so many young men,' she said. 'Think of poor Henry.'

'Who? Oh, yes, the gardener.' Just a week earlier they had heard he was missing in France. Young men who were described as 'missing in action' were seldom discovered alive.

Nothing will bring back Bertie or make Edmond the robust young man he once was, or Charles, Amy thought. *Even women have been killed, like poor Katherine. We have to make the best of the new situation.*

'No more young men will be killed,' she acknowledged thankfully. She picked up Beth and swung her around, as she cooed with delight. 'Finally we're at peace!' she cried. 'May you never go through anything like we have endured.'

Chapter Nineteen

London and Larchbury, November

There was a strange atmosphere in the hospital on the morning of the eleventh of November. Staff came into the ward, absentmindedly took temperatures or tended wounds, while discussing the possibility of the Armistice. A few minutes later some of them would come back to check they had completed the task properly. At eleven o'clock Charles heard bells ringing from two or three nearby churches, followed by the sound of car horns. Lieutenant Warner had managed to be sent on to a convalescent hospital, but Lieutenant Parker, the other officer in his ward, was sitting up in bed. Frustrated at not being able to move nearer his comrade, Charles shouted across to him. 'The Armistice! The war's over!'

Parker, who was recovering slowly from exposure to mustard gas, climbed out of bed and shook his hand.

Charles was overcome with a moment of disbelief. Was it really all over, or could it be a mistake? Then a nurse rushed into their ward to confirm the news.

There was a mood of euphoria. Sometimes he could hear excited cries from outside. Would he receive a visit from Isobel, Charles wondered, or even from Lavinia?

Nurses had accounts of crowded streets and swarming traffic as the jubilant public celebrated. In the confused, surreal atmosphere, some staff had to stay beyond their shifts because their replacements could not reach the hospital.

He waited impatiently but the afternoon passed without any visits.

By evening the cries on the streets had become raucous, and an orderly showed them a special edition newspaper that was circulating. Late into the night there were occasional rowdy cries.

The following afternoon he sat beside his bed, reading a newspaper. The Armistice had been signed in a railway carriage at Compiegne, in France, he discovered.

Then Isobel arrived in her smart winter suit. 'Isn't the news simply marvellous?' she asked. 'I'd have come to see you yesterday, but the streets were so crowded it was impossible. It's a little less frantic today and I managed to go and buy a new hat.' Strands of her dark hair, curly like his own, were visible beneath it.

She went on gossiping about some friends, and their celebration dinner the evening before. He remembered now how her frivolous chat had irritated him somewhat before the war, and even when he was on leave, after the first day or two. Would Beatrice have come to annoy him like that, he wondered suddenly. He was almost relieved when Isobel left.

'What a charming young woman she is, your sister,' said Lieutenant Parker.

'Yes…' Charles said dubiously. *There's a new breed of young women out there*, he thought, *who've performed demanding war work in difficult situations. They have a capable, independent air. The social butterflies, however attractive, are beginning to seem shallow in comparison.*

An hour later Lavinia arrived, stepping excitedly into the ward. 'Isn't it wonderful, Charles!' she exclaimed. 'I wanted to come to see you yesterday, but it was useless trying to get across London!'

'So I've heard.'

'You should have seen it – everyone was so thrilled. There were cheering crowds of soldiers, women waving flags, bands parading, people climbing lampposts…'

He smiled at her excited description. 'I wish I'd been able to go out.' A picture in his newspaper had given him an idea of the atmosphere of rejoicing.

'Let me take you to see the street,' she said, fetching the invalid chair from the corner of the room. The nurse she had met on her earlier visit turned around from taking Lieutenant Parker's temperature, and helped her manoeuvre Charles carefully into the chair then held the door open as she wheeled it outside. She took Charles to the end of the corridor, where there was a window with a view of the road outside.

Through the misty late afternoon he could make out a handwritten poster in a window opposite, proclaiming *To Hell with the Kaiser*, and gaudy Union Jacks festooned on doors and railings. Passers-by had a noticeable spring in their step.

'I'll remember this view forever,' he told her. He fell silent, recalling the men who would never return, and grieving for his own lost vigour.

She seemed to sense when he was ready to return to the ward. Nurses generally found the invalid chairs heavy to move, but she steered him efficiently to his ward and helped him back on to his bed. She pulled up a spare chair beside him.

'What do you think you'll do now it's over?' he asked her. 'Will you go on nursing?'

She looked surprised. 'It's so soon I haven't thought,' she said. 'I'm not sure how long they'll keep us on, those of us who are VADs. I imagine they'll need us while so many men are still being treated, and while the flu epidemic continues. Afterwards I could go back to being an art student, I suppose.'

'It's very soon to decide, as you say.'

'I'd prefer to go on nursing, or working in some worthwhile profession,' she said resolutely.

'You should take a few days' leave when you can. You've worked so hard.'

'As it happens, I'm going on leave tomorrow. Father has a few days' leave, so I'll go home for a while. So I shan't be around to visit you, maybe till next week.'

He reached for her hand, warm, though not as soft as Beatrice's dainty one. He looked at it curiously, noticing the slight roughness and occasional uneven nail, from less frequent manicuring. This was the hand of a woman who took on serious work, rather than being pampered at home.

'Enjoy your leave, Lavinia, but come and see me when you can. You know how I enjoy your company.'

–

The following afternoon, while Beth was taking her nap, Amy had some unexpected visitors. Mr Westholme and Lavinia had arrived. 'I hope you don't mind us calling in to see Amy,' he told Mrs Derwent.

Greetings were exchanged, for she was acquainted with him. Beatrice, who was out visiting, had been at school with Lavinia, though the young women had little in common. Mrs Derwent was content to welcome the distinguished surgeon. 'Let me send for some refreshments,' she said, ringing the bell. 'Amy, will you fetch my husband?'

She brought Pa from his study to greet their visitors.

'It's lovely to see you,' Amy said to Lavinia. 'Do you think you'll be in London for some time?'

'Probably.' She was smart in her coat with a fur collar, telling Amy the hospital where she was working; it was not St Luke's or the one where Edmond had been sent and where Charles was now recovering.

'I came over with some wounded,' Mr Westholme told them. 'I have to return the day after tomorrow, for even now many casualties in France aren't well enough to send home.'

'Florence came to see me yesterday afternoon, after she'd finished teaching,' Amy told Lavinia. 'She's so excited that the war's over and James should find it easier to get leave.'

'I'm glad for her,' Lavinia said. The three of them had kept in touch regularly through the tense final days of the conflict.

They all exchanged polite conversation for a few minutes.

'We came to discuss a matter with Amy,' Mr Westholme said soon. 'Don't look anxious, it's not bad news. Is there somewhere we can go and talk?'

She did not want to take them to her bedroom, and the garden would be cold on a November afternoon. 'Let's go to the conservatory,' she said.

They followed her in there and settled on the wicker chairs. Some of the little palms and orange trees were wilting, for the gardener was inexperienced in tending them, but as the afternoon was sunny it was warmer there than sometimes in the winter.

'I notice you're still limping,' Mr Westholme said. 'Lavinia told me your operation wasn't entirely successful.'

'No. I can get around, but it's not ideal.'

'May I examine your leg?'

She went outside to remove her stocking, then put her left foot up on a chair.

He felt around her ankle joint gently. 'The surgeon hasn't set it quite right,' he said. 'I couldn't operate on you that day as I was dealing with a very urgent case. I seem to remember it was at a time when conditions were very hectic.'

'The hospital was overflowing with wounded.' Some had been lying on the floor on stretchers, still waiting for a bed, she remembered.

'How do you feel about having it reset?' he asked.

'Oh,' she said. She had often wondered whether that would be effective. 'Do you think there's a good chance of improving it?'

'I'm afraid we'd need to operate again to realign the bones,' he said, looking at her seriously through his glasses.

'You'd be in pain again,' Lavinia warned her, with a steady gaze from her dark eyes. 'You'd need to wear a cast for a few weeks, but in the end the result should be worth it.'

'Oh, goodness – I would like to get around more easily,' she said, trying to decide what to do.

'Even when it's set and they've taken off the plaster, it'll take a while longer to strengthen,' her friend said.

Amy turned to her, remembering her wide medical knowledge. 'What would you do, if it was you?'

'I'd have it done,' she said without hesitation. 'I'd definitely recommend it for you.'

'I could take you back to London with me and operate tomorrow,' Mr Westholme told her. 'After that I have to return to France.'

She had to decide quickly, she realised. 'I'd like to talk to Edmond about it,' she said. 'In an hour or so he should be back from College, and his friend should be too. I can ring Horace and ask him to tell Edmond to ring me urgently.'

'Listen, Amy, Lavinia and I are going to call on the family in Alderbank,' he told her. 'I can be back here by about seven and take you with us to London in the car. I can take an X-ray of your ankle, to confirm what I think needs doing. You can stay overnight in the hospital, ready for the operation tomorrow.'

In her head excitement mingled with doubts. 'It's extremely kind of you to offer me this,' she said, 'but I would like to discuss it with Edmond first.'

'Very well. We'll call back at seven. Be ready if you're going ahead with the operation.'

The sunshine was beginning to fade as they left. Amy rang Horace's number as soon as he might be home, but there was no reply. She was expecting Edmond to ring her from a public phone, to confirm that she and Beth were able to move to Cambridge at the weekend. Now, if she went ahead with the operation, they would have to postpone their reunion once more. Generally he did not ring until half past seven, when their dinner would be finished, so it was vital that she contacted him earlier.

She had got Beth up now from her afternoon nap and she was crawling across the tiled floor as Amy hovered in the draughty hall beside the telephone. 'What am I to do?' she asked her daughter distractedly but the only reply was a gurgle.

Mr Derwent came out to the hall now, asking her what was going on. She told him of the opportunity to have her ankle fixed properly.

'You should probably have the operation, if you're prepared for the pain and inconvenience,' he advised her.

'Yes,' she said, though still unwilling to delay her move to Cambridge again.

Beth had crawled to a chair and was trying to pull herself to her feet.

Amy rang Uncle Arthur and asked him to pass on a message to her mother, asking her to pick up Beth and look after her for a few more days.

'How I'm imposing on her!' she said to Pa, who was still there in the hall.

As she looked around, Beth made a determined effort to get upright.

'Look!' cried Amy. 'She's properly on her feet!' Beth let go of the chair and took three unsteady steps towards her before collapsing on to her bottom. She looked surprised, but gave a little laugh and began to crawl back to the chair.

'Did you see that?' Amy asked Pa. 'She actually took her first steps!'

'She certainly did,' he said, chuckling as the child launched herself across the room again on her plump little legs and travelled a bit further this time. 'You're determined to get around, aren't you, young lady?' He smiled indulgently at his granddaughter. '…I wish we could care for Beth here, but Ma's still frail from the flu and Bea seems to lack much inclination to be a supportive aunt. It's cold and getting dark outside. If it's all right with your mother I'll fetch her to collect Beth, and drive them back.'

Amy picked up her daughter, who struggled for freedom for a moment before she settled. 'You're doing so well, darling,' she told Beth. 'I wish your daddy was here to see you… It's all the more incentive for me to walk better, now she's becoming so active,' she told Pa. She tried again to phone Horace, but without success.

'If only we'd got a phone installed in your house in Cambridge,' her father-in-law said.

Soon Amy's mother phoned to say she was happy to take Beth, and Pa set off to fetch her.

When she arrived in her tweed winter coat to collect the child she looked anxiously at Amy. 'Are you quite sure you want to put yourself through this again?' she asked.

'Beth actually started walking just now,' Amy told her. 'I'd love to be able to get around quickly when I'm looking after her.' All the same, she would prefer to have Edmond's blessing.

She hugged Beth and passed her to her mother.

'I'll be thinking of you, darling,' Mrs Fletcher said.

When Pa was back from driving them to Sebastopol Terrace, Amy still had not succeeded in contacting Horace. 'I'd better get ready, on the assumption that I'm going ahead,' she said.

'I'll get Cook to send you up some tea and something to eat,' Mr Derwent said.

The maid had lit a small fire in her room, but it was less cheerful there now with Edmond away and their favourite belongings sent to Cambridge. She packed a small suitcase and ate most of the food Cook brought. If only she could speak to Edmond.

It was nearly time for the Westholmes to collect her. She stood in the hallway with her coat and hat and her luggage, making one last attempt to phone Horace.

He was still not home. Beatrice came into the hall to see whether the telephone was free. Now that peace was restored she was making arrangements to meet friends and hoping lively social events would resume.

'Are you really going back into hospital?' she asked. 'What does Edmond think?'

'I haven't been able to reach him,' she said, reluctantly hanging up.

She stared at Amy. 'Is it true you'll be back in plaster? You'll be handicapped again?' Her green eyes probed Amy's face.

'I'm afraid so, for a while.'

'How do you know it'll work this time? It could leave you in a worse state than before!' Beatrice had been hostile towards her in the past but now she looked concerned. 'Do you think Edmond would want you to have another operation?'

'I don't know for certain, but Mr Westholme is a much respected surgeon and I'm lucky he's offered to do my operation.' She supposed he was still grateful that she had behaved well during her appearance in court, all those years earlier, not betraying Lavinia as ringleader of their civil disobedience.

'I hope you're doing the right thing,' Beatrice said.

Cook came to say that dinner was served. Beatrice postponed making her call and went to join the others in the dining room.

The doorbell rang: Lavinia and her father had come for Amy.

Mr Derwent interrupted his meal to see her off. 'I'll go on ringing Cambridge to tell Edmond what's happening,' he said.

'He'll probably ring here at seven thirty.'

'The very best of luck, Amy.' He carried her suitcase to Mr Westholme's car.

As they drove off she found it hard to join in conversation with the others, as she anticipated the ordeal of another operation.

–

Lavinia was encouraging as Amy settled down that night on the ward in a major central London hospital. The other women there were routine surgical cases.

Mr Westholme had used his influence to get an X-ray of her ankle taken outside the usual hours and said it would be developed in time for him to consult it the next day.

'While you're in I'll be able to visit you,' Lavinia said. 'I've agreed to go back to work tomorrow, as Father is returning to France. I can come here by bus when I'm off duty.'

Pa should have spoken to Edmond by now, Amy thought. *What will he think when he hears what I'm doing? We were planning to be together this weekend.*

–

So here I am again, Amy thought next morning, *lying with a dozen other patients being attended by nurses in starched caps and aprons, in a ward smelling of antiseptic.* She had passed a restless night. Once she had even dreamt that she was back in the hospital in Ypres, with Edmond desperately ill.

If only I'd been able to speak to him, she thought. *And yet, I've always said a woman should be allowed to make her own decisions. I still believe that: it's just that this decision affects all of us. Suppose the operation goes wrong and I'm left worse than before? Even if it goes well, I'll need to spend some weeks in plaster, and I'll be of very little help to Edmond or Beth in that time.*

As they wheeled her along to the operating theatre she reminded herself of Mr Westholme's acclaimed skills.

Chapter Twenty

As Amy began to return to consciousness she was aware of her aching leg. Then she noticed the figure beside her bed. It looked like Edmond, but he was in Cambridge. As she became wider awake she looked again. There was no mistaking him.

'Is it really you?' she cried. 'Why aren't you at College?'

'I found out last night that you were having the operation.' He leant over the bed, enveloped her in his arms and kissed her. 'I had to see you. I set off early this morning. How are you feeling?'

Her leg was not giving her agony, as it had over a year before, when she was first injured, but it might be worse when the anaesthetic had completely worn off. Feeling beneath the blankets her fingers located the new plaster enclosing it. 'I won't know if the operation is a success for weeks yet,' she said.

'My sweet, brave girl!'

'Did you bring those roses?' she asked him, gazing at the large bunch of pink blooms in a vase by her bed.

'Yes.' He held the vase nearer for her to smell their fragrance.

'How did you find such beautiful ones at this time of year?'

He smiled. 'I discovered a high-class florist's. You deserved a lovely bouquet.'

'I wanted to ask your advice before I decided on the operation,' she told him, 'but I couldn't contact you in time.'

'I was angry, but not with you. Have Ma and Beatrice been mean about your limp?'

'Beatrice might have been, occasionally, but I don't pay much attention. Actually, she's been more understanding lately.'

'I hope they didn't persuade you to have another operation. So long as you weren't pressurised I'd have wanted you to go ahead, providing you can face all the pain again.'

'I won't be able to look after you or Beth properly for weeks now. What are we to do?'

'We'll think of something.' He smiled in the way that always reassured her.

'I'm still a bit woozy,' she said. 'I expect I look a mess.' She reached for her bag and found her mirror and comb.

'Let me, darling.' He took the comb and gently ran it through her hair, before showing her her reflection. 'There! You're lovely as ever.'

Then Mr Westholme came to see her. 'I'm confident the operation went well,' he told her. 'Are you comfortable?'

'As much as I can expect, so soon after. Thank you for everything.'

He looked at his watch. 'You'll have to excuse me. I need to catch a train.'

Edmond stayed with her, holding her hand and telling her of the various celebrations that had taken place at university to mark the end of the war. 'Something weird happened when the news first came,' he said. 'Some students made for Bertrand Russell's rooms on Trinity Street and smashed them up.'

'Why did they do that?'

'He'd said the war was wrong. They said it had been right, and anyway we won it.'

'I'll never believe the war was justifiable,' she told him.

Presently the ward sister arrived to remind him it was time he went.

'Sister is right – I should leave you to sleep and get over the anaesthetic,' he said. 'It's Friday, and I don't need to be back at College till Monday. I thought I'd go to Larchbury and call on your parents to see Beth – Pa told me she's walking!'

'Yes – she suddenly took off – your father was actually there when it happened.'

'She's a determined girl, like her mother… Then I'll go to The Beeches and see how Ma is getting on.'

'She'll be thrilled to see you.' It would probably even help her recovery.

'I promise I'll call here on Sunday before going back to College.'

–

On the Saturday Lavinia had a half day and began the afternoon by visiting Amy, who had been considerably cheered by Edmond's visit. Then she went to the other hospital to see Charles. *Is it too soon to visit him again?* she wondered. But he always seemed to welcome her.

He was sitting up in bed reading a letter. He smiled and reached for her hand. 'It's kind of you to spend your time visiting me.'

She enquired after his progress, then told him about Amy's operation.

'She's a brave young woman,' he said. 'I hope it's been successful this time.'

He turned back to his letter. 'I heard from Frank Bentley this morning. He's still in France. He says how eerie it seemed when the artillery finally went quiet. And when they marched into the town the nuns came and stuck flowers into the barrels of their guns.'

Her thoughts hovered between delight and concern for the months ahead. 'Somehow we have to put it all behind us and look to the future.'

'Lavinia, do you think you could wheel me out of here again, down the corridor to that place where we can look out on the street?'

'Yes, of course.' He must welcome a change of scene.

'I'm sorry the chair is so heavy for you to move,' he said as she helped him into it.

Lieutenant Parker had two comrades visiting, and a well-built officer in uniform volunteered to push Charles. There was a spare chair in the corridor and she sat next to him as the lights began to come on in the dim street outside, where Union Jacks still fluttered.

'Thank you.'

After he had enjoyed the street scene for a few minutes he turned his dark eyes on hers seriously. 'How lucky Edmond is to have a devoted wife like Amy! Whenever you come to see me I wonder if you could become close to me like that.'

Heavens, he sounds almost as if he cares for me, Lavinia thought. His eyes continued to linger on hers. 'Do you think you might ever be tempted into marriage?' He pursued. 'I'm not the good-looking man I used to be, of course.'

'You mean – you and me?' she said, scarcely able to pronounce the words, for there must be some kind of mistake.

'I'm no great catch,' he said sadly.

'I didn't mean that, Charles. Of course you'll make someone a fine husband. But it's not long since you were engaged to Beatrice. I can understand how dreadful it was when she broke off the engagement, but you mustn't rush into another commitment.'

'Perhaps I shouldn't even suggest it,' he replied uneasily. 'You're so valuable as a nurse and maybe you wouldn't even want to be a wife.'

'I have sometimes considered it,' she admitted, 'though no-one has ever asked me.' She had become resigned to the way people viewed her. 'I'm simply not a pretty young woman, the kind who attracts admiration at parties and would manage her servants to run a beautiful home.'

'I used to believe those kind of talents were important,' he said, 'but I've learnt that they aren't all that matter. We're living in a different world now from the one we knew five years ago.' He squeezed her hand.

She sat, confused. A life with Charles – sometimes when her thoughts became unruly she had allowed herself to dream of such a future. But it was all so sudden. Was he anxious to find a wife now Beatrice was no longer available? Was he imagining her in the role because she was experienced at helping the wounded?

'Perhaps you don't know everything I've done in the past, Charles. Before the war I used to be active with the Suffragettes.'

'I know about that,' he grinned. 'It was common knowledge in Wealdham and Alderbank.'

'I suppose it must have been,' she realised. She had paraded wearing the white, green and violet sash. 'But you probably don't know the worst part. I was with Amy when she went into the cricket pavilion in Larchbury – in fact I was the one who broke in and painted the slogans that were hard to remove.'

'I wondered if you were there that day,' he said, apparently unshocked.

'You don't understand how serious it was. Amy got sent to prison, but I was the one who should have been punished.' When she recalled the incident, remorse still plagued her. 'On the day of her wedding – well, the day she should have been married – I couldn't get time off from the hospital where I was training. So I wasn't there when she was arrested.' The old guilt flooded back. 'If I'd been there, I'd have owned up and been arrested. Once they'd sentenced me and realised I was the ringleader they'd probably have been more lenient with Amy.'

'It was dreadful for her, I can see that,' he said, serious now.

He had been there as best man, she remembered.

'There was evidence she'd been inside the building and she was determined not to implicate anyone else,' he said. 'But you didn't know she'd get caught and blamed for the incident.'

'No, I only found out afterwards. When I offered to confess she said there was no point in both of us being punished.'

'She's a very understanding young woman. But listen, Lavinia, that all happened years ago. You shouldn't go on blaming yourself.' His hand left hers and his arm came around her shoulders. 'Tell me you'll consider taking me on as a husband, at least when I've had the chance to learn to use appliances on my legs.'

She hesitated. 'Charles – you're a very dear friend…'

'Just a friend? That's wonderful, but I was hoping for more.'

'I'm concerned you might rush into something too hastily,' she said. 'Please think about it for a while longer, to be certain what you want. And I assure you, whatever happens, I'll always value your company.'

'Let me at least kiss you.' He leant across and as his warm lips met hers she felt giddy with happiness. They stayed in their embrace a while longer.

When they heard footsteps, echoing down the corridor from the far end, he let her go. As she wheeled him back to his ward she hoped the sister had not noticed how close they had been.

When she left her mind was spinning. Could he possibly love her, the way she felt about him? It would be unfair to encourage him to rush into a new engagement. Even so, she could not prevent herself dreaming of such a glorious future.

–

Saturday and Sunday morning passed slowly for Amy. Nurses checked her recovery from the operation, juniors brought her food, and she waited impatiently for Edmond's Sunday visit.

At last he arrived. 'You look much better,' he said, 'apart from the leg, of course.' She was sitting in the chair beside her bed, her bare toes poking out of the plaster.

'Beth was pleased to see me,' he told her. 'Your parents are looking after her very well.'

'The hospital might be discharging me on Friday,' Amy said. 'If only I could go to Cambridge, but I'd be a burden to you, instead of being useful. If I'm at The Beeches I can have Beth with me, though she's getting to be a handful.' With her bad leg she could not even imagine carrying her daughter upstairs. Events seemed to be conspiring continuously to keep her and Edmond apart.

'Pa says you're not to worry,' he told her. 'He's engaged a new maid, called Daisy. It's going to get easier gradually to get staff now the war's over. And with your approval he'll take on a nanny for Beth.'

'Oh – that hadn't occurred to me. It would save me making constant demands on Mother.' She thought for a moment. 'I never considered having a nanny. I want to bring up Beth myself.'

'We all had a nanny when we were small. She was strict but looked after us well.'

'Ask your father to engage a nanny on a very temporary basis,' she told him. 'As soon as my leg is back to normal I won't need her any more.' She was still longing for the time when they could all be together in their own house.

'Keep getting better,' he told her when he had to leave. 'In just a few more weeks it'll be the vacation and I can join you at The Beeches.'

Late on Thursday afternoon Amy was sitting in the chair by her bed, becoming a little bored, for she had finished reading the book she had brought, the latest one in the saga about the Forsytes. She reached across to her few belongings, piling them up as best she could, so she was ready to leave the following morning.

'Hello – how's the leg?' came a voice, and there stood Lavinia. 'It's still painful, I imagine.'

'Yes, but it'll be worth it if I can walk better than before,' she said, glad to have a visitor. If only she could be certain the operation had been a success.

Her friend fetched another chair and sat beside her.

'What about you, Lavinia? The war's over but you'll go on nursing, won't you? You're so skilled.'

'I'm not sure how long I'll continue,' she said. 'I have new plans.' She smiled, her dark eyes shining with excitement. 'There's a man who's asked me to marry him.'

'Lavinia! How wonderful.' She had not expected this.

'Do you remember I once told you there was an officer I admired?'

'Yes – but he wasn't free.'

'He was badly injured and his fiancée didn't want to marry him any longer.'

'Oh – that's like Beatrice and Charles Shenwood,' Amy said.

'The man is Charles Shenwood.'

Amy gasped.

'I nursed him when he was first injured,' Lavinia said. 'He was engaged at the time and I don't believe he thought of me, except as a nurse. I couldn't help caring for him even then, though I assure you I behaved properly,

273

concealing the depth of my feelings. Tell me, has Beatrice got any regrets at breaking her engagement?'

'I don't think so.' Amy's mind raced at the idea of Charles transferring his affections so quickly, and to a woman completely different from Beatrice.

'I came back to England, escorting Charles and some other wounded. I was impressed with his courage in adjusting to the loss of part of both legs. He was an example to the other men.'

'Edmond told me how brave he is.'

'It was a slow journey, as we had to wait for a ship. Gradually he and I were growing closer. Eventually we reached London, and I was sent back to Flanders. Then I came back here with some other wounded and was told to stay in the London hospital. By then Beatrice had broken off their engagement. Charles was in poor spirits, though certain he'd done the right thing. I could scarcely believe it when he began to show me affection, to court me, even.'

Amy was concerned: Charles's change of heart did seem sudden.

'But it's become clear he really cares for me!' Lavinia said, with a tender smile that was unlike her usual resolute expression. 'I visit him every few days, whenever I'm not on duty in the afternoon. He assures me he's certain he wants to marry me. I never knew I could feel so blissful.'

'Have you met his parents?'

'Yes – they were visiting on Monday when I went to see him. I offered to leave them alone with him, but he asked me to stay. They were surprised at first when he told them of his plans, but they were very kind to me. I'm planning to tell Mother tomorrow, and write to Father in France – they'll be overjoyed. We're planning to announce our engagement soon. Charles has to go to the hospital at Roehampton before long to be fitted for artificial limbs. It'll take him some time to get accustomed to them, so we'll have to wait a few months, then we'll get married.'

'That's wonderful news,' Amy cried. At the same time an image flitted through her mind of Lavinia driving around France on her motorbike.

'I've even reminded Charles about my Suffragette activities,' she said. 'I was anxious what he might think if he suddenly found out I'd broken the law, but he was understanding.'

'You won't need to take action like that again, now the law has gone through Parliament about women getting the vote.'

Lavinia looked serious now. 'We both know that's not enough,' she said. 'We should get the vote long before the age of thirty, and without any need to own property. But I'm going to restrict my activities to within the limits of the law.'

'You'll make a wonderful wife for Charles,' Amy said. 'Edmond will be delighted when it's official.'

'It'll be difficult for us to visit you at The Beeches,' she said. 'I can hardly confront Beatrice with her former fiancé.'

'You'll both be able to visit Edmond and me in Cambridge.' She reached out and hugged her old friend.

Chapter Twenty-One

Larchbury and London, November to December

Soon Amy was back at The Beeches, with crutches, limping around on her plastered leg as she had done over a year earlier.

On the Monday afternoon she was bouncing Beth on her lap, thankful that they were reunited again, when Florence called in after school. 'How are you managing?' she asked as Amy got up awkwardly to ring for tea and shortbread.

'Better than I expected. We've two new staff, you see.'

Daisy, the maid, was young but hardworking. Ellen, the nanny, was in her thirties and efficient-looking in her striped dress and apron.

'She and Beth have taken to each other,' Amy told her friend. 'Ellen's previously worked with other families and she's remarked on my habit of spending much of the day with Beth. Apparently in her last family the parents only dropped into the nursery for an hour or so each day, but I made it clear that I'm determined to be close to my daughter.'

Presently Florence took Beth on to her lap. 'I've hardly seen you since the Armistice,' she said. 'I was so thrilled about it when I wrote to James, and then I wrote to Caleb too.'

'Who on earth is Caleb?'

Florence looked confused, as though she had said more than she intended.

'He's an American I met in France,' she explained. 'His ambulance unit helped me get back to the coast – I'm afraid I got sick travelling on Lavinia's bike. Anyway, he was kind to me and asked me to write – he's so far from his family. So I've written – this is only the second time.'

Amy was concerned. Would this man be a rival to James?

'I'm not encouraging him,' Florence said quickly. 'I haven't given him my address, so he can't write back.'

'Is there any prospect of James coming home?'

'Not for a while, though he may be allowed leave, which will be wonderful.' Florence's cheeks dimpled at the prospect.

'It'll certainly be good to see him again.'

–

It was a Friday, a few days into December, when Peter arrived home. He was concerned for his mother and relieved to find her much better. She was more particular now about how her hair was arranged and what clothes she was wearing, a clear sign of her recovery.

Peter was jovial, thankful that the war was over and he need not return to France till New Year's Eve.

'How's Edmond now?' he asked Amy, later that afternoon, when the curtains had just been drawn as dusk fell. They had already assured him he was enjoying life at Cambridge, but Peter seemed to sense that Amy would have a better assessment of his wellbeing.

Ma was in the kitchen speaking to Cook, and Beatrice was in her room having a new gown fitted by her dressmaker. Amy could speak freely in front of Pa.

'He's much better physically,' she reassured Peter, 'though even now he tires easily. I'm worried that he still has nightmares about France, and his broken nights may make it harder for him to study. That's one reason I'm especially anxious to be with him permanently.'

'I must go to Cambridge to see him,' Peter said.

At that moment Amy thought she could hear the growl of a motorbike from the direction of the drive. A minute later Edmond burst in.

'How did you get here!' Pa cried. 'You'll tire yourself, coming on the train, especially having to cross London. And how much time have you missed at College today?'

Amy reached for her crutches and limped across to allow Edmond to embrace her.

'I came on the bike,' he said grinning. Amy knew he had left his old motorbike in France. After he had been wounded he had arranged to pass it on to a fellow officer. 'I've bought a new bike,' he told them. 'It's first rate for getting around. I only had one lecture this afternoon, so I excused myself and set off at lunchtime and I was able to complete most of the journey by daylight.'

Peter rested his hand on his brother's shoulder. 'Trust you to find a way,' he said.

Amy was concerned, but could scarcely contain her delight at his unexpected arrival. 'Come and sit down,' she said, 'you must be exhausted, and frozen.' She felt one of his hands, which was less cold than she expected.

'I wrapped up well,' he told her.

She rang the bell and asked Daisy to bring tea and cake. There would be time later to question his mode of transport.

'Where's Beth?' he asked.

'Ellen's getting her ready for bed.' He rushed off to greet his daughter before returning for the tea.

—

Dinner was a merry occasion, for Edmond was still triumphant at joining them.

'Peter can stay till New Year's Eve,' Ma told him. 'He'll be here for our party.'

'Invite any of your fellow officers who are over here,' Beatrice implored Peter. 'It's been so dull with all the men away.'

He flung her a critical look and Amy guessed he had been displeased at her treatment of Charles.

'Can you leave the party till just before Peter returns?' Edmond asked. 'You'll have your plaster removed soon after Christmas, won't you, darling? I'd like you to be able to dance again.'

If only my leg has healed properly, Amy thought as Cook removed the dishes from the main course. 'It's not that easy,' she told him. 'When the plaster comes off my ankle's still likely to be swollen and I'll need to rest it a good deal. My dancing will be quite limited.' She had the feeling that Mr Westholme and Lavinia would advise against it altogether.

'Should we invite Colonel Fairlawn, if he's back from France, and his son Wilfrid?' asked Ma. 'They used to come to our parties, before the war.'

279

Across the table Beatrice dropped her knife noisily. Amy gasped and tried to conceal her dismay. She could not think of two people she was less willing to meet again. Beatrice had gone pale and was looking at her imploringly.

'I think it would be completely wrong to invite the colonel,' said Pa. 'He was responsible for getting Amy sent to jail.'

'She had actually committed an offence,' Ma pointed out.

Edmond's face was white, his eyes staring. Amy had never seen him so angry.

'The colonel uses his position to bully anyone who crosses him,' Pa retorted. 'I'd like you all to remember how much Amy has done for us. She nursed Ma back to health at great risk to herself.'

Edmond stood up. 'Let me make it clear: if you invite the colonel here I shall take Amy away for the evening to a hotel,' he said.

His mother shuffled. 'I'm sorry,' she said, 'I shouldn't have suggested it.'

'As for Wilfrid, he's still in France,' Peter said, looking at Amy sympathetically. He was the only other one there who knew exactly what had befallen her in Ypres, and Amy was the only one who knew of Beatrice's humiliation at Wilfrid's hands.

'And he's in serious trouble,' Peter went on. 'He's been accused of molesting nurses.'

'Surely not!' his mother exclaimed.

'He's denying it, but more than one young woman has complained.'

Amy looked across the table to Beatrice, who was trembling. It could not be long before one of the others noticed.

'I think Wilfrid is about to face charges,' Peter told them. Amy felt a rush of satisfaction that the man would be confronted with his actions.

'I had no idea he would do such a thing,' Pa said. 'That makes it inappropriate to welcome him here, however impressive his war record.'

Beatrice looked a little calmer and began eating again.

Now a sudden, frightening thought flashed through Amy's head. Might she be called upon to give evidence?

'The complaints were hushed up during the war, I'm sorry to say,' Peter said, 'because of Wilfrid's courage at the Front.'

No more was said of inviting the Fairlawns. Beatrice hurried away as they all got up from the dinner table. Amy asked Peter for a private word. 'It's about someone I know who was assaulted by Wilfrid,' she explained for the benefit of the others.

'It's all right,' he told her when the others had left the room. 'They won't call on you to give evidence, though your complaint was valuable for backing up what the others said. They were afraid Wilfrid would mention that his father had been instrumental in having you sent to jail. The other two nurses are still in France and so can give evidence conveniently. On one occasion he was surprised as he attempted to molest the young woman.'

She was sorry for the other women, but relieved. 'I'm glad I helped to bring him to justice,' she said.

When they rejoined the others Edmond looked very tired and was easily encouraged to retire with her to their bedroom.

'You really are very naughty, riding all this way,' she told him as she unbuttoned her dress.

'Ma didn't approve, I know, but you must understand the freedom it gives me.' His eyes shone with enthusiasm. 'I'd almost forgotten how much I love motorbikes.'

'I'm terrified of you having an accident,' she said. 'Imagine if you sustained more damage to your chest.'

He put his arm around her as she stood there in her undergarments. 'I suppose I should get a motor car,' he said. 'I'll start looking for a second-hand one which is reasonably priced.'

—

When they reached church in good time that Sunday, the first person they saw was James, smart in his uniform, waiting outside to greet them, with Florence at his side, wearing her best hat.

'How long have you been home?' Amy asked, hugging him.

'I only got back yesterday afternoon,' he said.

'It was such a lovely surprise when he called at my house,' Florence said.

They could not talk for long, as the service was about to begin. James went to sit in the vicarage pew, and later got up to read the lesson. There was an air of relief now as parishioners gave thanks for the end of the war.

Afterwards several crowded around James to greet him. Ma and Beatrice were anxious to return home. 'I'll take them, then come back for you,' Pa said to Amy and Edmond. They had left Beth with Ellen.

'I'll take them back in the pony trap,' Uncle Arthur told him. As other churchgoers set off home, he invited them to the vicarage, along with Florence, and Amy's parents.

–

It was a merry group who sat in the vicarage parlour drinking sherry.

'How much leave have you got?' Amy asked her cousin.

'Only four more days, but I might be able to get some more around Christmas or the New Year.'

'We'll spend time together when I'm not at work,' Florence said, her face dimpling.

There was much to talk about, for James was interested to hear about Edmond's experiences at university.

'Is Frank Bentley still in France?' Edmond asked. 'It'll be good to see him when he can come home.' He had been one of his first comrades.

'Yes, he's still there – his unit is further east now, of course. He's managed to get through the war, though he got some shrapnel in his leg at Passchendaele. What about Captain Shenwood? Is he recovering well now he's in Blighty?'

'He's making good progress,' Edmond said.

There was an uneasy silence. Amy suspected James had heard about Beatrice breaking their engagement, but restrained himself from criticising Edmond's sister. Amy would have liked to tell him about his new involvement with Lavinia, but the news was not yet official.

As lunchtime approached Uncle Arthur took them back to The Beeches in the pony trap.

'People are more tolerant of James now,' Amy said.

'They've heard how brave he's been,' her uncle said.

'Gradually some of them are coming to share his view that the war was wrong,' she said.

'Not wrong, exactly,' Edmond said. 'Once it started, once the Kaiser's troops began to invade other nations, I believe we needed to fight. But it should never have been started. The statesmen should have foreseen that it would be catastrophic and come to some agreement to avert it.'

Edmond had to leave immediately after Sunday luncheon to get back to Cambridge. 'Not long now to Christmas vacation,' he said to Amy.

'Don't forget I'm coming to Cambridge to see you next weekend,' Peter said, just before he roared off on his bike.

–

The following morning Ellen brought Beth down and went to eat in the kitchen with the staff. In between eating mouthfuls of her own breakfast, Amy began spooning food to Beth. Peter was completing his meal.

'Pa's rushed off to his study to work,' he said, looking up from the newspaper. Beatrice and her mother were normally last to appear unless one of them had an appointment.

'We had a long talk on Saturday night,' Peter told Amy. The brothers would have sat drinking port with their father. 'Edmond is able to unburden himself of his memories when he's with me, and Pa tells us not to spare him our accounts of the war.'

'Edmond was very calm when he came to bed that night,' she said. 'I think talking about it helps him come to terms with everything that has happened.'

'I've only been to the Front as an observer, not actually had to face the enemy or live in those conditions,' Peter said, 'but I've heard a great deal about life there, enough to listen to Edmond without flinching from the details.'

Just then Beatrice came in and sat down languidly. She rang for Cook to bring her coffee. Her mother soon followed her into the room.

'There's some news to interest you, Bea,' Peter told her. 'There's an engagement announcement in the paper. Charles Shenwood is to marry Lavinia Westholme.'

'What!' Beatrice cried, breaking off from nibbling an apple.

'It's hardly any time since he was engaged to Beatrice!' said her mother.

'Lavinia told me about it while I was in hospital,' Amy said, 'but I was not at liberty to mention it until the official announcement.' For a moment she dreaded Lavinia wearing the same ring Charles had given Beatrice, but her sister-in-law had dainty hands, so there was little chance it would fit.

'I suppose it'll be good for Lavinia that she has a husband,' Mrs Derwent said. 'She's such a gawky young woman.'

'At least Charles will have a wife who's accustomed to looking after invalids,' Beatrice observed, but for a moment she looked regretful.

Ellen arrived to take Beth up to the nursery. The baby's energetic walking was an annoyance to Mrs Derwent if they occupied the same room. Amy relied on the nanny to carry Beth, for she needed her hands free to go around on her crutches.

'I'll come upstairs in a minute,' she told Ellen.

When she had finished her breakfast, Peter followed her out of the room.

'I don't think you should worry too much about Edmond,' he said. 'You saw how happy he was when he surprised us on the motorbike. He's getting his old spirit back.'

—

Amy was listening for the sound of the bike when Edmond returned for Christmas. She hurried to the front door to greet him, more accustomed now to her plaster. Beneath it her leg was hurting less and she was growing optimistic that the ankle might be better.

'At last you're home!' she cried. 'And in the New Year, surely nothing can stop me and Beth returning to Cambridge with you.'

In high spirits they set out for church on Christmas Day morning. Pa was making two trips in the car, and Amy and Edmond were in the first group.

She walked up the path outside St Stephen's while Edmond carried Beth, well wrapped up in her shawl. Someone touched Amy's arm, and there stood Florence, who must have rushed to catch them up.

'Won't this be a joyful service!' Amy said. 'All the fighting is over!'

Once inside, they found the church more lavishly decorated with greenery than in recent years, and blazing with light from dozens of candles. All the same, she detected a slight edge to the atmosphere, as though something was wrong.

On the way to the Derwent pew near the front she stopped to greet her parents.

'Have you heard about Philip Brownlee?' Mother said. 'The young airman?'

'Yes, poor chap. He crashed his plane two days ago. He was on a routine flight to an airfield nearer the coast. They say he's badly injured, but should recover.'

Florence was beside Amy and had heard the news. Her face looked frozen with shock. 'He was convalescing at the same time as James, in the converted casino,' she said. 'How dreadful that he's had another accident!'

Amy caught sight of the young man's parents and sister, Caroline, standing hunched and subdued in a nearby pew.

Edmond looked drawn, equally upset that another young man should suffer, just when the conflict was over. 'It all seems so pointless,' he said. 'And Henry Smith is still missing, isn't he?'

The brother of George and Joe had gone missing in action near the end of the war, and there was still no sign of him.

What should have been an exultant service needed once more to include a prayer for a badly injured man in the forces and one who was still unaccounted for.

–

Just after Christmas Mr Derwent took Amy and Edmond to London so she could have her plaster removed. Mr Westholme was back in France and it was arranged that she would see the doctor who had attended to her the previous year.

Ma was still lethargic from the flu, but recovered enough for Pa to feel confident at leaving her for the day, with Beatrice and Daisy to give her any help she needed. He dropped them outside St Luke's hospital and went to meet a business contact, after arranging a time to return. As they walked towards the sombre brick hospital Amy could not hold back her tears.

'Are you frightened, darling?' Edmond put his arm around her.

'It's not that. I was thinking of Katherine. We both trained here, and she met me here last year when I had my plaster removed.'

'I'm sorry, darling. She was a great loss.'

They walked into the main entrance. The hospital seemed less busy now the war was over. Amy limped along the tiled corridor towards the Fracture Clinic, sniffing a little but trying to compose herself for Edmond's benefit.

After a short wait they were called into the treatment room. Edmond sat in a chair, smiling at her encouragingly. The orthopaedic surgeon chatted to her as the nursing staff carefully cut off her plaster.

'I remember you from last year,' he said, looking a little concerned.

Her leg and ankle looked swollen, as they had done the previous year.

'How does it feel?' he asked her.

'My ankle's stiff – well, I expected that – but the shape of my leg looks normal now.' She felt confident that the bones were correctly aligned.

The nurse took her arm while she put her foot to the floor. It felt reassuringly normal. 'It's so much better!' she cried. Edmond broke into a grin.

She removed the shoe from her good foot and walked across the room. At last her left foot could go flat on the floor with little strain. She felt her face ease into a smile as she turned and walked back again. 'It's much improved from last time!' she cried.

She sat down and put back her lace-up shoe on her right foot. She went behind a screen to put a stocking on the injured foot. Edmond got up and gently helped her ease her other shoe on to the left foot. He laced it very loosely, just enough to hold it over the swollen area.

The medical team looked delighted as she left the clinic. She and Edmond set off back to the lobby, to wait for Pa, and found Lavinia there, anxious to see how the appointment had gone. She took off the shoe to inspect Amy's leg and was satisfied.

'Thank your father for making it almost as good as new,' Amy said.

'Promise me you'll rest it for most of each day until it's completely healed,' Lavinia urged her.

'I'll make sure she behaves,' Edmond said. 'Lavinia, I'm so pleased to hear about you and Charles. You'll make a fine couple.'

Amy was thankful he was not looking too surprised at how rapidly Charles had moved on.

'Have you heard about Philip Brownlee?' Lavinia said suddenly.

'Yes, everyone in Larchbury is talking about his accident,' Amy said.

'Alice, Charles's younger sister, has become very attached to the boy,' Lavinia said.

'Your father is over there, I imagine,' Edmond said.

'He's at a hospital some distance away from Philip, unfortunately.'

Pa arrived and invited Lavinia to lunch with them. 'Where shall we go?' he mused.

Edmond reminded him that the hotel where Amy and he had spent their all too brief honeymoon was nearby. 'Might we go there?' he asked.

They all set off in excellent spirits.

'Remember how we had to rush away last time!' Amy could not help saying as the glass doors were opened to admit them to its smart foyer. After she and Edmond had married at their second attempt, he had ignored an order telling him to return early to France, so that they could spend their wedding night together.

'I got soundly punished for my disobedience,' he reminded them. 'They stopped my leave for months afterwards.'

'Yes – it was almost unbearable that we had to spend so long apart.'

They sat down once more in the elegant restaurant. Several officers were dining there, some with members of their family. The waiter recommended the roast lamb.

As Lavinia removed her gloves, Amy noticed her pretty but modest ring with three small diamonds. 'It's all right,' she said. 'The ring Beatrice wore was a family heirloom, and someone in the family has it back. Charles had a few rings brought to the hospital from Hatton Garden and we chose one for me.'

As they began with soup Lavinia told them that he had been to Roehampton to be measured for artificial limbs. Then he had spent two weeks at a convalescent hospital before going home to his family.

'I stayed with them over Christmas,' she said. 'On fine days we went out riding. Charles needs help to mount but he loves to go around on horseback.'

'I should go over and see him one day,' Edmond said, as the lamb was served. 'There's not much time before I go back to Cambridge.'

Chapter Twenty-Two

Larchbury, London and Alderbank, December

Next morning Florence phoned Amy and was thrilled to hear that her leg was much better.

'Will you be able to dance?' she asked. The party at The Beeches was only two days away.

'I hope so,' she said, 'but everyone is telling me not to take any chances.'

'Perhaps you should do as they say. How long will it take for the pain and swelling to go?'

'It should be noticeably better by the time we go to Cambridge. Is there any chance James will be back on leave in time for the party?'

'Yes! He should be on his way by now. I'm hoping he'll arrive today.' What a joyous occasion it would be.

Soon after her phone call, Florence was sitting in the parlour when the post arrived. 'There's a strange letter for you,' her mother said, passing her an envelope with unfamiliar dark blue handwriting. It had come from France and was addressed simply to

Florence Clifford, Larchbury, Sussex, England.

She tore open the envelope, curious to see its contents, and gasped when she read who it was from.

'*Dear Florence*', it said,

How wonderful that the war is over now! Thank you so much for your letters, which cheered me in our last difficult days fighting the Huns.

My unit is still stationed near the Marne, but we are to be allowed leave. I'm planning to come over to England, with a comrade. We are longing to visit London.

And while we're there, dear Florence, I'm planning on coming to see you! I can't wait to see where you live, and spend some time with you.

Your admirer,

Caleb Fawcett

Florence sucked her lip.

'Who's it from, dear?'

'An American soldier I met in France,' she said awkwardly, wishing her mother had not seen it arrive.

Mother frowned. 'An American? You mean you've been writing to him as well as to James?'

She explained the limited extent of her correspondence. 'I didn't expect to hear from him. As you see, I never gave him my address.'

Why had she revealed that she lived somewhere called Larchbury? She tried to remember him from that brief afternoon in his company. He had been friendly and confident, she recalled, and had seemed quite determined. Would he really come here looking for her?

She put the letter back in its envelope. Mother was more prepared to accept James now. Probably she had realised that Florence's marriage prospects were poor, now so many young men had been lost. She seemed satisfied with Florence's account of her meeting with Caleb and did not pursue the matter.

There was a knock at the front door. Mother went to answer it and a moment later James strode into the room, carrying a vivid amber-coloured bunch of chrysanthemums.

'Oh! It's you!' Florence rushed into his arms. 'I didn't expect you so early.' As he kissed her, his lips were cold from the chill December morning. His embrace threatened to squash the flowers. 'What lovely chrysanths,' she said, taking the blooms from him. 'Mother, we should light the fire in here.'

'Of course! I'll see to it.' Normally they left lighting it to slightly later in the day.

Florence placed the flowers carefully on the side table, hoping he would not notice the strange form of address on the envelope containing her letter.

'We reached the port in good time and came back overnight,' James told her. 'I haven't even been home to my parents yet.'

She snuggled into his arms. 'You'll need a warm drink in a minute, or maybe some sherry,' she said. She needed to find a vase as well. Mother was fetching coal as their maid did not work that day.

'I'm thrilled to be back with you again,' he said.

'How long can you stay over here?'

'I've got a whole week!'

She wished she had put on a newer dress and paid more attention to her hair. She sat down on the sofa and he sat beside her and put his arm around her as she basked in the delight of seeing him again.

When Mother returned with the coal James insisted on building the fire and starting it for her. Then Mother went to make some tea.

'I'll never forget that day you arrived at the convalescent hospital to see me,' James told her gently, sitting beside her once more.

'It was a shock, visiting France in those conditions, but I'll never regret coming to see you… But James, have you heard about Philip Brownlee?'

'Yes,' he said sadly, 'they're doing what they can to help him but I hear he's badly smashed up.'

'I was appalled that he'd been in another accident!'

'Yes. He'd recovered, so he was flying again, then he crashed. They say it was foggy that day. It's desperately sad.' He leant across and kissed her.

This should be a happy day, Florence thought. *I must put those gorgeous flowers in water.* She reached for the nearest vase, arranged them hastily, and hurriedly went for water for them. *I must savour our time together.*

As for Caleb, I won't mention him. If he ever reaches England he'll arrive in London and with luck he'll have such a good time there he won't actually come out to Sussex.

–

'I want to drive over to see Charles today,' Edmond said next morning. It was not far to his family home near Alderbank. 'I can go on my bike.'

'I'll come with you!' Amy cried.

'Do you think you should?' He hated to question her enthusiasm, but her leg was still a little swollen and he knew some of her shoes were uncomfortable. 'Perhaps you should rest your ankle again.' She was meant to spend some time each day on the sofa with her leg raised.

'I suppose so,' she said, unwillingly. 'I must be fit for the dance tomorrow.'

He knew she was determined to attend, at least for part of the evening.

The day was cold again, with the sun appearing only fleetingly. On his bike the journey took only a quarter of an hour but he could feel the cold air sharply in his scarred lung.

Alderbank had a small village centre, surrounded by several large houses and estates. Slightly to the west of his route lay the turreted stone house which was home to Colonel Fairlawn and his family. The Westholmes lived near the railway station, while Charles's family lived between the village and the outskirts of Wealdham.

He reached the Shenwoods' handsome house, set in ten acres of grounds. The butler admitted him and led him towards the drawing room. As he approached there was the sound of someone playing the piano confidently, though not as proficiently as Beatrice. When he went in he saw it was Lavinia. Charles was sitting on the sofa, his legs covered.

They both looked pleased he had come. Charles looked healthier than when Edmond had last seen him, just after Beatrice had ended their engagement. Now his eyes were lively and sparkling again. He and Lavinia were casually dressed.

She enquired after Amy, and Edmond was able to reassure her that the swelling on her foot was subsiding gradually.

'I came here for Christmas,' Lavinia said, 'and as you can see, I'm back again. I managed to arrange another day off.'

'We were just about to go for a ride in the grounds,' Charles said. 'I try to go out most days, though it's been cold lately. You'll join us, won't you?'

They put on outdoor riding clothes but it was chilly as they made their way to the stables. The gardener, who looked a little too young to have been called up, brought out three horses and saddled them. With Edmond's assistance, and some difficulty, the young man helped Charles into the saddle of his favourite bay. There was a grey for Edmond, and a slightly smaller one for Lavinia, who mounted with the appearance of a confident horsewoman.

They set off along a track which led through an avenue in the grounds. 'I've always loved riding here,' Charles said, 'and now it makes ideal exercise.' They continued down a lane for a while before turning back.

How well he's managing, Edmond thought, though a wind was getting up and they were all a little relieved when they were heading back towards the stables.

They warmed up by the fire in the drawing room and he felt his cheeks begin to glow as they sipped glasses of sherry before lunch.

Edmond gave him an account of his life at Cambridge. 'It's stimulating to be back there,' he told them, 'but I'm impatient for Amy and Beth to arrive. In less than two weeks we should all be at home there.' Sometimes it seemed like an impossible dream, for there had been so many delays and setbacks.

'I'm determined to follow your example and overcome my problems,' Charles said.

'Do you plan to study or find an occupation when you're fitter?'

'It's too soon to decide yet,' Charles said, 'but I need some worthwhile activity. As for Lavinia, I want her to have some life outside the home.'

'I'm prepared to give up work for a while if we have children,' she said, more gently than he had heard her speak before. 'Bringing up a family is a vital role for a woman, though she should pursue other interests if possible.'

'Yes, of course, dearest, you have a worthwhile vocation and may wish to return to it one day.'

'Amy talks of that too,' Edmond said, 'though she's not in a rush to work again.'

'Apart from her nursing, I've always imagined Lavinia taking a lead in some way,' Charles said. 'I believe politics might suit her now there are more opportunities for women.'

His future wife's eyes lit up at the suggestion and Edmond agreed he could visualise her in that kind of capacity. *We would never have talked of such a possibility before the war*, he thought.

Then the butler summoned them to lunch. They helped Charles into his invalid chair and Lavinia wheeled him through to the dining room.

They joined his mother and two sisters at the table. The cook served them a pie and winter vegetables, while Mrs Shenwood made a predictable apology about shortages. 'Let's hope the food supply is back to normal soon,' she said.

Isobel, the older sister, was elegantly dressed and enquired if Edmond had attended the theatre recently. She reminded him somewhat of Beatrice, and did not seem especially eager to talk to Lavinia. Alice, the younger sister, was friendly and livelier. The parents were kindly and ready to praise Charles's fiancée for the care she lavished upon him.

Amy will be glad to know that Lavinia is appreciated by most of her new family, Edmond thought. *How good she is for Charles!*

'How is Philip progressing?' Edmond asked Alice.

'They say he should recover,' said the slender younger sister. 'Knowing him, he'll be determined to fly again!' she added ruefully.

A servant came in and banked up the fire with fresh logs.

'My family begged me to return before the daylight begins to fade,' he told the others. 'The evening may bring a frost.' They were still not resigned to him travelling on the bike.

'My motorbike is still in France,' Lavinia said nostalgically. 'I wrote and told another nurse she could use it, and as far as I know she's still out there.'

Before long it was time for him to leave. 'Tell Amy to go on taking plenty of rest,' Lavinia said. 'She's not still determined to dance tomorrow, is she?'

'I'll try to persuade her to be sensible,' was all he could say.

'She'll want to join in, won't she?' Lavinia said, sounding frustrated.

'Amy has always taken up challenges instead of favouring a quiet life,' he said. 'I suppose we all have.'

Amy was excited at the prospect of the dance. On the day, Edmond's cousin, Vicky, joined them for lunch and commented favourably on Amy's new confidence at walking. 'I'm so glad it's all working out for you and Edmond,' she said.

'I hope soon we'll be together for good,' Amy said.

Peter had invited his friend, Robert Lambert, who Amy remembered meeting in France. She was a little embarrassed that he knew what had happened between her and Wilfrid Fairlawn, but felt she could rely on him to keep her confidence. He was sitting next to Beatrice, who was eager to talk. Amy imagined she was hoping to find a successor to Charles. Beatrice would have no idea that Robert was involved in prosecuting Wilfrid, and he would have no inkling that she was another of his victims.

Vicky was beautiful now she was a poised eighteen-year-old. 'Have you made any progress with your plans for the future?' Amy asked her. Vicky had shown an interest in nursing.

'I wondered whether to find work in an office,' she said. 'But I'm still eager to do nursing, like you. They'll need nurses, even though the war is over.'

Beatrice looked in their direction. 'What do your parents think of your plans?' she asked her cousin. 'I daresay they'd prefer you to stay at home and enjoy social events.'

'They might, but now that way of life seems dull,' Vicky said firmly. She told them about her visit to a London hospital to discuss training for the profession. Beatrice looked bored, but Robert seemed interested.

As the afternoon wore on Beatrice's concerns turned to her hair. She was sorry Janet had left to look after her relatives, for she had been gifted at styling hair. Eventually Mrs Derwent had asked the former maid to return to work just for the evening, to arrange Beatrice's hair and help serve the buffet.

'She might arrange Amy's hair as well,' Ma suggested.

'What about Vicky?' Amy asked. 'Would you like her to put your hair in ringlets or make curls on top of your head?'

'Oh, I should love ringlets,' the young girl said.

Beatrice insisted that Janet spent sufficient time arranging her chestnut locks to her complete satisfaction. Amy was content with two well-placed curls upon her head and then passed on the maid to Vicky.

Amy's new gown, made especially for the party, was a simple style in pretty blue satin. 'You look wonderful, dearest,' Edmond said, fastening her amethyst pendant around her neck; he had given it to her for Christmas. 'But you mustn't overdo the dancing.'

'My ankle's just better enough to wear dancing shoes for an hour or two,' Amy insisted.

—

They were soon meeting the guests downstairs. Vicky looked enchanting in her ivory-coloured dress, with auburn ringlets cascading onto her shoulders.

'We used to have a huge pine tree from the forest decorating the ballroom,' Edmond said.

'Yes! It's one of the things I remember from that evening when I first attended the dance here!' Amy said.

'We used to dig up suitably sized pine trees and sell them each year,' Pa said. 'Lately there's been no demand for them and we've had to stop having our own Christmas tree. They became very unpopular during the war, because they're regarded as a German tradition.'

'Perhaps we can start having them again in a year or two,' Amy said.

There was an air of excitement, for almost all those invited had made an effort to attend this year, as a token that better times were on the way. Yet few could completely feel free to enjoy themselves, aware of all the losses that had been suffered.

Florence arrived, escorted by James. *How lovely she looks*, Amy thought, *with her hair becomingly arranged*. Her turquoise-coloured evening gown was not new, but she had trimmed it with some fresh velvet ribbon. Amy's parents joined the couple, acknowledging their increasing closeness, seeming to accept that, while Florence would never forget Bertie, she was ready to find happiness elsewhere.

Amy followed her parents as they went to talk to Mr Leadbetter, who had decided to come, although it was not many months since he had lost his wife to the flu. Peter joined the group, keen to talk to Amy's father, his former tutor.

'It's too bad you'll have gone back to France by Beth's birthday,' he said to Peter.

'Can't be helped, I'm afraid. I gather you're entertaining on the first to mark the occasion.'

'We've invited your family,' Amy's mother said a little nervously.

The Derwents had briefly employed Mr Fletcher as tutor when Peter and Edmond had been boys. They had only once visited the little house in Sebastopol Terrace, soon after Edmond and Amy had become engaged. Amy wondered if Mrs Derwent was prepared to visit again, but her husband was determined they should all go.

'I'd love to help you prepare for Beth's party,' Amy said. 'I can make the cakes and jellies.' She knew there was much packing to do before they set off for Cambridge, but Mother deserved some support.

'I won't have you do any such thing,' Mother replied. 'It's not long since you were in hospital, and you need to rest your leg, besides getting ready for your move.'

'But you've given up so much of your time to looking after Beth for me!'

'Mrs Johnson has promised to help me with the cooking,' her mother said.

Soon they moved into the next room for supper. Now Vicky was with a few others around her own age and there were stifled giggles from their direction.

'They're ready to move on from the war, aren't they?' Florence said. 'There are young men who were born just too late to have played any part in the conflict, and women too young to have served in any important capacity. Unless they've lost someone close they're eager to have fun.'

'You're right,' Amy said.

Then someone mentioned Philip Brownlee. There was fresh concern about him.

'His family have gone to Flanders to see him,' Mr Leadbetter told them. 'I gather he's suffered a setback.'

Edmond looked tense at the news.

With the more mature guests, the chief topics of speculation were how soon their surviving relatives could return from France, and how they might settle back to peacetime occupations.

'They say some men will remain abroad for a while,' James said. 'There's to be an army of occupation in Germany. They'll begin to plan it as they start to negotiate the peace treaty at Versailles next month.'

For those with relatives who would never return there was seldom much to be merry about, and excessive frivolity was soon met with stern glances. They discussed the memorials to the dead that were proposed.

Mr Derwent had managed to assemble a quartet of musicians for the evening, as he had for the parties a few years earlier. Soon they were tuning up and guests began moving back into the ballroom. The younger ones were expected to dance, while others were prepared to watch.

Edmond's parents started the ball as usual, though his mother was still not in full health and probably would only dance once or twice. As other guests joined them on the floor Edmond seized Amy's hand and they began to glide around the floor together. He held her firmly and she put as little weight as possible on her bad foot. Somehow she managed to complete the dance, thrilled at her newly revived ability.

At the end of the first dance she and Edmond exchanged contented glances.

Mother hurried around the dance floor to speak to her. 'Are you all right, dear?' she asked. 'It's very soon after your plaster has come off.'

'Yes, I know I mustn't overdo it,' she said. 'Don't let that stop you dancing, darling,' she said to Edmond.

Nearby James was holding Florence close. They seemed to be oblivious to the guests around them.

Peter's friend Robert engaged Beatrice for a waltz, but then turned his attention to Vicky, who practically sparkled with excitement. As Robert continued to dance a lively polka with her, Beatrice stood, without a partner, looking sour. This time last year she had just announced her engagement to Charles. For a brief moment Amy felt sorry for her. Her sister-in-law must be the most expensively dressed woman in the room, but the layers of lace now looked excessive, for most women had turned to simpler styles in the years of war, when there were other issues claiming their attention. There had been a trend to more comfortable garments when women were taking war work, but Beatrice was still fiercely corseted. She was nearly twenty-six, and with her indolent life what did she have to talk about, apart from her occasional visits to the theatre and her shopping expeditions?

Between dances James hovered by Florence's side, but he seemed content for Edmond to claim her for a waltz.

Amy stood beside Beatrice. 'Edmond's looking well, isn't he?' she said. 'I believe he'll stay up for most of the dance tonight.'

There was a pause between dances, but Robert remained at Vicky's side. 'What a little minx my cousin is!' Beatrice said. 'She's planning some busy future involving nursing but she doesn't hesitate to flirt with an eligible man.'

Amy made no reply, delighted to see Edmond's cousin enjoying the evening.

Mr Leadbetter now approached. 'I wasn't intending to dance this evening,' he said, 'but I believe my late wife would not have wished me to retreat from social encounters altogether. Beatrice, would you care to take the floor with me?' he asked her.

For a moment she hesitated and Amy could imagine her deciding it would be preferable to be dancing with a man who was not her first choice of partner than to remain a wallflower. She let him lead her into the waltz and responded with her usual grace and style.

Soon Edmond was back. 'Can you manage another dance, darling?' he asked her. She wished she had concentrated more on resting her ankle earlier in the day. Could they actually repeat that magic circuit of the dance floor?

'It had better be another waltz,' she said, anxious not to embark on anything vigorous. When another one began, he took her in his arms. How good it felt as he led her around the floor.

'Remember four years ago, when I first danced with you?' he said.

'I'll never forget that evening, though it seems like a lifetime ago. I was very worried about what your family would think of me, but I knew you were the man I should be with.' Florence and James drifted past them. This time they were the ones who were entwined in an enchanted world of their own.

As the music ended Edmond held Amy close and kissed her tenderly.

Chapter Twenty-Three

Larchbury, December 1918 to January 1919

The following day Peter had to return to Headquarters in France. Ma stayed at home while Pa drove Beatrice into Larchbury village for some shopping, then took Edmond and Amy to see Peter off at the station.

He wished them all a warm farewell and climbed into his train. Soon Pa was driving them back. As they travelled along the High Street they saw a couple emerging from the tearoom. It was Mr Leadbetter, whose term had not yet started, and Beatrice, in a smart coat and large feathered hat.

'I didn't know she was meeting him,' Edmond said.

'She just asked me to drop her off outside the shoe shop, so she could look for new boots,' Pa told them, shouting over the noise of the car. 'I hadn't expected Bea to show much interest in him. She seems determined to seek a husband.'

'He can't decently remarry for a while yet,' Edmond said.

Beatrice still had a beautiful pristine wedding dress in her wardrobe, Amy remembered. 'There's still time for her to meet some officer returning from the war,' she said.

On the first day of the New Year Amy's parents were holding their little party to celebrate Beth's first birthday. Beatrice said she had rather not come, as she had a headache, but Pa drove the rest of them into Larchbury.

Amy held her daughter in her arms, as she wriggled, anxious to escape the confined space. She was learning to speak a few words now, and developing a mind of her own. Her dress of fine wool was trimmed with a small panel of Belgian lace, for Pa had driven Amy into Wealdham one day and she had spent some more time with Madame Rousseau.

Beth's first year had flown past, and for Amy and Edmond it had been full of incident, with more than its share of tragedy. On the very last day of the old year they had heard that Philip Brownlee, the young airman, had died of his wounds; so another local family had been plunged into mourning, along with Alice Shenwood, just as they were thinking the terrors were past.

Amy had spoken on the phone to Lavinia about this latest loss. 'They called Father to examine him two days ago,' she told Amy. 'Outwardly his wounds were healing but they had failed to notice some internal bleeding. It was too late to save him.'

'Let's hope he's the final victim,' Amy had said, determined the New Year should start on a promising note.

When they arrived at the party the parlour was decorated with branches of pine that Edmond's father had sent them. Aunt Sophie was playing an old-fashioned Victorian ballad on the piano. Amy's father greeted Edmond's parents. Beth looked around, bewildered by all the relatives. Edmond's parents were greeting her own relatives, enthusiastically in Pa's case and more vaguely by Ma.

Father steered Ma to the most comfortable chair and Pa to the one beside it. The little parlour looked crowded. Amy and Edmond settled next to Florence and James on upright chairs brought from elsewhere in the house.

'I'd have liked to invite Aunt Louisa,' Mother said, 'but goodness knows where she'd have sat.'

Perhaps it was as well, after all, that Beatrice had not come.

Ma, slightly flustered, dropped her handkerchief on the floor. 'Look!' cried Beth, pointing to it, and Amy sent her to return it to its owner. She toddled across to retrieve it and reached up to the sterner of her two grandmothers, who bestowed a smile as she took it back.

Guests were producing little gifts now. Amy encouraged Beth to help undo them. She and Edmond had bought their daughter a lovely doll, but now there was a stuffed cat which Mother had knitted, for her to take to bed, and a cloth book from her aunt Sophie. Florence had knitted Beth a jacket to wear, in an intricate lacy pattern.

Pretty in her new woollen dress, Florence was darting to and fro, talking to James, clearing up wrapping paper and taking her turn at cuddling Beth.

Soon it was time to take their places in the dining room. There was only room for Beth on someone's lap, and she was passed around from Amy to Florence and then to Edmond as Mother served tea and Mrs Johnson offered the guests slices of pie and other savouries.

When Amy asked Mrs Johnson about her family she sighed. 'Poor Elsie is so concerned about Henry,' she said.

Amy remembered seeing the young girl with him during his last leave.

'He's been missing for two months now,' Mrs Johnson said, shaking her head. She went back to the kitchen, returning later with cakes and a tray of jellies.

To one side of Amy, on top of a bookcase, the old photo of Bertie smiled down on them. Florence was sitting opposite it and Amy saw her gaze at it more than once.

Father seemed to read her thoughts. 'He'd want you to be happy and make a fresh start,' he told her gently.

'Perhaps it's time you told everyone your news,' Uncle Arthur said.

James was next to Florence, and now he stood up. 'I'm very proud to say that Florence has agreed to become my wife!' he announced. She grinned happily as he kissed her.

Everyone congratulated them. 'How wonderful to hear some good news,' Pa said as Father poured glasses of wine to toast the couple.

Amy hurried around the table to her friend and embraced her. 'That's wonderful!' she said.

'One day we'll both go to visit Bertie's grave near the Somme,' James said.

'Me too,' Amy said. Many of the fallen were in makeshift graves, but there were plans now to provide well laid out cemeteries near the battlefields to honour them.

'I'll need to serve in France for a while longer,' James told them, 'for many young men are still out there, too ill to come home yet.'

'And what'll you do afterwards?' Pa asked.

'I'd like to study at university, like Edmond, if I can secure a place,' he said.

'So you'll be trying to support a wife, while studying, like Edmond,' Ma said, with a note of concern. Ma knew the vicar, of course, and Aunt Sophie from their Working Parties. She had never paid much attention to James.

'Yes, but I hope to join a profession or find a worth-while occupation as soon as possible,' he told her.

'Young men have had to serve abroad and many are in this position,' Pa said. 'They're returning as heroes. Why should they be forced to wait to get married?' He seemed to be aware of James's bravery, even as a medical orderly.

'He's our only child,' Uncle Arthur said. 'Fortunately we're in a position to give him some support.'

Ma seemed at last to be warming to Amy's family. 'At least the hostilities are over now,' she said, smiling. 'I wish you all the best for the New Year.'

–

Two days later Florence went with James's parents to see him off on the train. A cold wind blew along the platform.

'If only there had been time to choose you a ring, darling,' James said, his arm around Florence while his parents stood a little way away. 'I'll request some more leave as soon as possible and we'll choose you one.'

'I can hardly bear to see you returning so soon,' she said.

'When the situation becomes clearer we must fix the date for our wedding,' he promised. 'You won't mind living at the vicarage for a while, until I come home for good? There are some spare rooms there we can use.' It was a sprawling building, intended for an incumbent with a larger family.

'Amy and Edmond have managed,' she said, smiling. She had once told the vicar and his wife of her former involvement with the Suffragettes and they had seemed to understand. She felt sure they would be easier to get along with than Amy's mother-in-law and Beatrice had sometimes been.

The train had not yet appeared: it was running late. Florence snuggled up to James. 'You know how I always look forward to your letters,' she said.

'I love writing to you and imagining you beside me,' he said. 'By the way, I didn't tell the others something I want to do now the war is over…'

'Go on…'

'I want to write down my experiences out in Flanders. You're not encouraged to keep a diary there but I did manage to write one.' She remembered taking him an exercise book and wondering what it was for. 'They're saying this was the war to end all wars, but in a few years from now there'll be young men thinking that it all sounds a huge adventure, like some of my old schoolmates did when it started. I'd like to remind them of the huge losses, and some of the ghastly effects of the war.'

'You should do that.' She admired him now for his determination to oppose war.

There was the sound of the train approaching in the distance, and a puff of smoke was visible. Her future in-laws hurried to wish him well. The train drew into the platform and the vicar helped James into a carriage with his kit. James leant out of the window and she enjoyed a final embrace and kiss.

Then the whistle blew and she stepped back and waved as the train clanked off. She accompanied his parents back to their pony and trap.

In a few days school would begin again, to distract her. 'I'll miss James terribly while he's abroad,' she told the others, 'but at least we can live normally now, without dreading the arrival of a telegram.'

They took her back to her family home. *How fast James's leave has passed*, she thought. It occurred to her that Caleb Fawcett had not, after all, arrived. She was thankful he had stayed away.

-

The following Monday Beatrice asked her father to drive her to the station to catch a train to Wealdham, where she did some worthwhile shopping. As she returned, alone, in a first class carriage, she reviewed her friendship with Ernest Leadbetter. The man admired her, that much was clear. He could talk intelligently on a number of subjects, and as headmaster he held a respectable position. He was tall, but his steely blue-grey eyes and lank hair did not appeal. She had hoped she might grow to care for him, but was beginning to find him dull. Only the lack of healthy young men returning from the war had made her consider him as a suitor.

The train slowed down as it drew into Larchbury. The stationmaster would allow her to telephone her father and ask him to collect her. As she stepped out on to the platform a young officer was alighting from a second class compartment. It was almost dusk, but she was fairly sure she had not seen him before. He reached the ticket barrier at the same time as she did and courteously indicated that she should go first. She was curious about his uniform, which did not look quite like a British one. She handed her ticket quickly to the familiar man at the barrier and went through into the ticket office. The newcomer followed her, and she began to dawdle, interested to discover who he was.

He was soon by her side, raising his cap to reveal sandy-coloured hair. It seemed he was anxious to speak to her.

'Excuse me,' he said in an extraordinary accent which she thought might be American, or possibly Australian. 'My name's Caleb Fawcett, and I'm looking for a young lady called Florence Clifford. Would you happen to know where I might find her?'

Florence – where had she met this confident, good-looking young officer? Beatrice supposed it must have been during her escapade in France during the summer.

She decided to postpone phoning her father. 'Yes,' she said, 'I do know where she lives. It's not far from here. Shall I take you there?'

'That's extremely kind of you.' For a moment his gaze lingered on her, and she was glad she was wearing her smart coat, well-fitted to show off her tiny waist, and her feathery hat. She had always known she was right to take care of her appearance, when some young women had been so absorbed in war work they had neglected their looks.

He followed her out into the High Street, and insisted on carrying her shopping bag as well as his own suitcase. They set off through the dusk in the direction of Florence's home. *Will she be there*, Beatrice wondered. *Has the school term started yet?* She thought Ernest had told her school was starting the following day. Even if she was wrong, by now classes would have finished for the day and Florence would be home.

'Have you heard that Florence is engaged now?' she asked, suddenly remembering that recent piece of news. 'She's to marry the vicar's son.'

'Is that so?' He sounded disappointed. His steps slowed. 'Have you come far to see her?'

'From France, on leave, but I've been seeing London for a few days,' he said. 'I guess I'll need a hotel to stay in while I'm here.' He hovered, indecisively, under a lamp.

What attractive light blue eyes he has, Beatrice thought.

'Now I'm here I think I should at least go and see her,' he said. 'I'd like to renew our acquaintance.' They continued on their way.

–

At last Amy was packing ready to move to Cambridge on Friday. It was late on Wednesday afternoon and Florence had called in after school to help her.

'Is Beatrice still seeing Caleb?' she asked, an amused twinkle in her eyes.

'Yes – he's staying at the inn.' Amy paid attention for a moment to folding some of Beth's little dresses. 'When Beatrice introduced him to us I was worried at first, as he said he'd come to see you.'

'I'm engaged to James, and nothing would induce me to change my mind. Caleb was never more than an acquaintance.'

'He keeps calling to see Beatrice.' The pair of them had just returned from a walk and he was invited to stay to dinner.

'Caleb was friendly when he called to see me,' Florence said, 'but he had just met Beatrice, and he was gazing at her as though he had never seen anyone quite like her.'

'Maybe he hadn't.'

'She was looking at him the same way, and before long they left so she could take him to the inn.'

'I think he's going back to London soon for another few days before he returns to his unit in France. Beatrice is planning to go to London and stay with a friend while he's there.' She was on poor terms now with Harriet and her family, but had found another hostess.

Florence went on folding Beth's spare sheets. 'I wonder – does she know Caleb is just a Warrant Officer?'

'I've no idea.' She wondered if Beatrice would ever consider going to live in America, and could not imagine whether or not that would work out satisfactorily.

'I suppose I'd better go home for dinner now,' Florence said.

'I'll see if Pa can take you in the car.'

Florence hugged her. 'I'll miss you so much when you've gone,' she said.

'You'll be one of the first to stay in our spare room, I promise.'

—

On Friday they set off in the car with Mr Derwent so Edmond would be ready for the new term. Ellen, the nanny, was accompanying them to Cambridge. Meanwhile a removal firm was taking the last of their belongings to their home.

'There's not much room at our house,' Amy warned Ellen. 'We've bought a small bed for the nursery so you can sleep there.' The nanny was content with this arrangement, for they planned that she should only work for them for a few more weeks.

Ellen sat in the front of the car, while Amy held Beth in the back, well wrapped up against the chill wind. Edmond sat beside them pointing out cows and sheep to his daughter as Pa drove them. Beth began to doze as they made the tedious journey through London, before stopping at an inn for lunch. There was thin sunshine as they continued their journey in the early afternoon, finally approaching Cambridge. *Now I'll be able to look after Edmond properly*, she thought.

He reached for her hand. 'At last I'll have you and Beth here to care for,' he said. 'This is just the start. I need to get my degree and a good job so I can support all of us decently.'

'You'll find a way!' Certainly, if courage and devotion were enough he would achieve his aims. And perhaps one day they would have another child or two.

'I've imagined this day for so long,' he went on. 'When we were first married I used to look forward to carrying you across the threshold of our own house.'

'Well you can't now,' Pa said firmly, 'you're not sufficiently fit for that.'

'Better take Beth and carry her instead,' Amy said. Edmond unlocked the front door and ceremonially carried his daughter as they all went inside.

Grace, the maid, had lit the fire and there was a delicious aroma as she prepared a meal for them to eat later.

'It's really cosy here,' Amy said. She caught sight of a china bowl of bulbs in the middle of their table. 'Oh, look! Hyacinths!'

He smiled. 'When I wrote to Grace I asked her to get some, ready for your arrival.'

'They'll be in bloom in a day or two. Look, already you can see a petal showing pink at the tip.' She even detected a faint perfume.

The removals van arrived and they had to instruct the men where to take the last of their belongings. Ellen followed Amy as she took Beth up to the nursery and let her help position her toys around the room. Amy's walking was improving day by day.

At last they settled in the little dining room as Grace dished up their meal. There was another surprise: a new photograph was hanging on the wall. Amy took a closer look.

'It's that lovely one of the three of us at Beth's christening!' she cried. It had not been there when she last visited.

'I was determined to have it in place for when you arrived,' Edmond said. It was hanging from the picture rail in a silver frame.

'It's perfect,' she said.

They ate their meal with Pa, who would drive back the following morning. Soon it was time to put Beth to bed. Grace left and Ellen retired to the nursery. Pa told them he was tired and went to settle down in the spare room.

There had been so many frustrating delays that living together in their own home had sometimes seemed like an unattainable dream. But here they finally were!

Edmond took Amy to their own room and drew her into his arms. He leant his warm face against hers.

'At last we're together for good,' he said, 'for tomorrow and all the other days!'

A Letter From Rosemary

It's wonderful to see *Until the War is Over* published. I'm thrilled to have the backing of Hera Books, and that you have chosen my historical romance to read.

Once my first book, *Until We Meet Again*, was published I began getting mail asking me what happened next to Amy and Edmond. I wanted to continue their story in 1918, with their new daughter Beth. Already their world had changed significantly from the life they knew in 1914. Edmond had to adjust to his severe war wound, intending to continue his studies and then begin to support his family.

By this time the war had lasted over three years, and it must have seemed as though it would never end. Edmond and Amy continued to need all their courage and devotion to deal with further challenges.

By now others in their circle were facing major struggles too. Edmond's friend, Charles, was caught up in one of the most desperate battles, while James, Amy's cousin, faced censure for only serving as a medical orderly.

In the wards Lavinia had to nurse without such modern aids as antibiotics.

One historical event of 1918 was the horrific flu pandemic, and as I wrote a chapter where it affected one of my characters I had no idea that a modern epidemic was about to strike. We can see now how frightening it becomes when a new disease spreads rapidly. Fortunately, medical experts assure us that the current epidemic should be much milder.

I hope you enjoyed this second story about Amy, Edmond and their friends. If you did, I would love to hear your impressions in a review. I welcome readers' feedback, and it helps others to discover my book.

Amy and Edmond will be back before long in the third book in the series, so you can discover what lies ahead for them!

If you would like to talk to me directly about *Until the War is Over*, you can find me on my social media pages:

Twitter:
@RoseGoodacre

Facebook:
Rosemary Goodacre Author

LinkedIn:
Rosemary Goodacre

Thank you again for choosing my book, and for your support. It is lovely to receive your comments, and encourages me to write further stories.

Best wishes

Rosemary

Acknowledgments

I am very grateful to Keshini Naidoo and Lindsey Mooney at Hera Books, for believing in my stories and guiding me through the process of being published.

I have learnt a good deal about the Great War through the moving memoir of Vera Brittain, in *Testament of Youth*. (Virago Press, ISBN 0 86068 035 5.)

I have also referred to *A Nurse at the Front*, based on the First World War diaries of Sister Edith Appleton, edited by Ruth Cowen. (Simon & Schuster, ISBN 978-1-84983-366-0.)

I have a great respect for the women who lived through the First World War and, besides fulfilling traditional tasks, turned their hands to difficult and demanding work they would not otherwise have tackled. Sometimes they filled the places of men who had joined up, by serving in restaurants or acting as bus conductors. Others were particularly respected for driving ambulances and training as nurses. Some travelled to France, at risk of mines in the Channel and bombs aimed at railway lines near their hospital. Their courage helped demonstrate their right to be allowed the vote.

I must also extend my sincere thanks to all who helped me on my path to becoming a published writer. Here I must include the Romantic Novelists' Association, a valuable source of advice and encouragement for novice writers. Formed to promote romantic fiction and encourage good writing, this year (2020) it celebrates its sixtieth birthday.

Books By Rosemary Goodacre

Until We Meet Again